THE GIRLS

LISA JEWELL

ISIS
LARGE
PRINT

First published in Great Britain 2015
by
Century

First Isis Edition
published 2017
by arrangement with
Arrow Books
Penguin Random House Group

A catalogue record for this book is available
from the British Library.

ISBN 978–1–78541–308–7 (hb)
ISBN 978–1–78541–314–8 (pb)

Published by
F. A. Thorpe (Publishing)
Anstey, Leicestershire

Set by Words & Graphics Ltd.
Anstey, Leicestershire
Printed and bound in Great Britain by
T. J. International Ltd., Padstow, Cornwall

This book is printed on acid-free paper

Dedicated to all my neighbours on
the C&G Gardens

5 July, 9p.m.

Pip stands behind her mother in the tiny bathroom. She's not sure what to do. She's never seen her mother being sick before.

"Urgh, God, Pip. I'm so sorry. I am *so sorry*."

"That's OK, Mum." Pip tentatively touches her mother's head, and strokes her fine blonde hair just once.

Her mother doubles over and is sick again. She judders afterwards and rocks back on to her heels, staring up into the halogens buried in the ceiling.

Pip passes her a beaker of water. "Here," she says, "drink some."

Her mother does as she is told.

"Do you think that's it? Do you think you've finished?"

Clare shudders and says, "Yes. I think that's it." She rests the beaker of water on the floor by the toilet with shaking hands and unfolds her legs, leaning back against the side of the bath. "Pip," she says, taking her hand, "I am so so sorry."

"Honestly, Mum, it doesn't matter."

"It does matter!" Her mother's words are slightly slurred. Her pale skin is waxy, her mascara smudged under her eyes. "It matters because I'm your mother and it is my job to look after you and how can I look after you in this state." She points at herself. "You shouldn't have to be looking after me. You shouldn't have to deal with anything you've had to deal with these past few months. You've been the best, most amazing girl. I don't know what I'd do without you. I don't."

Her mother pulls Pip to her and holds her tight. Too tight.

"I need to go to bed now. I have to . . ." Clare gets uncertainly to her feet, holding on to the sink for balance. ". . . I have to sleep."

The back door is still unlocked. All the lights are on. And Grace is still outdoors somewhere, roaming the communal garden with her friends. Pip resists the urge to say, "But what about Grace? What about me?" She's twelve years old. She can handle this.

Her mother stumbles from the bathroom and falls face down on to her bed. Pip pulls the duvet from under her small body and covers her properly. "Thank you, baby. Thank you. I love you so much. So, so much."

Pip sits on the edge of her mother's bed for a while, until she hears her breathing change to a sonorous bass. It is just past nine. She moves to the living room and sits there, perched uncertainly on the edge of the sofa. Beyond the back door, across the gardens, the party is still going on. She can hear it in snatches of laughter and high-pitched screams of over-excited children out

2

long past their bedtimes. She doesn't know what to do. She is all alone. And soon it will be dark. She phones Grace, but, unsurprisingly, her call goes straight through to voicemail. Grace has been outdoors since two o'clock and her phone will be out of charge.

Then she hears something at the back door: footsteps. She looks up, her heart racing. She sees a tall shadow move past the window. The footsteps are closer now, and suddenly there is a man standing by the door. Pip clutches her heart and hides herself behind the sofa.

"Hello? Clare? Pip?"

She breathes a sigh of relief. It's Leo. She goes to the door, where he stands with his golden dog, Scout. "Just checking on your mum," he says, looking behind her. "Is she OK?"

Pip nods. "She was sick. And now she's gone to bed."

"Ah." He nods.

Pip crouches to stroke the dog, mainly because she is embarrassed to be here, alone, talking to a grown-up.

"Are you coming back out?" he asks. "The party's still going on. Loads of kids still out there."

"I don't think I should," she says. "I don't want to leave Mum. In case she's sick again."

He nods approvingly. "Fair enough," he says. "If you need anything, come to ours: we'll all be up for a good while longer."

Then he goes, the golden dog following behind, and disappears into the shadows of the encroaching dusk.

By ten to ten it is dark and Pip wants to go to bed. She looks in on her mother who is asleep on her back, her mouth hanging open, her arms above her head, snoring.

Pip looks out into the darkness beyond her garden gate. The party has finished but the garden is still alive. Clusters of people sit on the grass or on arrangements of folding chairs, their faces lit by storm lanterns, by candles flickering in jars, by the red embers of disposable barbecues. She needs to find Grace, so that she can lock the door and go to bed. But she doesn't want to wander these gardens in the dark on her own, however lively they are.

The security light at the back of a neighbour's house goes on and she sees a stream of twenty-somethings pass through the garden and back door, each holding something: rolled-up blankets, empty wine bottles, bin bags full of the detritus of a day in the sun. The sudden brightness and the wholesome chatter of her neighbours and their friends makes Pip feel brave for a second and she grabs the key to the back door and locks it behind her.

The table on their terrace is still bedecked with balloons from Grace's birthday party earlier in the day, bobbing mournfully in the warm night breeze.

She sees children in the playground: big children. She heads towards them, hopefully. She sees faces she recognises: Leo's older daughters, Catkin and Fern, mucking about on the swings. And Tyler and Dylan, side by side on a bench. But no Grace.

"Have you seen Grace?"

They all look at each other and shrug. Dylan sits up straight. "Isn't she at home?"

Pip feels a cold chill of dread pass down her spine. "No," she says. "I haven't seen her for hours."

"She said she was going in," says Catkin. "About an hour ago. She must have changed her mind. Have you checked our flat? Maybe she's hanging out with our parents?"

Pip wanders across the lawn, through the remains of the party, bunting fluttering darkly from trees, bin bags in piles ready to be removed the next morning, piles of folded chairs and dismantled gazebos stacked under trees. She can see the light from the Howeses' garden apartment glowing from here, empty now after a day-long party, the party that she and her mother had been at earlier, where her mother had drunk too much wine and had had to excuse herself, barely able to walk in a straight line.

Then she cries out and clutches her chest when a figure appears at her side. It is Max, the football-mad loner of the garden. He's only nine, three years younger than her. She can't believe he's still out here, wandering alone at this time of night. As ever he is holding his beloved football, squeezing it tight against his stomach. He looks at Pip, his eyes wide and appalled. He looks as though he's about to say something, but no words come. He turns then and runs, down the hill, towards the lights.

Pip watches him go, feeling that something is wrong. "Grace!" she calls out. "Grace!"

There is something on the brow of the hill, a strange shape emerging from the hedge that encircles the Rose Garden. She heads towards it.

"Grace!" she calls again. "Grace!"

As she nears the shape she can see it is a foot. She holds her breath deep inside her body and rounds the corner timorously.

The foot is attached to a person. Pip passes the beam from her mobile phone across the figure: a girl, half-undressed. Shorts yanked down to her knees, floral camisole top lifted above small naked breasts. Her hair is spread about her. Her face is a bloodied mass.

Grace.

Pip drops to her knees. "No," she mutters, "no. No. No. No." She pulls Grace's camisole down, she pulls her shorts up. Then she runs down the hill, runs and runs, towards the warm safe lights of the Howeses' apartment, towards grown-ups, her heart thumping piston-hard in her chest.

Before

CHAPTER
ONE

Dear Daddy,

We moved into the new flat this weekend. It's nice. It's on a quiet street with little houses. You walk into a narrow hallway and if you turn right there are two bedrooms. I have to share with Grace but I really don't mind. You know I never liked sleeping on my own in the old house anyway. Not really. Do you remember? I don't really know how much you remember about things from before. I don't know if you've lost all your memories or if you're just the same except with all the other problems.

Anyway, our room is really cute. We put our beds in an L shape so that our feet point together and our heads are furthest apart and I can see Grace when I'm in bed. It's like this:

It's weird how I'm eleven and I should be wanting my own room and I just really don't. Remember how I used to say I wish we lived in a caravan? So we could be all snug together? Well, this is a bit like that, I suppose. Then Mum's room is next door to ours. It's quite small but she's got a little shower room attached, which is nice for her. Then on the other side of the hallway there's a kitchen which is square with white units with silver handles and white tiles and Mum says it looks like an operating theatre. It kind of does. Well, it's totally different to our old kitchen, that's for sure. Do you remember our old kitchen? Do you remember those crazy tiles around the sink with the bits of fruit on them? Grapes and stuff? I sort of miss those now.

So the kitchen has a breakfast bar, which is good, I like breakfast bars, and a window that looks over the garden. And next door is a tiny living room. It's all painted white with that kind of shiny wood flooring that's not really wood and whoever lived here before must have worn very sharp heels because it's full of little dents, like a Ryvita. There's a door in the living room that takes you into the back garden. It's tiny weeny. Just big enough for a little table and some chairs. And maybe it's just because it's winter but it does smell a bit damp out there and there's lots of moss all over the walls.

And it has a little wooden gate and when you go through the gate there's a totally massive garden.

We were not expecting it. Mum didn't even tell us about it before. I was just thinking what a cute little flat it was and then suddenly it's like Narnia, there's all these tall trees and pathways and a lawn that takes you up to all these big white houses with windows that are as tall as two men and you can see the chandeliers and the big splashy paintings on the walls. At night when you look up the hill and the houses have all their lights on it's so pretty. And in the garden itself there are all these pathways and little tucked-away places. A secret garden which is hidden inside an old wall covered with ivy, like the one in the book. A rose garden which has bowers all the way round and benches in the middle. And then there's a playground too. It's not particularly amazing, just some swings and a clonky old roundabout and one of those sad animals on a spring. But still, it's cool.

This is what the garden looks like.

Mum says I can't tell you the name of the garden, or where it is. I totally don't know why.

But it is still in London. Just a different part to where we lived.

So, all in all I quite like it here. Which canNOT be said for Grace. She hates it. She hates sharing a room with me, she hates the tiny rooms and the narrow hallway and the fact there's nowhere to put anything. And she hates our new school (I can tell you it's a girls' school and there are two baby goats and a Vietnamese potbellied pig in the playground. But I can't tell you what it's called. I'm really sorry). Anyway, she hates it. I don't really know why. I really like it. And also she hates the communal garden. She says it's weird and scary, probably full of murderers. I don't think so. I think it looks interesting. Kind of mysterious.

I have to go now. Mum says she doesn't know if they'll give you any letters or even if you'd be able to read them anyway. But I always told you everything, Dad, and I don't want to stop now.

Love you. Get better!

Your Pip (squeak) xxxxxxx

"Look," said Adele, standing in the tall window of her living room, her arms folded across her stomach. "More new people."

She was watching a young woman with a soft helmet of pale blonde hair wearing an oversized parka with a huge fur-trimmed collar that looked as though it had eaten her. She was walking along the perimeter of the Secret Garden, followed by two biggish girls, Adele couldn't really gauge their age, but she thought roughly eleven, twelve, thirteen, that kind of area. The girls had matching heads of thick dark curls and were wearing similar-looking parkas to — she assumed — their mother. They were tall and solid, almost, Adele couldn't help herself from thinking, verging on the overweight. But hard to tell in the winter coats.

Leo joined her at the window. "Oh," he said, "them. I saw them moving in a few days ago."

"Whereabouts?"

"The terrace," he said, "about halfway down."

The garden was formed in the space between a long row of small, flat-fronted Georgian cottages on Virginia Terrace and a majestic half-moon of stucco-fronted mansions on Virginia Crescent, with a large mansion block at either end.

Adele had lived on Virginia Crescent for almost twenty years. She'd moved into Leo's flat when she was twenty-one, straight from a cramped flat-share on Stroud Green Road. She had been immediately overwhelmed by the high ceilings and the faded grandeur: the foxed mirrors and threadbare sofas, old velvet shredded by the claws of a dozen long-dead cats; the heavy floor-length curtains patterned with sun-bleached palm fronds and birds of paradise; the walls of books and the grand piano covered with a fringed chenille throw. They'd long since taken out the opulent seventies-style bathroom suite with its golden bird-shaped taps and green porcelain sanitary-ware. They'd ripped out the expensive, claret-red carpets and taken down the curtains so heavy they'd needed two people to take the weight. Leo's mother had died twelve years ago and two years later his father had moved to some land-locked African state to marry a woman half his age. She and Leo bought out his two brothers and room by room they'd made the flat their own.

Adele felt as much a part of the garden as her husband, who had grown up on these lawns. She had seen babies become adults. She had seen a hundred families come and go. She had had dozens of other people's children in and out of her home. The garden became a mystery during these winter months: neighbours becoming shadows glimpsed through windows, their children growing taller and taller behind closed doors, people moving out, people moving in and people occasionally dying. And it wasn't until the onset of spring, until the days grew longer and the sun shone warmer, that the secrets of the winter were revealed.

She looked again at the new arrivals. Gorgeous girls, tall and big-boned, both of them, with square-jawed faces like warrior queens. And then she turned her gaze to their elfin, worried-looking mother. "Was there a man?" she asked Leo. "When they moved in?"

"Not that I noticed," he said.

She nodded.

She wanted to wander out there now, accidentally cross paths, introduce herself, make sure they realised that there was more to the garden than it might appear on a dank January afternoon such as this. She wanted to impart some sense of the way the garden opened like a blossom during the summer months: back doors left open; children running barefoot in the warm dark of night; the red glow of tin-can barbecues for two in

14

hidden corners; the playground full of young mothers and toddlers; the pop and thwack of ping-pong balls on the table wheeled out by the French family along the way; cats stretched out in puddles of sunshine; striped shadows patterning the lawn through fronds of weeping willows.

But right now that was all a long way off. Right now it was January and in an hour or so it would be getting dark, lights switched on, curtains pulled shut, everyone sealed up and internalised. The garden itself dark and shabby; lines of bare-branched trees, dead-faced backs of houses, pale gravelled paths covered in the last of autumn's leaves; an air of desolation, melancholic whistle of wind through leafless tendrils of weeping willows, cats sitting listlessly on garden walls.

"I wonder where those girls go to school," she muttered mainly to herself. The girls' school up by the Heath, maybe? Or maybe even the hothouse place on the other side of the main road? She tried to work out whether they had money or not. You couldn't assume anything in this community. Half these houses were owned by a charitable trust and the mansion blocks at either end were affordable housing for service workers. There was even a halfway house on the terrace, home to an endless succession of recently released female offenders and their children, its back garden cemented over and sprouting weeds, with a never-used solitary plastic rocking dog.

There was no single type of person who lived here. No neat social demographic catchment. Everyone lived here. TV presenters, taxi drivers, artists, teachers, drug addicts. That was the joy of it.

"You're starting to look a bit creepy there, Del."

She jumped slightly.

"Those girls will be going: *Mum*, have you seen that weird woman over there who keeps staring at us?"

Adele turned and smiled at Leo. "They can't see me," she said, "not in this light."

"Well, that makes it even worse! *Mum*, there's a ghostly shape in that window over there, I don't like it!"

"OK."

Adele turned one last time, before moving away from the window.

CHAPTER
TWO

Dear Daddy,

How are you? When can we see you? I miss you so much. Well, we've been here for ten days now. Granny came for lunch on Sunday. She made lots of weird faces. I don't think she liked it very much. She said that Mum shouldn't let us out in the garden on our own, that there might be murderers and paedophiles hiding in the bushes! She said she'd heard a story about a young girl being found dead in a garden like ours a long time ago. And that everyone would be looking in our back windows all the time. She's so silly sometimes!

We went for a walk around the garden after she left and me and Grace mucked around on the swings and stuff. There was nobody out there. But then yesterday after school I could hear voices in the garden. Children's voices. And I looked out the window and I could see kids running about, some others on bikes.

Anyway, me and Grace went out, just to look. We stood under the tree outside our house so that nobody could see us and we spied on them. They were kind of our age, I think. Mainly girls. Some of the girls looked a bit strange, wearing really weird clothes, patterned things, one had really really long hair, literally down to her bum, another one had shaved off bits and another one had dreadlocks. There was another girl who was much smaller than the others but she acted like she was probably the boss of the gang. She was really pretty with silky blonde hair that looked like it had been straightened because it was so shiny. She was wearing normal clothes, jeans and stuff. And then a boy. Mixed-race. Kind of good-looking.

This is what they look like:

They weren't really doing much. The smaller girl was on rollerblades. The boy was on a bike. The other three girls were just kind of hanging about and then one of them got on to the back bit of the boy's bike and they were cycling around and I said to Grace, Let's go to the playground. Let's go on the swings. Because I really wanted to get closer to them all and see them properly. But she said, I'm going indoors. I hate it out here. It's cliquey and full of stuck-up kids.

But I don't think they are stuck-up really. I think they're just all different kinds of kids, that's all. And they probably think the same about us. Stuck-up girls! Hiding under trees! Staring at them!

So we went inside then because I felt too shy to stay out there on my own. It's raining today so the garden's empty. Is it raining where you are? Do you have a garden? Are you allowed out of bed?

Are you even in a bed? I wish I knew more. I wish I could understand why you're there and what they're doing to you and how you're feeling. I wish we could come and see you. Are you lonely? Do you remember? Do you remember anything? I've drawn you a picture of me in case you can't remember my face any more.

And if you can't remember what Grace looks like, it's basically the same as me except her lips are fuller and her hair is two shades darker. And she's got a little freckle by her eye that looks like a teardrop.

I love you, Daddy. Get well soon.

xxxxx

"OK, girls." Adele put out her hands to gather up the exercise books handed to her by her children. "Lunchtime."

"What are we having?" asked Fern, uncurling herself from her usual position on the blue armchair, scratching at the stubble of her shaved temples.

"Soup," said Adele.

"What sort?" asked Willow, uncrossing her legs and getting to her feet.

"Chicken noodle."

"Can I go to the shops and get myself a sandwich?" asked Catkin, her hands folded into the cuffs of her jumper and held to her mouth, pensively.

"No."

"Please. I can buy it with my own money." Her blue eyes were wide and beseeching.

"No. I don't want you going anywhere. We won't see you again."

"Oh, come on, where the hell am I going to go in the middle of the day?"

"I have no idea, Catkin. You are an eternal mystery to me. But I'm not letting you go to the shops. And you should be saving your money for things you actually need rather than wasting it on expensive sandwiches."

"It's my money."

20

"Yes. I know. And it's good for you to learn to budget and prioritise. And while there's a huge pan of perfectly good soup on the other side of that door, it is crazy for you to waste your money on crappy shop-bought sandwiches full of additives."

Catkin rolled her eyes and dropped her baby-animal stance, her arms falling angrily to her sides. "Fine," she said. "Bring on the fucking soup."

Adele and her girls had their lunch in the kitchen, loosely arranged around the big farmhouse table that was one of the few things left behind from her in-laws' inhabitation.

It was the same table that Leo and his brothers had sat around as boys and it still bore scars and marks left there forty or more years ago, added to now by Leo's own children.

Catkin sat with her long legs stretched out along the bench, her back a C-shaped hump, causing her to turn her head forty-five degrees in order to reach her soup bowl. Fern sat straight-backed as always, rhythmically spooning the soup into her mouth, her body language giving nothing away, her ears taking in every last thing. Willow, meanwhile, kept up a running commentary, her soup getting cold in front of her, a habit she'd had since toddlerhood. In fact, until she was about nine years old Adele had spoon-fed her, slipping the spoon between her lips every time she paused for breath just to get the blessed food into her.

"What's for pudding?" she asked now.

"Pudding?" said Adele. "You haven't started your soup yet."

"Yes, but the thought of pudding will incentivise me to eat my soup."

"No, stopping talking for more than thirty seconds is what you need to do. And anyway, there is no pudding."

Willow gasped and put her hand dramatically against her heart. "Are you serious?"

"Well, there's crumble but you won't eat crumble, so . . ."

"Not even any biscuits?"

"Just those oaty ones you don't like."

"I'll eat an oaty biscuit," she said. "If that's all there is."

"That's all there is."

"Right then." She picked up her spoon and started shovelling soup into her mouth.

Fern looked at her in horror.

"Slow down," said Adele, "you're splashing it everywhere."

"What can we do after lunch?" asked Willow, wiping soup splashes from her cheeks with the back of her hand.

Adele looked at the time. Then she checked the timetable taped to the front of her folder. "Well, it's double maths this afternoon, so it might be good for you all to burn off a bit of energy. Why don't you go out in the garden for half an hour?"

"It's wet," said Catkin.

"No," said Adele. "It's damp. If you were at school it would be deemed playground weather."

"Yes, but we're not at school, are we? Precisely because you didn't like the way mainstream schools herd children around like cattle."

Adele sighed. "In which case, do whatever you want. But no TV. And back here at one fifteen please. *With your brains switched on.*"

The girls left the table, grabbing oaty biscuits and apples on their way. Adele tidied up the soup bowls and wiped the crumbs from the ripped-apart bread rolls into the palm of her hand before dropping them in the bin.

Adele had been home-schooling her children since Catkin was five. She and Leo had decided to take her out of school halfway through her reception year when she'd come home in tears after being told off for running in the playground. For a while they'd seriously considered moving to the countryside, putting Catkin into one of those wonderful little schools with woods and fields and pigs and goats. But Leo's revolting father had refused to sell them his half of the flat: "It's my little bit of London! I couldn't sleep at night without my little bit of London!"

They'd been to see Montessori schools, Steiner schools, some of the woollier local private schools, but they hadn't managed to make the finances work. So Adele had given up her job as an education coordinator at an arts centre — it had barely paid her anything anyway — spent a month familiarising herself with the foundation stage of the national curriculum and become her child's teacher.

Then had come Fern and then Willow and what had started off as an experiment became a way of life. Not everyone approved. Adele's sister Zoe, for one, thought it verged on child abuse. "But they won't know how to play with other children," she'd said. "And they won't know what's in and what's out and everyone will think they're weirdos!"

"Do you think they're weirdos?" Adele had asked in reply.

"No. Of course not. I think they're lovely. But I'm a middle-aged woman. I'm not another child!"

"They've got the garden," Adele would counter. "They can do all the peer-to-peer stuff they need to do out there. It's just like a playground."

"Except it's not. It's just not. It's just another weird thing that makes them different from other children. I couldn't live like that." She'd said this more than once. "Everyone being able to see in. Never being able to go and sit in your garden, on your own, in your bra. Always having to talk to people."

It was an acquired taste, Adele supposed. Sometimes she did wish she could take a blanket and a book outside and sit and read undisturbed. Sometimes she did resent other people's children running through her freshly hoovered flat. But the benefits far outweighed the difficulties. And for the girls it was crucial, the lynchpin to their entire existence. Without the garden her sister would probably be right, they would be odd and out on a limb. The other children were their connection to the mainstream world. And, of course, as a world heard about only through the anecdotes of friends, school did sometimes become a romanticised concept and each of the girls had on occasion begged her to let them go to school. When she was eleven years old, Fern had even taken to walking up the hill to Dylan's school to meet him at three thirty just to feel that she was experiencing the first flush of independence like other children her age.

Yes. Home-schooled children. Communal living. All very alternative. Verging on controversial. But to Adele, entirely and completely normal.

At 1.15 p.m. she went to the back gate and called the girls in for afternoon school. They came, her brood, her gaggle, with their unkempt hair and their unworldly clothes, their brains filled with everything she'd ever taught them, their stomachs filled with food she'd cooked from scratch. The babies that she'd never had to hand over to the world.

For half an hour they studied mindfulness. It had appeared on the national curriculum this year. Adele had been delighted. She'd been effectively teaching them mindfulness skills for years; she'd called it meditation although that hadn't been quite accurate.

The girls arranged themselves into their usual layout, long legs outstretched in wash-faded leggings and hand-me-down jeans, scrubbed faces in mindful repose, wearing holey old jumpers and unbranded sweatshirts from the charity shops along the Finchley Road — nothing from Primark, nothing from New Look, nothing ethically unsound. The girls understood. They'd watched the documentaries about the sweatshops, seen the news reports about the factory fire in Mumbai that had killed all those people. They knew fashion wasn't as important as people. They weren't vain. They weren't shallow. No smartphones. No Facebook. No Instagram. All too likely to turn them into narcissists. They understood. They sneered at the posturing and posing of their contemporaries, the twelve-year-old girls in mascara puckering into camera lenses, the misguided fools on talent shows. They got it, her girls. They absolutely got it.

They weren't weird, Adele thought now, looking at them in turn. They were magnificent.

CHAPTER
THREE

Pip stared up at the girl standing in front of her, squinting against the low sun. It was the blonde girl, the one who looked like the leader of the garden clique. She'd been watching them from a distance and then suddenly got on her bike and cycled towards them with some urgency. "Hi."

"Hi," said Pip.

"Have you just moved in?" the girl asked in a flat monotone.

"No," said Grace. "We moved in last month."

"Oh. Right. Haven't seen you before. Who are you?"

"I'm Pip."

"Pip?"

She nodded.

"Is that your real name?"

Pip blinked.

"Seriously? You're called Pip?"

She felt her cheeks fill with warm blood.

"It's her nickname," said Grace. "Short for Pipsqueak. What we called her when she was a baby."

"So, what's your real name?" The blonde girl stared at her impatiently as if this conversation had been going on for long enough even though she'd been the one who'd started it.

"Lola," she said.

"God, that's a much nicer name. Why don't you ask to be called that instead?"

Grace spoke for her again. "The woman next door where we used to live had a really yappy dog called Lola. It put us all off."

"But still," she said, "you don't live there any more. You could change it back now."

Pip shrugged. She still thought of the yappy dog when she thought of Lola. She still thought of the woman next door and the thing that had happened and, besides, she'd always been Pip. She *was* Pip.

The girl stood astride her bike, a big black thing with gears. Her fine blonde hair was tucked behind one double-pierced ear; her thin hands gripped the handlebars possessively. She wore denim shorts with pocket bags hanging out and a grey sweatshirt that was as wide as it was long; she had narrow feet in bright white Converse and blunt-cut fingernails.

"What's your name, then?" Pip asked her.

"Tyler."

"Tyler like the boy's name?"

"Yeah."

Pip nodded. She looked like a Tyler.

"Where do you live?" asked Tyler.

"That flat there," said Grace.

Tyler nodded again. "Where do you go to school?"

"Mount Elizabeth."

"Are you twins?" She narrowed her eyes at them.

"No."

"You look like twins. Are you sure you're not twins?"

"Positive," said Grace.

"I know someone at Mount Elizabeth. She says you're allowed to smoke. Is that true?"

"No!"

"Or maybe she said swear. Are you allowed to swear?"

"I don't think so."

Pip tried to think of something to say. But Tyler had lost interest, and was scouring the gardens from left to right. She stopped when she saw a boy in the distance; then she pressed her feet to the pedals and propelled the huge bike across the garden towards him, her hair blowing out behind her.

Pip watched for a while. It was the good-looking boy, the tall one with bobbly golden-tipped Afro hair and green eyes. The boy's gaze fixed on to Tyler. Pip watched him pull off his school tie and absentmindedly roll it into a ball which he tucked into the pocket of his posh school blazer. Tyler said something to him and dismounted from the bike. Then they walked slowly in the opposite direction, towards the square of benches at the furthest end of the garden, Tyler wheeling the bike, the boy strolling with his hands in his pockets, the pair of them deep in conversation.

Pip and Grace looked at one another. Grace shrugged. "What was that all about?"

"Maybe she was just being friendly?"

Grace shook her head. "Weird."

"She's pretty."

"Skinny," said Grace dismissively.

"I guess."

Pip stared into the anemone-shaped head of a clover flower growing by her feet. She pinched it between her thumb and index finger arid then brought the honey smell to her nose. A sharp breeze circled the half-moon of the garden, feathering the tendrils of weeping willows, biting through the wool of Pip's jumper. The last slice of setting sun fell behind a chimney stack and the temperature dropped.

"I'm going in," said Grace.

"Me too."

Pip turned briefly to look at Tyler and the boy again. They were sitting side by side on a bench. The bike lay flat on the grass, its back wheel still turning lazily. Tyler's legs were pulled up into her body and the boy was laughing at something she'd said. Pip wondered how old he was, where he lived, if they were boyfriend and girlfriend. As she watched, the back gate of one of the flats across the lawn opened and three tall, thin girls emerged. One after the other. It was the strange sisters with the weird hair. They walked in height order, louchely, scuffing at the gravel on the path with old sneakers. The smallest one picked up her pace as she neared Tyler and the boy; the other two trailed behind. And then, virtually telepathically, they arranged themselves into a horseshoe huddle around the bench, a silent choreography. Pip saw Tyler nod in their direction; the boy and the sisters all turned to look at them and then they looked away again.

"Come on," said Grace. "I'm cold."

Pip followed her big sister back across the lawn and down the gravelled path that led to their back gate, and as she did she heard the garden whisper in their wake. It talked to itself about the things it knew, the secrets it held close within its pathways and crannies, its bowers and corners. It whispered about the people who lived behind the closed doors and the insular group of children on the bench, and of the days yet to come when the warmth of summer would bring it all back to life.

Clare watched her girls through the kitchen window. It was the first time they'd gone out into the garden without her, just to hang out. She'd seen a young girl come and talk to them. Hard-faced. Pretty. It had looked like something of an interrogation. Not exactly friendly. Then the girl had cycled away and joined up with her little gang at the other end of the garden, three slightly alternative-looking girls who looked like sisters and a tall, mixed-race boy in a dark school uniform. She saw her girls now, casting backward glances at the gang on the benches, then heading back indoors. The sun was getting low. She saw Grace hugging herself to keep warm. It was nearly five o'clock. Time to think about tea.

"What do you fancy?" she asked, meeting her daughters at the back door. "I can do spaghetti with peas?"

The girls dropped their garden *froideur* as they came indoors and said yum, and yes please. Spaghetti and peas. A favourite family staple. And cheap too, which was just as well now that Clare was living off a finite sum of money.

The girls joined her in the small kitchen where they sat side by side on bar stools at the breakfast bar. Hard to tell them apart sometimes, especially when they were seated and you couldn't see the two-inch difference in height. The same big square faces and almond eyes. The same mass of brown curls and bright hazel irises. They both looked just like him. Just like their dad.

"So," said Clare, bunching raw spaghetti into her fist and forcing it down into a pan of boiling water, "did you see anyone out there?"

"A girl came and talked to us," said Pip. "She's called Tyler."

"Oh," said Clare, "was she nice?"

"Not really," said Pip.

"Bit of a bitch," said Grace.

"Oh," said Clare again, prodding stray sticks of spaghetti under the surface of the water with a fork. "That's a shame. By the way, I forgot to tell you: your onesies came today. From Next. They're in the hallway. *But don't rip the bag open!*" she yelled after Pip who was already halfway out of the door. "In case we have to send them back!"

Pip brought the parcel through and together the girls pulled out the clear plastic bags. Pip handed Grace the one in her size and then they both tried them on. Clare watched her girls undressing, absorbed their shapes: broad and strong, already dipping at the waist, Grace in her junior bra, Pip still flat-chested, the pronounced S-bends of their bodies and the small doughy tummies that neither girl was as yet at all concerned about. Their father's bodies, too. Not Clare's. Clare had been a painfully skinny child, flat-chested well into her teens, and was still slight and bordering on bony. It would not be long, she mused, until both her girls towered over her, until they could carry her around like a child.

They zipped up their onesies and stood before her, striking poses to make her laugh. "You both look adorable," she said, pulling open the freezer door. "Like lovely overgrown babies."

The day became dark and Clare began the process of pulling shut the blinds and curtains, of running a bath for the girls, stacking the dishwasher; the girls clean and glowing in their onesies doing their homework side by side, the sound of the TV going on, a mug of camomile and all three of them together, warm and safe in their tiny flat.

At nine thirty she came to kiss the girls goodnight. They were reading by the pale light of table-lamps, Grace leaning against her bedhead, her knees brought up to her chest, Pip curled foetal-style with her book held on its side. Pip glanced up at her and smiled. But there was something brittle about the upturn of her mouth and Clare realised that she was on the verge of tears.

"When can we see Daddy?" Pip asked.

Clare sighed and brushed Pip's forehead with the palm of her hand. "I truly don't know."

"When will he reply to my letters?"

"I really and truly don't know."

Grace lifted her head from her book and peered disdainfully at Pip over the top of her knees. "Why do you keep going on about it? I mean, seriously, he's just scary. I don't care if I never see him again."

Clare sighed again. They were treading familiar ground.

"I want to go to see the house," said Pip.

"Oh, God." Clare pushed Pip's hair off her forehead. "I really don't think —"

"Please. Please, Mum. I'll go on my own . . ."

"Don't be silly. You can't go on your own. You wouldn't even know how to get there."

"Yes I do. I'd get the bus."

"I really don't think you'd want to see the house, Pip. I think it's too early."

"But . . . *why?*" Pip was crying now. "I want to, Mum! I want to see the house. Please!"

Clare exhaled deeply and took Pip into her arms. She felt her shuddering and shivering inside her embrace. For days and days on end they could act like everything was normal, like they were on a lovely little adventure together. And then the reality of their situation would crash through the façade and they'd emerge like a straggle of pile-up survivors crawling from the wreckage. "Fine," she whispered into Pip's hot ear. "Fine. We'll go after school tomorrow."

"I'm not going!" said Grace. "I never want to see that place again. I never even want to think about it."

Clare dropped her face on to the crown of Pip's head. She kissed her hard, breathed her in. What was worse? Denial or fascination? She didn't know.

"Do you promise?" said Pip, looking up at Clare through wet eyelashes.

"Yes. I promise. We'll go straight from school. But, Pip, be prepared for a nasty shock."

Pip nodded her head against Clare's chest, tightened her arms around her waist, whispered *thank you*.

The house was still shrouded in scaffolding and plastic sheeting. It looked monstrous between the immaculate houses on either side. The insurers still hadn't settled and, given the circumstances, it was possible they never would. It was possible in fact that their beautiful house might sit shamefully like this forever.

Pip's hold on her hand tightened. "It looks scary," she said.

"It is scary," said Grace.

She'd come, in the end. At breakfast time she'd said, "It would be weird if you two had seen it and I hadn't. I don't want to. But I think I have to."

"Do you remember . . .?" Pip began. But she didn't finish the sentence. She didn't need to. Because they all remembered — painfully, clearly. The late autumn night when the three of them had walked home from dinner at a local restaurant and found their house ablaze, their father standing on the pavement in his scuba-diving suit, waving his arms towards the flames, shouting out profanities and nonsense, his eyes wild with madness.

Clare pushed open the metal gate and the girls followed her up the path towards what used to be the front hallway. She pulled back the plastic sheeting and swallowed hard. There it was, her home. A charred, buckled, disfigured nightmare.

Luckily they'd had a joint account, she and Chris. Luckily everything Chris earned as an independent documentary maker was paid straight into their bank account and was easily accessible. But it wasn't infinite. It would run out one day. And then what? Clare had no skills. No work experience. She could get a job at the school like some of the other mums, but that wouldn't cover rent in central London. That wouldn't keep the three of them fed and clothed. So she eked it out. Pound by pound. And hoped that at some point before it ran out Chris would be well enough to work again.

The girls pushed open the front door. The ceilings were propped up here and there by long scaffolding poles. Clare could barely remember what they'd lost now. She saw blackened lumps of furniture that meant nothing to her any more.

"I hate this, Mum," said Grace. "Can we go now?"

"No," said Pip, "not yet. I want to see it. Properly." She walked ahead purposefully, looking this way and that as though evaluating the situation, as though preparing a report.

Grace turned sharply towards Clare when Pip was out of earshot and said, "Why did you marry someone who was mad, Mum?"

Clare swallowed. Neither of her girls had ever used the "M" word before to talk about their father. She'd told them it was politically incorrect. That their father was mentally ill. She resisted the urge to reprimand

Grace for the transgression and said, "I didn't know he was."

"Yeah you did."

"Well, I didn't know how deep it ran. I didn't know how bad it would get. I thought it was a phase."

"You thought you could save him."

"What?"

"You thought you could save him," she repeated.

Clare blinked at her eldest daughter. "Where on earth did you get that from?"

Grace shrugged. "Nowhere," she said. "I just think it."

What did a twelve-year-old girl know about the intricacies of adult relationships? Clare wondered. And was she right?

"I wish I had a different dad," Grace said.

"Oh, Grace, that's so unfair . . ."

"No. It's not unfair. It's true. I wish I had a *normal* dad."

"But then you wouldn't exist. You and Pip. You wouldn't be here."

"Yeah, well, I wouldn't know, would I? So it wouldn't matter."

Pip appeared then, looking pale and shaken. She turned to face the door. "Can we go now? I've seen enough."

Clare watched as her daughter strode past her and through the front door. She and Grace followed behind. Pip did not speak the whole way back down Fitzjohn's Avenue, and when they got home she headed straight into her bedroom without saying a word.

Dear Daddy,

Mum took us to see the house yesterday. It was my idea. I thought it would make me feel better. But it didn't. All I could think was that it was like a nightmare. All of it was like a nightmare. I try not to think about it. Try to pretend that that wasn't you on the pavement that night. Just some crazy man we don't know. Usually that works. But yesterday it all felt really real again. Like it had only just happened.

At the house I went into the kitchen. The table and chairs were still there. They looked like they'd been painted black. There was a vase of flowers on the table. The vase was black and so were the flowers. Everything was black. It looked like it had all been cut out of black paper. Like one of those silhouette books. Except for one thing — the calendar on the wall, the one with the photos of me and Grace on all the months. It was just hanging there. Like nothing had ever happened. And it was stuck on November. It was a photo of me and Grace on the terrace in that house we stayed at in Turkey last year. In our pyjamas. And we looked so happy. And there was stuff written on it, stuff that was going to happen that week. And one of the things was that we were going to go to the animal-rescue centre to look at kittens. And I know it's not like everything was perfect before that night. I do know that. But things can't have been so bad if we'd been thinking about getting a kitten. And now I don't suppose we'll ever get a kitten. Because only normal families get kittens. And we're not one of those any more.

I can't write any more today because I'm feeling too weird.

I still love you though,

Pipsqueak

xxxx

CHAPTER
FOUR

"Do you want the bad news or the really bad news?"

Leo stood in front of her by the hob, his mobile phone in his hand, looking sheepish.

Adele tapped a lump of mashed potato off the masher and stared at him. "Oh God." It was going to be something to do with his father. She had guessed by the tone of his voice. The very particular flatness of it, as though he was talking in his sleep.

"He's coming. To stay."

"Oh. *God*." She poured more milk into the mashed potatoes and stirred them hard. "When?"

"Well, that's the first instalment of bad news. The second is, he's on his way. Now."

"What!"

"He's just landed at Heathrow. He said he'd been trying to call for days. I reckon he'll be here in about an hour and a half. Maybe less."

"You are kidding me! Why!"

"Urgh, Christ, something to do with a hospital appointment. Some kind of operation. I didn't really catch the detail."

Adele envisaged her spare room full of Gordon and his things, and not just that but an *ill* Gordon, a

Gordon with dressings and medications and tiresome requirements around the clock. "Tell me Affie's coming. Please!"

"It doesn't sound like it."

"Oh. Jesus Christ. Why not!"

"I don't know. He didn't say. There were tannoys going off in the background and I just wanted to get him off the phone before he asked me to come and pick him up."

It was six forty-eight. The girls were in the living room with their new friends from the garden, the tall sisters with the curly hair. Dinner was almost ready. She'd intended to invite the two sisters to stay. The five girls seemed to be getting on so well together and it was the first night of the May half-term and the evening air was warm around the edges and the sky was still blue and she'd been going to suggest they could put on a movie after dinner and have a kind of sleepover without the sleepover. But now she'd have to ask the sisters to leave, they'd all have to scoff down their supper and then be on best behaviour for the arrival of the man the girls called Puppy, although he was far from adorable. She'd have to clear out the spare room of all her teaching stuff and find fresh towels and, oh *God*, send someone out for cows' milk because he wouldn't countenance the almond milk they drank at home, and some white bread because he claimed bread with bits in it was a pneumonia risk.

Gordon Howes.

Horrible old pervert.

His first words to her had been, "Your cups runneth over, young lady," as he peered down her dress and into her cleavage. He was a handsome man, taller then than Leo with the same head of thick dark hair and chocolatey eyes. But even back then, when he was still only in his fifties, he'd had the porous red nose and rheumy eyes of the heavy spirit drinker and the swollen overhanging belly of a man who enjoyed rich late-night suppers in fabled London restaurants where the staff knew him by name. He had diabetes now and apparently his feet looked like rotten cauliflowers. But in his time he had been a force of nature, a sex-fuelled party animal and carouser. His reputation still lived on in the garden. "Oh, *Gordon*," people would say and then regale her with some terrible tale of breast-fumbling or skirt-lifting or bum-cupping. And according to this reportage, age hadn't been much of a barrier to Gordon's attentions. Fifteen or fifty. It didn't seem to matter as long as there was something to grab hold of.

And now here was Adele, forcing a five-pound note into her eldest daughter's hand, saying, "Go, quickly, you need to get Puppy some milk and some bread. And, oh" — even though he didn't need it, did not deserve it — "one of those Mr Kipling chocolate-cake things he likes, you know, with all the layers." She'd seen him devour a whole one of those in an evening last time he was here. Every ten minutes or so, stretching himself from the sofa, as if about to go somewhere; Adele or Leo saying, "Everything OK? Can I get you something?" And Gordon, crumbs of cake still embedded in the cracks around his mouth, saying,

"Thought I might just sneak another bit of that delicious cake."

"We're killing him," Adele had whispered loudly to Leo in the kitchen as they slid the last slice of cake off its cardboard bottom and on to Gordon's plate.

"Yes," Leo had whispered back. "I know."

A taxi drew up on the kerb beyond their front door exactly an hour from Gordon's phone call. They all glanced at each other in panic, all apart from Willow who had no truck with her Puppy and couldn't understand why everyone else was getting so worked up. The taxi's engine rattled and banged, matching Adele's heart rate, then there was the sound of the taxi door being slammed shut, a cheery farewell from the taxi driver (for all his many faults Gordon was an excellent tipper) and the ominous rumble of suitcase wheels up the front path. Nobody moved until the doorbell rang.

"Hello, Dad."

"Hello, hello. Christ. Hello."

Adele pasted on a smile and popped her head around the kitchen door into the hallway. "Hello, Gordon," she said, smoothly.

"Yes," said Gordon, "hello."

He looked worse than ever. He was bursting out of a red linen blazer and a mint-green shirt splattered with whatever he'd had to eat on the plane. In one hand was his stick, a gnarled African thing carved from wood with a bird's head on the top. In the other was the handle of his case, a vast, battered affair, held together in places with parcel tape, and a bulging bag of duty free that clattered together like a milk float. His awful feet were encased in oversized green rubber Crocs. And he was wearing a peaked leather cap on his head of the type favoured by men in 1970s gay bars.

"Christ," he muttered, "I need to sit down. Dear Christ, let me sit down."

Leo snatched his suitcase and his duty free and Adele held open the door to the living room. He lumbered past her and landed on the nearest chair, not noticing the dog asleep on it. "What the bloody hell?" He peered behind his bulky self at the animal he'd almost killed and said, "Was this here last time I came?"

The dog leaped from the back of the chair and ran to the kitchen to soothe itself with food.

"We've had him for eight years."

"Have you? Good grief."

He pulled off his odd leather cap and stroked his dyed brown hair back into place. He grimaced and then seemed to remember himself. He smiled from granddaughter to granddaughter and said, "Now. Let me see. You all look so similar and you've all got those blooming flower fairy names but I'm pretty sure that this is . . . Fern." He pointed at Willow and winked.

Willow shook her head.

"Then you must be Willow? And you — my goodness, look at the size of you — you must be Fern."

Fern nodded shyly.

"Good grief. You were a child last time I saw you and now you're, well . . . remarkable. And Catkin. Taller than your mother now. Taller than your father too probably." He turned and chuckled over his shoulder at

Leo, who at five feet ten had historically been the smallest of the Howes men. Nobody had yet been brave enough to point out to Gordon that he had shrunk substantially and Leo was now a good inch taller than him.

"Extraordinary." He nodded, smiling blandly at the three girls. "Like trees. Like bloody trees."

Adele fetched Gordon a mug of tea and a slice of the chocolate cake.

"This hasn't got that godawful fake milk in it, has it?" he asked in his raspy Big Bad Wolf voice as she passed him the mug.

"No," she said. "Proper gold top."

"Good," he said. "Good."

He put the tea and the cake on a side table and twisted awkwardly to remove his linen blazer. The golden lining was torn in places and stained with old sweat. Adele took the jacket from him gingerly and retreated to the hallway to hang it up.

"Put it on a hanger will you, Mrs H.?" he boomed after her.

Mrs H. It was what he'd called Leo's mother. And what he now called Affie. Adele sucked her breath in deep and hard. She found a hanger and slipped the ancient old jacket on to it. Please, she thought, please let this just be one night.

In the living room she could hear Gordon regaling Leo and the girls with the details of the "sub-par" service he'd experienced at the hands of cabin crew on the way here: "Bloody fifteen-year-old poofs and dolly birds. Not a brain cell among them."

The dog sat by her feet and she patted his head. "I know, Scout, I know. Maybe we didn't feed him enough cake last time, eh? Maybe we should have bought two."

Dusk was falling on the gardens as Clare came to her back gate and peered across the lawn. She saw the mixed-race boy on his bike, a blur on the path behind her. The girls had told him he was called Dylan. Tall for his age, tawny skin, green eyes and a way about him. Grace was besotted and even Pip was in the throes of some kind of pre-teen crush, even if she didn't yet know it. Dylan was the same age as Grace, apparently, and went to one of the many private boys' schools in the area, the ones housed in converted Victorian mansions, which had little liveried buses to take them up the hill to the village and bring them back down again.

Another whizz of rubber against gravel. This time it was the girl called Tyler. She was wearing cut-off dungarees over a cropped T-shirt, her fine blonde hair in plaits, windows of pale flesh exposed on her narrow waist with every turn of the wheels. She stood against the pedals, wiry muscled legs pushing hard to catch up with Dylan at the top of the hill. Clare appraised them. They seemed worldly, for children their age. The way they patrolled these gardens for hours on end, often long after dark, never seeming to eat, never seeming to sleep, as if they inhabited a world without grown-ups.

She remembered something her mother had said, when she'd come to see the flat for the first time: "You won't be able to let the girls out here on their own, you know." She'd thought it a ridiculous statement of paranoia at the time. But as she wound her way through the so-called Jungle, the Secret Garden, the Rose Garden, the playground, and the network of paths that ran around the demi-lune perimeter of the garden, without any sight of her children, she began to wonder if her mother might have been right.

She glanced at the time on her wristwatch. Six fifty-eight. She took the outer path again, this time peering into the back windows of her neighbours' houses. She saw people laying tables for dinner, changing babies' nappies, reading papers, staring into laptops, reaching to put things into tall cupboards. She saw a woman standing in a bath towel, eating a chicken drumstick while staring at the seven o'clock news. She saw a child scoop up a cat and kiss its neck. She saw two men side by side on a sofa with matching beards, eating their dinner off wooden trays.

And then, as she passed one of the big flats in the centre of the crescent, the ones with the twelve-foot windows and big south-facing terraces, she saw a golden dog lying stretched out on its stomach with its legs splayed out around him like a collapsed table. He got to his feet when he noticed Clare looking at him and came to greet her at the garden gate. She crouched to his level and offered him her hand to smell. Through the open French windows, Clare could see into a huge rectangular living room patterned with yellow chinoiserie wallpaper, walls hung with unusual art, a seventies-style glass chandelier, a giant modular sofa upholstered in patchwork fabrics and there, for all the world as if they lived there, she saw her daughters sitting on it.

She rose to her feet and stared incredulously. She felt disarmed. Like unexpectedly encountering her reflection in a shop window. Her children. In a stranger's house. As she looked she saw more children. It was the other sisters. The wild-looking ones who didn't ever seem to go to school. The ones whom her own girls had declared "weird". Yet here they were, ensconced in their living room, looking delighted to be there. Pip looked across and caught Clare's eye. Her face opened up into a smile. She waved and came to the door.

But Grace glanced at her furiously and shook her head. It was code for *keep away*. It meant she was having a good time and did not want it to end.

"Pip," Clare said, "I've been looking everywhere for you."

As she said this the living-room door opened and the girls' mother walked into the room. She wore a clingy black T-shirt dress with a scooped neck and lots of ethnic jewellery. She looked cross and anxious. She said something to her daughters and then she noticed Clare and smiled. "You must be psychic!" she sang, coming to the door. "I was just coming in to tell them they should probably head home because you'd be getting worried." She tossed her head back and laughed. She had those teeth, those big white teeth that looked as though they could withstand anything, and one of those full mouths that was naturally red. She was an attractive woman, sexy and earthy, maybe even a bit dirty. A man walked into the room then and stood behind her. He was attractive in the same way as her: his body was strong and rangy, his face open and honest, his mouth full, his teeth white, his hair thick and tousled. He wore a sludge-green linen shirt with the sleeves pushed up and a pair of stone-coloured shorts. He had a tan and bare feet.

They introduced themselves. She was Adele. He was Leo. They'd love to invite her in for wine but they'd just found out they had an unexpected house guest on the way and it was such a shame because they'd been about to suggest the girls could stay for dinner and they could all watch a movie together. But never mind, maybe next time, they've all been having such a nice time together, and where is it you live? On the terrace, lovely.

They were distracted but friendly and a minute later Adele and the girls were heading back to the flat.

"Seriously, you two, you can't do that. You can't just disappear. Or if you do, at least take your phones with you."

"But we weren't expecting it," said Pip. "We didn't know they were going to ask us to come inside. We didn't know we were going to stay for so long."

"Oh God, their flat is so cool," said Grace. "It's, like, massive and they've all got huge bedrooms and, get this, they're home-schooled."

"Yeah, their mum teaches them. And the younger two have never been to school in their lives!"

"Yeah, and they go on spontaneous trips to museums or, say, if they're learning about World War Two, their mum takes them to, like, Normandy for the night to look at the soldiers' graves . . ."

"Yeah, or once she took them to Berlin to look at where the wall was, for a project they were doing."

"And they can go on holiday whenever they want. Like, literally. You know, like they can wake up in the morning and go: Oh, it's a nice day, why don't we drive down to the seaside."

"Or go to Thorpe Park."

"Yeah."

"So, they're not so weird after all?"

"Yeah, well, they are *quite* weird," said Pip.

"Yes," agreed Grace. "They are a bit."

"In what way?" Clare opened the back gate and let the girls go ahead of her.

"I don't know," said Grace. "They just are."

"But nice?"

"Yes." Grace shrugged. "They're nice."

"Friends?"

Pip nodded and Grace shrugged again.

"Maybe," said Pip.

"Yeah, maybe," said Grace.

"And what about their mum and dad? What did you think of them?"

"Nice," said Pip.

"Yes," Grace agreed. "I really like them. They're really good with kids."

"Good with kids." Clare laughed drily. She'd never been *good with kids*. Not in that playing-at-their-level way. She was good at looking after kids. And good at talking to kids. And good at loving kids. And good at putting her kids' needs before hers. But she'd never been good at playing or mucking about, chucking about, running about, role play, imaginative play. That was why she'd had her babies so close together. Company for each other.

"Yeah," said Grace. "It's like they're both really in touch with their inner child."

She thought of Chris, when they'd first met. She'd had children with him young because he'd had that air about him: that air of innocence and naïvety. She'd pictured him in her mind's eye leaving her to sleep on Saturday mornings, disappearing for hours with their brood of grubby, wild-haired children to have unplanned adventures, returning home later than intended, muddy, pink-cheeked and full of secrets. She'd thought he'd be their playmate.

How wrong she'd been.

"What's the dad like?" she asked, thinking of the smooth-skinned man with the dazzling smile.

"He's really, really, really nice," said Grace, with surprising enthusiasm.

Clare arched an eyebrow. "Really, really, *really* nice?"

She saw her daughter's face flush pink. But Grace didn't say a word.

CHAPTER
FIVE

It was a sunny afternoon, almost warm. Pip had put on a dress, a short one from New Look with a skater skirt. Grace was wearing a loose T-shirt and high-waisted leggings. They both had ponytails. And Grace, Pip had not been able to help but notice, was wearing mascara. There was an unspoken but concentrated effort from both of them to look nonchalant as they headed across the lawn towards the group of children sitting on the benches at the top of the hill. This was all still new. Although they'd hung out at the sisters' flat on Friday night that didn't mean they were automatically accepted into the gang. There was still a long way to go.

Tyler noticed them first. Pip went to put her hand up in greeting but Grace held it firmly down by her side.

Nobody said hello as they approached the group, but Willow inched across the bench she was sitting on so that Pip could sit down, and Catkin turned and smiled. Pip glanced curiously at the other person. He was standing next to Dylan, wearing earphones attached to an iPod. He was very tall, at least six foot, if not more, and he was sort of funny-looking. He seemed too old to be one of the gang, probably about twenty-five, but also too young to be an adult. No one introduced him or explained him and he didn't seem to be at all interested in either of them.

They were discussing the sisters' grandfather, the one who'd been about to arrive when they were there on Friday night.

"Our granddad has to have one of his feet amputated," Willow whispered in her ear.

Pip recoiled. "Ooh."

"Yeah. It's all swollen up and bleeding and his little toe's gone black and they told him in Africa they'd have to amputate it and he said no way, you're not cutting my bloody foot off, and he came to London because he thought they'd say they didn't need to cut his foot off, but they do."

"Yeah, and he is so pissed off," said Catkin.

"And it means he has to stay here for, like, a whole week."

"Maybe more," added Fern.

"And Mum's in a really bad mood."

"We're all in a really bad mood," said Catkin, with a roll of her eyes.

The tall man with the iPod made a strange noise just then and moved jerkily from foot to foot. Pip saw Dylan put a gentle hand on his arm and say, "You all right, Rob?"

The man called Rob nodded, over-emphatically, and adjusted the plugs in his ears.

Another boy appeared then, a boy Pip had seen around, red-haired, younger than the rest of them, probably about eight or nine. He was holding a football. "Wanna kick a ball?" he said to Dylan, flicking his ginger fringe out of his eyes. Dylan said, "Yeah, OK." The boy turned to Tyler. "You?"

Dylan and Tyler both nodded. Then Willow was on her feet and then Catkin. Soon it was just Fern and the tall man with the iPod left at the benches with Pip and Grace. Fern was the middle of the three sisters. She was the quietest and the strangest. Her hair was shaved above her ears and she had a whole row of tiny sleepers arced along one of her ears that looked quite painful. She always had weird stuff written on her hands and picked the skin around her fingernails until her nail beds bled. Her eyes were really big, almost too big for her face, and slightly red-rimmed as though she was constantly on the verge of tears. And she carried a piece of cream silk with her all the time that she ran across her top lip, obsessively. She sat now with her knees pulled up to her chest, watching the others as they scuffed the football around, pick-pick-picking at her fingernails, rub-rub-rubbing the piece of silk. Then suddenly Dylan turned to them and called out, "Grace. Pip. You playing?"

Pip felt her heart fill with blood and throb beneath her ribs. She turned to Grace. They nodded at one another and then at Dylan. Pip couldn't play football. She didn't even like football. But she didn't care. Dylan knew their names. He knew their names and he'd asked them to play. She could feel the nervous energy coming off her big sister in waves. It was coming off her too, coming off her so strong she was scared someone else might be able to see it.

She saw Tyler steal a look at her and then give the same look to Grace. Then she saw Tyler and Fern exchange a strange look. She ignored the smoke-signals, beamed at Dylan and ran towards the ball. She didn't even know where the goal was, she just knew this was sink or swim and if she wanted to be part of this gang she needed to get her feet wet.

Dear Daddy,

Today we played with the gang! At last! It all started on Friday. We were out in the garden after school and the sisters were out there and then it started to rain a bit so they went inside and then the youngest one, who's also the friendliest one, Willow, said why don't you come in? They have the best apartment on the garden. Totally. It's massive and all the rooms are huge. And we were there for the whole afternoon, until seven o'clock. They've got a really nice dog called Scout, and Willow's got a chinchilla in her room called Chester, and her sister Fern's got two rats called Kurt and Courtney. And they are home-schooled! They're about the luckiest kids in the whole world!

Anyway, Willow is really nice, except she never ever stops talking or moving. But the middle sister, Fern, is kind of strange. I think she might be depressed. Or maybe even a bit autistic. And their oldest sister, Catkin, she's OK, a bit full of herself, thinks because she's the oldest of the gang that she knows everything and that we should all kind of worship her. So, it's not like they're the greatest girls ever in the world or anything. But it's good to have got in with them because they know all the other children on the garden. So this morning me and Grace went outside and they were all there and this boy called Dylan — who I think Grace is in love with, but don't tell her I said that, she'd kill me! — asked us to play football and it was so much fun. I even scored a goal and all the kids rushed over and picked me up. Well, all of them except Tyler. I think she hates us. She's Dylan's best friend. They've been best friends since they were babies apparently. Willow told me that Tyler used to walk around the garden when she was a toddler screaming Dylan's name for hours, didn't stop until Dylan's mum brought him out. Everyone in the garden thought it was really cute and funny. And they went to the same nursery together and were in the same class at primary school for a while too. But Dylan got a bursary to a private school in year three because he's so clever. I think Tyler's a bit neglected — that's what Willow says anyway; her mum doesn't look after her properly. That's why she's always outside, because there's nothing for her at home.

Oh. And there was this other boy in the gang today. Except he's not a boy. He's twenty-six. And guess what? He's Dylan's big brother! He's called Robbie and he's learning disabled and special needs and he lives in a residential care home most of the time, but he comes home for holidays and stuff. He's kind of weird, but not scary-weird. Just like he's in his own little world. Dylan really loves him. Dylan really looks out for him. You know, I think Dylan is about the nicest boy I've ever met. Apart from you, of course!

Love you, Dad. When are you coming home?
Your Pipsqueak

"Mrs H.!"

Adele paused, mid-thought, and raised her face to the air like a squirrel hearing an acorn fall. Except this was no acorn. It was her enormous, soon-to-be-one-footed father-in-law. The girls were still on half-term and Adele had been planning to spend the week editing a neighbour's memoirs. Rhea, from the second-floor flat in the block in the corner. Eighty-four years old, a Holocaust survivor from Hungary. Rhea remembered Leo and his brothers as babies. Her own babies were already grandparents and she shared her flat with her nineteen-year-old grandson whom she referred to as her roomie.

Adele had been greedily awaiting this break from teaching the girls, but instead of spending her days sitting out on the terrace with a mug of tea and Rhea's manuscript, she was spending it tending to the needs of an old man with a very painful foot. The foot itself; well, she didn't want to dwell too long on the physical reality of the thing. How he could have got from Bangui via Casablanca on a combined thirteen-hour flight with a foot that was virtually rotten to the core and with at least one gangrenous toe, she had no idea. His wife, a former nurse, had been tending to his foot at home.

But his wife's mother was having cancer treatment and as much as Gordon had probably tried to bully and cajole Affie into travelling with him, she hadn't been able to. Adele had already said there was *no way* she was even going to look at the foot again, let alone touch it. So they'd arranged for a private hospital to send a nurse twice a day to dress it and medicate him. But in between times and while they awaited confirmation for the operation date, Adele was playing nurse.

She put down her mug and turned to look through the patio doors. Gordon was stretched out on the sofa, covered with a blanket, one hand in a packet of Cadbury's Eclairs, the other on the remote control. He was peering out of the window and as Adele walked into the room he said, "Ah, Mrs H. You came! Thank God!"

Adele forced a smile. "What can I do for you, Gordon?"

"Well, first of all can you show me how to get this blasted TV to show me something that isn't a load of middle-aged hags screaming about who does or doesn't do the housework?" He flapped the remote at the television, which was showing *Loose Women*. "And secondly" — he adjusted his position slightly and winced — "I'm afraid I do rather need to visit the bathroom again. If you wouldn't mind just giving me a hand out of this thing." He gestured at the sofa and grimaced.

Adele's teeth ground together with the effort of looking pleasant. "No problem." She offered Gordon her shoulder, wrapped her arm around his back and used her spare hand to pull him up by the elbow.

He puffed and gasped. "Christ," he hissed, finding his balance. "Christ."

He leaned against Adele for a moment. She gripped his elbow, helping steady him. Then she passed him his stick. He took it from her and sighed. "Never thought it would come to this, Mrs H.," he said, sadly. "Really never did." Then he brightened a degree, turned to look out of the window at the communal gardens, smiled and said, "Some of the best years of my life out there. All those endless summers in the seventies, the little ones running about, everyone up to God knows what. Did I ever tell you about the girl who streaked across the lawn with a lampshade on her head? Nobody did ever work out who it was." He chuckled, caressing the wooden bird on his stick. "And whatever happened to that lovely girl, what was her name? Little blonde thing. Mother was the headmistress of the girls' school up the road?"

"Cecelia?"

"Yes!" he clicked his fingers. "Cecelia. That was the one. Pretty, pretty little thing. Whatever happened to her, I wonder?"

"She still lives here," said Adele. "Her mum's in a home now. But Cecelia still lives in the same flat. And she's got a daughter now, same age as Fern. Tyler."

His gaze turned to the window again. He licked his dry lips. "Lovely girl," he murmured. He turned slowly and headed towards the bathroom, shuffling in his huge slippered feet, pausing every now and then to let the pain subside, singing creakily under his breath as he went: "'Cecilia, you're breaking my heart, you're shaking my confidence daily,'" giving a showgirl kick at the doorway and wiggling his large bottom just once before disappearing.

"Good morning, Mrs Wild, this is Don Feild, I'm your husband's treatment coordinator at St Mungo's."

Clare drew in her breath, fearing bad news.

"I'm calling because things are progressing very well for Chris. We've been trying him on a brand-new medication. And we're all completely amazed with the results. We've set up a meeting, later this week, for everyone in Chris's team. To talk about the future."

Clare pulled herself up on to one of the kitchen bar stools and said, "Yes?"

"We were hoping you might want to come along."

Clare fell silent for a moment. She'd kept her distance from Chris so assiduously these past few months that she'd almost forgotten she was allowed to be part of his life. "Not really. I mean, what's the likely outcome of this meeting?"

"Well, the way things are looking right now and going forward, my recommendations will be very strongly geared towards starting a discharge programme. Towards getting him home."

"Home?" She pulled her spine from a hump into a straight line.

"Mrs Wild, your husband is doing remarkably well. He's responded so well to the medications that he's barely the same man who came in here six months ago."

"But, home? What home? I mean, you don't mean here . . .?"

"Well, if not with you then another family member? Chris's mother for example." She heard the sound of papers being moved about. "Susan Wild."

"But she lives in Switzerland."

"Yes, right, I see. Anyone else? Closer to home?"

"No. I don't know. But I don't want him here. Under any circumstances."

"I really think it might be good idea for you to come and see him, Mrs Wild. To see how much he's changed."

"What, the man who set fire to his children's home without even knowing if they were in it or not?"

"Well. Yes. And I understand, obviously, why you haven't been to see him. But I also know that his main objective every day since he's been here has been to get well enough to be accepted back into his family."

Through the kitchen window Clare could see the girls. As with almost every moment of this warm and sunny half-term week, they were with the gang at the other end of the garden. They suddenly seemed unimaginably far away, as though they were on a boat drifting far from shore.

"And if he finds us? If he comes here?"

"Please don't worry, Mrs Wild, nothing bad is going to happen. I promise you. No one will give Chris your new address and you will be absolutely safe. If that's what you want." He paused, as though waiting for her to say something. "Anyway," he said after a moment. "I'll call again at the end of the week. Let you know the outcome. But if everything goes according to plan, your husband will probably be discharged straight away."

CHAPTER
SIX

Adele was standing at her back door holding a large wooden board piled high with wholesome-looking muffins and bars. She shouted out her daughters' names and then indicated that everyone was welcome to help themselves too. The whole gang trooped across the lawn and into the Howeses' back garden. "Fresh out of the oven," said Adele, pouring out plastic beakers of elderflower cordial.

Pip looked at the muffins and bars suspiciously. Were those raisins in there? And the bars looked as though they were full of seeds. She did not like seeds. Or raisins. "Help yourself, Pip," said Adele.

Pip smiled. She didn't want to be rude. She picked up a muffin and tore off a small piece.

Dylan and Tyler took their snacks to the swinging wicker chair in the corner of the patio and squeezed themselves together inside its bulb-shaped basket. Tyler hooked her legs across Dylan's lap. Crumbs from her muffin fell on to Dylan's legs and she pushed them off, nonchalantly, with the side of her hand. Pip watched, curiously, somewhat enviously. She couldn't imagine ever being like that with a boy, particularly a boy who wasn't her boyfriend.

The three sisters sat in a row at the garden table, Adele at the far end with her arm draped across Catkin's shoulders. They were tribal somehow, Pip thought, distinguishable only by their different haircuts.

"Sit down, girls," said Adele, smiling at Grace and Pip as though she thought they were quaint or amusing in some way. "Have some juice."

Adele was wearing a long-sleeved dress with a black and red pattern on it and old black plimsolls. Her thick dark hair was plaited and hanging over her shoulder. She had three holes in her left ear and a tiny pinprick golden stud in her nostril. The afternoon sun caught her cheekbones and the stud in her nose as she chatted with the children and Pip thought she was one of the most beautiful mums she'd ever seen, particularly as she was quite old — at least forty, she reckoned.

After they'd eaten the snacks, the children started to drift into Adele's flat.

"Where's your granddad?" Tyler asked, looking about suspiciously.

"Don't know," said Willow.

"He's having a nap," said Adele. "So try not to be too noisy." Then she disappeared, leaving the children alone in the living room. The sisters arranged themselves across the enormous modular sofa and Tyler and Dylan sat on the floor with their backs against the sofa edge and the dog nestled between them. Pip squashed herself against Grace in an armchair and wondered what would happen next. The atmosphere felt strangely charged. Nobody was really talking. She wondered for a moment if it was something to do with them. If maybe they weren't supposed to be here. She was about to whisper into Grace's ear: *Shall we go?* when Tyler suddenly fixed them both with her chilly gaze and said, "Is it true that your dad set fire to your house?"

Pip felt Grace's body stiffen. "Who told you that?"

Tyler shrugged. "My mum. She said she saw you lot in Waitrose the other day and she recognised your mum from the papers when it happened. Is it true?"

Pip caught her breath and waited for her sister to reply.

"No," said Grace, a moment too late, "it's not true. Our dad's dead. Your mum's wrong."

Tyler picked up her shoulders and said, "Whatever. I could always Google it."

"Feel free," said Grace.

"What's your dad called?"

"I told you," said Grace, "he's dead."

"Then what *was* he called?"

Pip saw Dylan nudge Tyler hard with his elbow. Tyler threw him back a dirty look.

"David," said Grace, again a beat too slow. "He was called David."

Tyler nodded, unconvinced. "So is that why you moved here, then?" she continued. "Cos your dad died?"

"Yes," said Grace.

"What did he die of?"

"Cancer."

"What kind?"

"Lung."

Tyler nodded again. Then she got to her feet and said, "Can we go and play with the chinchilla, Wills?" Her manner was affectedly bored and offhand. She yawned. But though she was feigning ennui, it was obvious to Pip that was she rattled.

After she and Willow had left the room, Dylan turned to Grace and said, "Sorry about that. She can be a bit . . ."

"Yeah," agreed Grace, "what is her problem?"

Catkin stalked across the room to the fruit-bowl and picked up a plum. "She's jealous," she said examining the plum in minute detail, turning it over and over in her hand before finally biting into it.

Grace frowned. "What of?"

"Jealous of everyone, really. But especially of you two."

"What? Why?"

"No particular reason. It's just, you know" — she waved the plum around the room in an arc — "this is her territory. You're the new cats."

Pip and Grace exchanged a glance. "That's really silly," said Pip.

"Yeah, well," said Dylan, getting to his feet and helping himself to a plum from the bowl as if this was his own home, "Tyler's got issues. I mean, her home life — it's quite difficult. She's very insecure."

Pip couldn't work out if he was being defensive or explanatory. Either way she felt strangely put out by the intimate tone of his explanation; there were infinite impenetrable layers of shared history behind his words.

A whole world that had nothing whatsoever to do with her or her sister. An emptiness opened up inside her, an out-of-placeness, and she felt almost as though she was about to cry. But just at that moment they heard the front door bang shut and a male voice and then Leo burst into the room and immediately the mood changed and the tension lifted. "Hello, cherubs!" He kissed Fern on the crown of her head and threw his arms around Catkin and spun her around. "Hello, Dylan, old man. How are you?" He greeted Dylan with a man-hug and a firm pat on the back which Dylan appeared to relish. "And you two." He smiled from Grace to Pip and back again. "Apologies: I can't quite remember which is which, you're so similar. Pip?" He pointed at Pip and she nodded, blushed slightly and Leo said, "Phew!" wiping his forehead.

"Where's Wills?" he asked then, looking around the room.

"She's in her room with Tyler."

"And Puppy?"

"Sleeping," said Catkin. "How come you're home from work so early?"

He flung himself down on the sofa beside Fern and kicked off his shoes. "I got bored," he said. "Kept thinking of my family all loafing about at home in the sunshine and couldn't bear not being part of it. So" — he switched his attention to Pip and Grace — "how are you two getting on in our garden? Do you like it?"

Pip nodded effusively. "It's really good," she said.

"How about you, Grace? How do you like it here?"

Grace shrugged and forced a smile. "It's OK," she said.

"Good," he said. Then he slapped his hands on to his knees and said, "Right, well, I suppose I'd better go and check on dear old Puppy. Make sure he's still all in one piece."

"Or alive," said Catkin.

Leo smiled. "Yes. That too."

He left the room and Pip saw Grace follow him with her eyes. She turned to see what her sister was seeing: a middle-aged man in coloured trousers and a rumpled blue shirt, very slim, nice brown hair, curls of which covered the nape of his neck. He walked with a looseness in his joints, as though his cartilage was made of rubber bands. He walked, she thought, like a teenager.

"Can I use your toilet?" Pip asked Fern, suddenly curious to see what lay beyond the door of the living room.

"Yeah, sure," said Fern, "it's in the hallway, by the front door."

The hallway was high-ceilinged with grey-green walls and black and white encaustic floor tiles. The internal front door, with its panels of glowing stained glass, was ahead of her, and the kitchen to her right.

"Hello, Pip!" said Adele who was sitting at the kitchen table reading a pile of paper with a pen in her hand and black-framed reading glasses on. "You OK?"

"Just going to the toilet," she said.

"Oh, OK, but don't use the one in the hallway, it doesn't flush properly. Use the one in the bathroom, over there." She pointed at the other end of the hallway. "Second door on the right."

"Thank you," Pip said, smiling widely.

There were numerous doors off this part of the hallway. She peered through them as she passed. The first had walls painted dark red, curtains drawn, bed unmade; she heard the scratch of small claws against plastic and thought it must be Fern's room. Opposite this was another bedroom. Here the curtains were open and there was a view across the gardens. A neatly made single bed, clothes hanging from a free-standing rail, inspirational posters on the wall — sunsets and dolphins — this must be Catkin's room. Then came the bathroom, and beyond that three more doors. Pip looked behind her, checking she was out of view of Adele sitting in the kitchen. The door at the far end was open so she went and peered through the door. This was clearly the master bedroom, where Leo and Adele slept: walls painted bright white with a giant futon, colourful artwork and family photos on the walls, an oversized linen light shade hanging from the ceiling and a free-standing bath in the corner with bottles of organic-this and homeopathic-that unguents arranged on its sides.

Hearing footsteps she turned and quickly headed towards the bathroom. As she passed one of the closed doors it opened, revealing a scene Pip hadn't expected to see. A child's bedroom: pink walls, fluff-covered fairy lights, a heart-shaped rug on white floorboards, a basket of soft toys, a white wrought-iron bedstead with twists and flourishes, and there, on the bed, Leo sitting

69

side by side with Tyler, her hand inside his, her head rested on his shoulder.

Willow, who had opened the door, looked at Pip in surprise. "What are you doing?" she asked softly.

"Looking for the bathroom."

"Just there." She smiled. "Next door down."

And then Willow left her own bedroom, where her father sat hand in hand with her thirteen-year-old friend, and she pulled the door shut behind them.

Dear Daddy,

I'm starting to think there's something not right about this garden. Seriously. Yesterday we went into the sisters' flat again, but this time with all the gang, and first of all Tyler was really rude to me and Grace. Well, particularly to Grace. She asked us if we were the girls whose dad burned down their house. But she asked it in a really nasty way, in front of everyone, and so Grace had to lie and say we weren't, but you could tell she didn't believe us and then she stropped off. And then the sisters' dad came home and a few minutes later I went to use the bathroom and when I walked past Willow's bedroom, he was sitting in there, on her bed, holding hands with Tyler. I'm not lying. It was the weirdest thing I've ever seen. And she was all snuggled up next to him. And when Willow left her room, she closed the door behind her, like she was giving them both some privacy or something.

Anyway, I was really freaked out and wanted to leave, but when I came back into the living room, Grace and Dylan were sitting next to each other, looking at something on Grace's phone and laughing and I could tell she was all excited to be sitting with Dylan and she wouldn't want to come with me. So I just left. And after that I walked around the garden on my own for ages. Trying to work it all out in my head. Like, why is Tyler so offish with me and Grace and what the hell is going on with the sisters' dad and Tyler? And what does Dylan's mum look like? And where does Tyler's mum live? And where are their dads? Stuff like that.

I walked past the halfway house. Mum says it's for women and their babies. I could hear a woman shouting at a child and it made me sad. It made me wonder what it's like where you are. Is there lots of shouting? Does it keep you awake at night? Are there scary people there? Do you get scared? I haven't seen you for six months now. I'm starting to forget what you look like . . .

Anyway, there was a woman sitting on a bench in one of the hidden-away corners. She was quite old and very thin and she had a cat sitting next to her in a cat box. The door of the cat box was open but the cat didn't try to get out. And then when I looked closer I saw that she had a huge rabbit on a lead by her feet. A real rabbit, not a toy one. So I couldn't help but smile and she said it was OK to come and stroke the rabbit. He was called Fergus.

He was so soft and calm. This is what he looks like (sorry, I'm not very good at drawing animals!):

The woman said her name was Rhea and that she'd lived on the garden since she was fifteen and she was now eighty-four! She said she'd seen everything there was to see. And then she said a strange thing; she said, "Best to keep yourself to yourself in these gardens. Don't get too involved." She said not to stroke the cat because he would bite.

Then I saw the boy with red hair. His name is Max. He was on his own, just kicking his football against a wall. He didn't say hello.

I went into the Rose Garden. There was nobody in there and I looked at the plaques on the benches. I noticed there was one for a girl called Phoebe. It said: "In Memory of Phoebe Rednough 1977–1992". She was only fifteen when she died. That made me feel so sad I nearly cried.

Imagine dying when you're only fifteen. When you haven't found out what you're good at. And you'll never know how tall you were going to be or how pretty or if you were going to be rich or poor or happy or sad. So I sat on Phoebe's bench for a while and thought about everything. About you. And what you did. And how we could all have died. And maybe then there would have been a bench for us somewhere — someone might have put one on Hampstead Heath. And how someone might have sat on it one day and said: Oh poor things, they were only eleven and twelve. They had their whole lives ahead of them. Next time I see Rhea I will ask her about Phoebe Rednough. I bet she knows what happened to her.

Then the man came into the Rose Garden, Dylan's big brother, the one with special needs. I was polite and said hello but I didn't really want to stay in there on my own with him so I left. After that I went back inside and watched telly with Mum. She was very quiet. I think she misses you too.

Love you, Daddy, more than words can say,
Your Pipsqueak xxxx

CHAPTER
SEVEN

"What do you think of those girls?"

Adele rested her chin on the edge of the roll-top bath and looked at her husband who was lying in bed reading a book.

"What girls?

"Pip and Grace. What do you make of them?"

Leo shrugged. "They seem like perfectly nice children. The older one's a bit frosty but the little one seems charming."

"Did Tyler tell you", she began, "what Cecelia said to her when she saw them in Waitrose last week?"

"No. She did not." He put down his book, showing that he was fully engaged with the conversation. "What?"

"She said that she recognised their mother, from an article in the papers a few months back. An article about a man with paranoid schizophrenia who set his house on fire because voices in his head told him it was infested with alien rats who were scheming to take over the world. Anyway. I Googled it earlier and I think she might be right. Two girls aged eleven and twelve. Mother aged thirty-two. House in Hampstead. Happened last November. The article I read said the mother and children had been taken in by relatives afterwards. It all adds up."

"Christ," said Leo, "those poor little girls."

"I know. Imagine it. Imagine having a parent just go completely and utterly crazy. You know, sectionable crazy. How would you deal with that as a child? How would you make sense of it? And I wonder if they've seen him? I wonder if they visit? Because I must say, I'm not sure, as a mother, if I could face you again if you'd put us all in danger like that."

"But don't forget," said Leo, "for all his faults, the guy did save the world from an alien-rat invasion."

"Leo!" Adele sat upright in the bath and looked at her husband, aghast. "That's not funny!"

"Oh, it is."

"It is not! And listen, you mustn't say a word to anyone. Apparently when Tyler asked the girls about it they totally denied it and Grace told her that their dad was dead. So pretend we never had this conversation."

Leo nodded sombrely. "I hear you."

"So sad." She thought for a moment. "We must make a special effort with those girls. And their mum. You know, maybe we should have them all over for supper?"

"Yes," said Leo, "why not? Maybe Friday next week? When Dad's in hospital?"

Adele smiled at the thought of Gordon being in hospital. "Excellent, yes, Friday week. I'll pop over tomorrow and ask them."

"How's the manuscript going?" Leo asked a moment later as Adele stepped from the bath and pulled a towel around herself.

"Slowly," she said. "You know, Dylan's school are giving them two-week half-terms now. I was half tempted to give the girls the same so I can work on it some more when Gordon's gone." She sat on the arm of the sofa and looked at Leo. "What do you think?"

"I think as long as Catkin's on track with her GCSE studies, then why not? The weather's so nice. I might even take some time off work too."

"Really?"

"Yes, why not? I can take the girls off your hands maybe, do a day trip or two. It's the least I could do to repay you for looking after my old bastard of a father all week. It's the least I could do to repay you for everything you do. Seriously."

"I really do love you sometimes, Leo."

"Sometimes?"

"Yes, sometimes. Sometimes I hate you."

"But right now you love me?"

"Yes. Very much."

Leo smiled, wolfishly, and patted her side of the futon.

Adele let her bath towel fall to the floor, and climbed in next to him.

The following morning Adele put Scout on a lead and walked him around the gardens for a while. The girls were all still sleeping; Leo was showering; she'd taken Gordon his morning toast and jam and water for his painkillers.

It was a pale, bland morning, no cloud, yet no sun, the lawn still dewy underfoot. Scout tugged at the lead and Adele checked the time on her watch. Not even eight thirty. Was it too early, she thought, to knock on Clare's back door? She decided to pass by, discreetly, see if there were any signs of life. The girls said it was the one near the halfway house, with the giant magnolia tree in the back garden. She stood, nonchalantly, on the path outside, pretending to adjust Scout's collar. The light was on in the kitchen, the curtains open in the living room. She saw a head pass the window and the steam of a boiling kettle blooming into condensation on the glass. She came to the back door and knocked gently. Pip appeared, in fluffy pyjamas, her thick curls in disarray.

"Hi," she said uncertainly, her hands tucked inside the sleeves of her pyjamas.

"Sorry," said Adele, "it's really early. I just wondered if your mummy was here."

Pip crouched down to pet the dog and called over her shoulder for her mother.

Clare, thankfully, was dressed. She looked both surprised and displeased. "Oh," she said, "hello."

She was a funny little thing, Adele observed. Made from tiny bones, with a pale, almost peaky face framed by an urchin cut of soft bleached hair. She wore no make-up apart from a coat of the kind of mascara that gives you unnaturally long eyelashes. The overall appearance was that of a newly born lamb.

"Hello, don't know if you remember me, I'm Adele, mother of the three girls . . ."

"Yes," said Clare, "I remember. From across the garden."

"Yes!" said Adele. "That's me and it was lovely to meet you the other day and I wanted to say I'm so sorry I couldn't ask you in or stop and chat but, like I said, we had a last-minute house guest on the way and anyway . . . we were thinking — me and Leo — the girls all seem to be getting along so well and we wondered if you might all like to come over for supper one night. We were thinking maybe Friday next week? My father-in-law will be in hospital then and we'll be a lot more relaxed. And nothing fancy. Just a pie or something?" Adele knew she was babbling, but she couldn't quite stop herself. It was something to do with the way Clare was staring at her as if she was waiting impatiently for her to get to the point. But the point had been reached and passed, yet still the words fell from Adele's mouth.

"Would you like that? And obviously if you have a partner or someone else you wanted to bring . . .?" Adele looked beyond Clare into her flat; it was immaculate. Horribly so. White walls, grey sofa with four carefully arranged red felt cushions, small square table with three wooden chairs, laminate flooring, nothing on the walls. It was the sort of clinical interior that chilled her heart. But of course, she realised, if Clare's husband had burned down her house then she'd have had to start from scratch. All her photos gone. All her clothes. All her children's drawings. Adele couldn't even begin to imagine what that would be like.

"Er, yes. Of course. That would be lovely."

"Good! Great! Come at seven. I'm sure I'll see you before. But if not, anything you don't eat? The girls?"

Clare shook her head and said, "We'll eat anything."

Pip looked up from where she was still crouched down petting Scout and said, "That's not true! I don't like meat. Or ravioli. Or any green vegetables. Apart from green beans. And I hate lentils and things like that. And coconut. And things with bits of —"

"OK, Pip, thank you," said Clare, smiling conspiratorially at Adele. "I think we get the message."

Adele laughed. "Great. I'll try to bear that all in mind. And I'll let you get on. Sorry to disturb you so early. Have a good day."

Adele tugged at Scout's lead and let him walk her home.

Clare didn't know what to make of it. An invitation to supper with the glamorous couple across the way. She'd said yes because it was eight thirty in the morning and she hadn't even had a coffee yet. Caught in the twin beams of Adele's shining brown eyes and dazzling smile, she couldn't work out how to say no.

Pip didn't seem too taken with the idea either. "Do we have to go?" she said.

"I thought they were your friends?"

"Yes, sort of. But I just don't really want to go there for dinner."

"No," said Clare. "Me neither."

She hadn't told the girls about their father yet. Pip would be delighted. Grace would be terrified. It could set her right back to where she'd been just after it had happened. Nightmares every night. Refusing to go to school. Refusing to eat.

She'd keep it to herself, for now. Because even if they did let him out and even if he did find his daughters, what would he do? He wouldn't harm them, she was pretty sure of that. He would just want to talk. He would just want to spend some time with them.

But even as this highly reasonable summation of the situation passed through her consciousness it was overwritten by the memory of him last November, standing, ridiculous in his wetsuit, oblivious to the crowd of people surrounding him, the dancing flames reflected in his crazed eyes, the dark, nonsensical words spilling from his mouth. She remembered her daughters' faces, golden and red in the light of the fire, pulling Pip back from going to her father, silent tears pouring down Grace's cheeks as she shuddered inside her arms, and then her whole body arching, tensing as she cried, "But my homework's in there! And my new jacket! And" — she'd clapped her hands over her mouth, eyes wide with horror — "my piggy bank with all my money in it!"

Three things amongst so many. Clare sometimes lay awake at night trying to compile a mental inventory of what had gone. She'd get 3 per cent into it before giving up. Baby teeth. Hairbrushes. Her favourite All Saints cardigan that went with everything. The cookbook with the recipe in it for chocolate birthday cake which was the only one she'd ever used. The book she'd been halfway through reading. Diaries. Hairbands. All her silk underwear. Linen. Towels. The vintage velvet cushions from her grandma's house. Six orchids in full bloom. Her laptop. Her camera. Passports. Half a box of expensive chocolate truffles. Her brand-new sunglasses. Her wedding dress.

They'd come to this flat with nothing and were building themselves back to normality sock by sock, cushion by cushion, spoon by spoon.

"I'll tell them we can't come," she said, her hand on Pip's crown. "I'll tell her something came up."

Grace walked in and caught the end of the exchange. "Tell *who* something came up?"

"Adele," said Clare, "the sisters' mum. She asked us over for supper next week."

"But" — Grace looked from Pip to Clare and back again — "I want to go. Why aren't we going? I really want to go!"

Clare regarded her daughter curiously. "Really?" she said. "Why?"

"I just do," she said. "I like it there. I like them."

Clare looked at her daughter's bright face and then looked about her at their flat. They'd come such a long way but this place was not yet a home. And maybe her daughter had found a place that felt, for whatever reason, like home to her.

"But, Mum, listen." Grace bit her lip. "I told the girls a lie. About Dad. I told them he was dead."

Clare rocked slightly on her feet. "Wow," she said. "Did you?"

"Yes. Tyler asked us if we were the people whose dad burned down their house and I just said we weren't. And I could tell she didn't believe me so I said he was dead. Just to shut her up." She cast her eyes to the floor and shifted from foot to foot. "I'm really sorry."

Clare took her daughter in her arms. She was the same height as Clare now, and a stone heavier. But there was still that residual smell to her, that essential perfume of the child she used to be. "That's OK. That's fine. I understand. We'll just change the subject if it comes up. OK?" She felt Grace nod against her shoulder.

Then she smiled and held Grace at arms' length, staring deep into her hazel eyes. "That's probably why they've asked us," she said. "They feel sorry for us!"

"I still don't want to go," said Pip.

"It's fine," said Clare, as much for herself as for Pip, "you and I will eat and run. And if Grace wants to stay on and play with the girls afterwards . . .?" Grace nodded effusively. ". . . then she can. We'll just say you've been ill and need to go to bed. OK?"

Her girls both nodded and smiled.

Clare felt a brief moment of parental satisfaction — a compromise painlessly reached — before it was overtaken by a wave of nervous energy that went straight through her gut like a storm. Dinner. With strangers. Her daughters finding safe places away from her. Lies to cover up. Secrets to keep. And all the time, as a throbbing, ominous backdrop, her husband, back to health, ready to re-enter the world. And possibly turn it upside down.

CHAPTER
EIGHT

Pip couldn't stop thinking about the giant rabbit called Fergus. All weekend she'd replayed the sensation of his soft fur beneath her fingers, the twitch of his nose, the big fluffy humps of his haunches. After lunch on Sunday she sought out the old lady called Rhea. Grace was indoors doing last-minute panicky homework. The sun was out but it wasn't that warm; there were people scattered here and there. Pip kept her fingers crossed inside her fists as she walked. *Please let the rabbit be there*, she chanted to herself, *please let the rabbit be there*.

At the far end of the garden she saw Dylan and Tyler sitting side by side on a bench, looking at Dylan's smartphone and laughing. Dylan looked up and saw Pip approaching; he beckoned to her to join them, but she didn't want to. She smiled and shook her head, pointing towards the Secret Garden.

She saw the toe of Rhea's trainers as she turned the corner. They were big, white, trendy trainers with fluorescent pink bits on them. She wore them with black leggings and a black polo neck jumper with a bright pink scarf and finger less gloves. Her white hair was pinned up in a wispy bun. She had a mug of tea by her side and was reading a book. She looked up when she saw Pip standing there and said, "Hello again."

She had a slight accent, a bit German-sounding, Pip thought, or maybe a bit Albanian or Kosovan like some of the mums at her old primary school.

"You've come to see Fergus?"

Pip nodded, resisting the urge to touch him, waiting to be invited.

"Come on then." She brought the giant rabbit up on to her lap and moved over so that Pip could sit next to her. "There you are." She smiled.

The rabbit didn't look at Pip. It seemed to be on a permanent mission to observe its environment in minute detail. "You can take him for a walk if you like," she said.

Pip beamed and nodded.

"There you go." She passed Pip the leads to the harness.

"Why is he so big?" she asked.

Rhea smiled, the fine white skin of her face folding into a lattice of Fortuny pleats. "He is a Giant Flemish Rabbit. They say they are bred from Labradors." She shook her head and laughed. "But I don't believe that. I think they just kept breeding very big rabbits together until one day they produced one the size of a dog. And then they thought: Aha! Look how big this rabbit is! It must be related to a dog! But look at him. There's no dog there. Look at his perfect little bunny bobtail!"

The rabbit tugged at the lead and Rhea smiled and said, "Go!"

Pip walked him into the Secret Garden. He lolloped and sniffed and twitched and jumped. He found some leaves that he liked the look of and began to nibble but Pip pulled him away, in case they were not the sort of leaves he should be eating. Then she walked him around the paths between the Secret Garden and the Rose Garden. A small boy watched her in disbelief and then ran to tell his mother that he'd just seen a really giant rabbit. She saw Fern sitting alone in the Rose Garden. She was reading a book, with earphones in, using her spare hand to pass the weird piece of silk back and forth across her top lip. She glanced up briefly at Pip with her big, damp eyes and then she looked away again. Pip paused, not sure if she should say hello or be friendly in some way. But then Fergus tugged again at the lead and she took him back to Rhea.

"Did you enjoy that?" she asked.

"Yes. He tried to eat some leaves but I didn't let him in case they were poisonous."

"Good girl," Rhea said. "How old are you?"

"I'll be twelve in a couple of weeks."

She nodded. "And have you been living here long?"

"Since January. Six months."

"Have you made many friends?"

"Sort of."

"The sisters?"

"Yes. And someone else called Tyler. And a boy called Dylan."

"Beautiful Dylan." Rhea smiled. "Very popular boy."

"He's kind."

"Yes," said Rhea. "He is a kind boy. He looks after his brother very well."

"Robbie?"

"Yes. Robbie. Poor soul."

"What's the matter with Robbie?"

Rhea cupped her hand over Fergus's head and left it there. The rabbit went completely still. "Ah, well, no one really knows. I don't think his poor mother even knows. Just one of those things. Her husband was an old man — sixty, I think, when Robbie was born — and a very, very heavy drinker. Not that I would want to blame him for what went wrong. He was a perfectly nice man. But it does make you wonder . . ."

Pip wasn't sure what it made you wonder about but nodded anyway.

"Anyway, Dylan's mum, Fiona, she couldn't cope after Robbie's dad died, it was all too hard, so she put Robbie into a nice place just outside London when he was about ten. And then suddenly Fiona is pregnant at forty-five and nobody knows who the father is and then there is this beautiful, beautiful little boy and still nobody knows who the father is. Nobody asks and she tells no one."

"Where does Dylan live?"

"Up there." The lady pointed at three tiny windows in the attic floor of the same house that the sisters lived in.

"And where does Tyler live?"

"She lives there." She pointed at the mansion block in the easternmost corner. "Her mother is a social worker so she gets the nice big flat for the good rent."

"And where do you live?"

"I live just here." Rhea turned and pointed at the mansion block behind her. "That one on the second floor with the balcony with all the flowers. I was a nurse, you see, so I too get the nice big flat for the good rent."

Pip nodded and stroked the rabbit from its crown to its haunches. She didn't really understand about the big flats and the good rents. But she was enjoying talking to Rhea, who seemed to know everything about everyone and was able to answer all of the questions she'd been too shy to ask the children in the gang.

"Who was Phoebe Rednough?"

Rhea glanced at her quizzically.

"Sorry," said Pip. "I think I pronounced it wrong. The girl whose name is on the bench in the Rose Garden?"

"Ah, Feebee Redknow."

"Rainbow?"

"No," said the lady, patting Pip's knee, "although that would have been a very suitable name for her. No. Her name was pronounced Redknow."

"Did you know her?"

"Yes. Yes. Everyone knew Phoebe. She was an adorable girl. A bit wild, but adorable. So cheeky, very clever. Very pretty. Everything sort of revolved around her."

Pip felt vaguely jealous of this dead girl. She sounded like everything she would like to be.

"There was a gang of children then too of course, there's always a gang on this garden. There were all the

Howes boys — you know, Leo and his two brothers. And there was Phoebe's little sister, Cecelia, you know, Tyler's mum —"

"Tyler's mum?"

"Yes. Phoebe would have been Tyler's aunty if she was still alive."

"Oh," said Pip. Phoebe Rednough felt suddenly brought to life. "What happened to her? To Phoebe?"

"Well, when she was fifteen years old she was found dead in the garden." Rhea shrugged. "I saw her from my balcony, covered in the morning dew, her hair all spread about, like Ophelia. Nobody ever really knew what happened. Drugs. Alcohol. Some kind of accidental overdose. *Inconclusive.* They had to bury her without ever knowing the truth. And of course the gossips went into overdrive." She stopped and looked at Pip from the corners of her eyes. "Is this too grown-up for you?"

Pip shook her head.

"Well, Phoebe was linked to two of the Howes boys at the time of her death. She'd been going out with Patrick, who was the same age as her, for a few months. They were love's young dream, Romeo and Juliet. But then, according to various gossips, the older brother had been involved with her too."

"Which one?"

"Leo. You know." She nodded towards the centre of the crescent. "That man over there with all the daughters. He was a good three years older than her. An adult!" She threw her arms out from her sides, then tugged at the edge of her pink scarf. "He said he was

88

not involved with her. Who knows if he was telling the truth? Only Phoebe knows what really happened that summer, and that poor child is dead."

"Do you like him?" Pip asked. She drew in her breath, feeling she'd asked an important question.

"Leo?"

She nodded.

"Oh, I don't know him all that well," she said. "But I knew his father. Gordon." She pronounced it as two words. Gore. Don. "And if his son is anything like him then ..." She rolled her eyes theatrically in their sockets. "Well, then, God save his soul." Rhea looked at Pip thoughtfully and said, "What about you? Do *you* like Leo?"

Pip smiled shyly. "I don't know," she said. "I think so."

Rhea picked up her rabbit and tucked him under arm. "Trust your instincts," she said. "You'll find they're nearly always right."

Dear Daddy,

So much to tell you, I don't know where to start. First of all we've been invited for dinner at the sisters' house. Mum and I really don't want to go but Grace really does so we're going to go and Mum and I will come back early. I think it's going to be so weird. Mum's not really ready for that kind of thing, she's still all thin and nervous after what happened and she hasn't really been out anywhere since we moved in here. Anyway, the really exciting thing happened yesterday. I went into the garden to find the old lady with the rabbit and she was there and she told me loads of stuff about the people on the garden. And I asked her about the girl on the bench, Phoebe Rednough, and she told me that Phoebe was found dead in the garden one morning and no one ever knew why!! She said there was drugs and alcohol but that it was all a mystery! And she also said that Phoebe was going out with Leo's (the sisters' dad) little brother when she died but also people thought she might have been going out with Leo too even though he was three years older than her! And also that Phoebe is Tyler's mum's sister! So the girl on the bench is actually Tyler's aunt.

I just can't believe that a girl could die and be buried and nobody knows why or what happened? I tried to get Grace excited about it but she was just, like, leave me alone, I'm trying to do my homework. And I won't tell Mum because she wouldn't get it. She doesn't get much these days. She's in her own little world really. I feel like I'm the only person in this family who's normal. The only one who's the same as they were before the thing with the house. If you were here you could help me find out about Phoebe. It's the sort of thing you'd be really good at. Maybe you could even have made a documentary about it. You could have called it *The Secrets of the Garden*. Or *Whatever Happened to Phoebe Rednough?* Maybe it would have won an award . . .

I thought I saw you today. When I was coming home from school. I saw a man who looked just like you. Except much thinner. With shorter hair. And a beard. He looked at me and I looked at him and I almost called out your name, but I managed to stop myself.

I love you, Daddy, and I miss you every minute of every day.

Be really good and maybe they'll let you come home?

Your Pipsqueak xxxxxxxxxxxxxxxxxxxxxxxxxxxxxxx

CHAPTER
NINE

Clare was trying to dress for dinner at the Howeses. She'd had to buy all her clothes from new after the fire. It had seemed mildly exciting at the time, the sort of experience her teenage self would have dreamed about: a five-hundred-pound budget and a whole new wardrobe. In reality it had been stressful and unsuccessful. Nothing really went with anything else plus she'd bought everything in a size eight and was currently closer to a size six and now it was June and everything was either too big or too warm.

She knocked at the door of the girls' room. "Girls, can I come in?"

Pip opened the door.

"I haven't got anything to wear. Would you mind if I had a quick look through your wardrobes?"

"I know what would look *great* on you," said Pip. "Hold on." She rifled through the wardrobe and pulled out a black lawn playsuit with wide shoulder straps and a drawstring waist. She held it up against Clare and appraised the effect. "You know, I think it might actually be too big for you. But try it on anyway. You look lovely in black."

Clare eyed the playsuit uncertainly. It was warm out, but possibly not quite warm enough for such a tiny thing. As if reading her mind Pip reached back into the wardrobe and pulled out a small black cardigan with a sequinned collar. "There," she said passing it to her. "Try it on."

Clare smiled and took the outfit to the full-length mirror behind the door where she was startled to see Grace sitting cross-legged on the floor, applying make-up. And not just her usual special-occasion coat of mascara, but lipstick, eye shadow and wings of black eyeliner too.

"Gosh," she said. "Grace, that's an awful lot of make-up."

Grace shrugged.

"No, seriously, Grace. You're not even thirteen yet."

"I'll be thirteen next month."

"But that's not the point. Even thirteen is too young for that amount of make-up."

"Says who?"

"Says every mother of a twelve-year-old girl!"

"That's not true. How do you even know that's true?"

"More to the point, Grace, we're only going across the garden for supper with another family. I could maybe understand if I was taking us out to the Savoy. Who are you making yourself up for?"

"Nobody," she snapped. "For myself."

"But there won't even be any boys there."

"What has this got to do with boys? I don't dress for boys, Mum. I dress for me. And given that this is the first time in, like, *six months* that we've been invited anywhere — you know, like even *left the house,* can you blame me for wanting to look nice?"

Clare breathed in. She had barely seen Grace this week. Every day after school she would change out of her uniform and head straight out into the garden. She didn't even come in for tea half the time. Clare would have to keep things warm for her under tea towels and tin foil or occasionally just admit defeat ("I am not eating cold risotto!) and give her a bowl of cereal. Most of the time she was on the benches at the top of the garden. Other times she'd disappear entirely and Clare would text her, plaintively: *Where are you? At girls' house,* would come the reply. And finally she would appear in the back doorway at seven, eight o'clock, smelling of fresh air and indifference.

"Fine," said Clare, "but you do not need make-up. And frankly, you look ten times better without it."

She stepped into the black playsuit that belonged to her eleven-year-old daughter. It fell off her. She took it off, looped it back on to its hanger and handed it to Pip. "Never mind," she said. "I'll just put my jeans on, I think."

At the door she turned to look again at Grace. She was angrily applying a second coat of mascara. She looked brittle and bizarre. Behind her, Pip shrugged, an adult gesture as if to say: *What can you do?* Clare shrugged back and headed to her bedroom where she sat down heavily on the edge of her bed and let her head drop on to her hands. There was something wrong with the shape and texture of her world. While her

94

children grew bigger and stronger, outgrowing clothes and shoes, outgrowing their own mother, she was shrinking to the size of a doll. While they spread their wings, found new friends, new places to spend their time, new ways to look, she was turning into a recluse.

She pulled on her too-big jeans and a black lacy tunic top. She fluffed up her white blonde hair and put on a coat of red lipstick. She faced herself in the mirror: Clare Wild. What would Leo and Adele make of her? A young mum. A single mum. A thin mum. Would they find her engaging? Peculiar? Hard work? Would they like her?

"Girls!" she called into the hallway. "Are you ready? Time to go!"

She almost didn't recognise her own daughter as Grace appeared before her. She was thrown momentarily, unnerved by the presence of what appeared to be a second grown-up. Her brown curls were plaited tightly away from her temples, bursting out into a voluminous cloud behind. She wore skintight jeans and a fitted grey T-shirt showcasing her small high breasts and her flat stomach. When had she lost that roll of puppy fat? Clare wondered. Her liner-winged, almond-shaped eyes appraised her coolly as if to say: *Don't dare say a word.*

Clare didn't. Instead she smiled and picked up the bottle of wine she'd bought earlier and a small potted orchid and said, "OK, girls. Let's go."

Adele greeted them at the kitchen door in a patterned chiffony thing over a black vest and leggings. Her dark hair was twisted into a big bun on top of her head with a pair of black-framed reading glasses nestled into it. "Hello! You came!"

She leaned in and kissed Clare on both cheeks. Then she grasped the girls' hands and told them to "go straight through, the girls are waiting for you!"

Pip followed Grace into the living room where they found Catkin and Willow behind a drinks trolley, mixing up cocktails.

"No," Catkin was saying, pulling at the neck of a bottle of vodka in Willow's hands, "that's way too much. *No! Stop!*" She snatched the bottle fully from Willow and said, "Now pass the vermouth. No, not that one, *that* one."

Pip watched curiously. Were they going to be drinking cocktails tonight? Nothing much would surprise her about this family. Then Adele walked in and said, "How are those vodka martinis coming along?"

Catkin pushed a lid on to a metal flask and began shaking it up and down. "Nearly done," she said, "but they might be a bit strong." She threw Willow a withering look.

Pip watched as Catkin carefully poured the cocktails into wide-topped glasses and arranged olives on the rims. Then Willow placed them on a tray with small plates of nuts and crisps and subserviently offered it around. Pip thought back to the old days when they still lived in Willoughby Road, before her father had got ill and gone mad, when their lives were relatively normal. She thought of nights when people had come round for dinner and she remembered how she and

Grace would stay in their bedrooms for as long as possible or hide in the living room until it was all over. This was another world entirely.

"What can we get you girls to drink?" said Adele. "We've got the usual: cordials, water, smoothies."

"Have you got Coke?" she asked.

Adele's face folded with disappointment. "I'm so sorry," she said, "no. We don't."

"OK." Pip shrugged. "I'll have a smoothie."

Fern walked in then. She was wearing what looked like a man's shirt unbuttoned over a black vest and low-crotched trousers with multi-coloured high-tops. Her hair was in a towelling turban and her face was streaked blue.

"Fern," said Willow, "what the . . .?"

"I've dyed it," she said offhandedly. "Just the ends."

Pip waited for a reaction. She waited for Adele or Leo to say: *What do you mean you've dyed it? What the hell have you done?*

But instead Adele smiled that contented smile of hers and said, "Oh how lovely, I can't wait to see it."

Then they all changed the subject.

"How's your father?" Clare asked Leo.

"Well, they finally operated yesterday," Leo replied, fixing Clare fully with his dark eyes.

"So the foot's gone?"

"Yes, the foot is gone."

Leo was looking very puffed-up, Pip thought, as though he was trying to be really cool. Pip looked at her mother. She looked quite pretty tonight, she thought. Not in the same way as Adele, with her piles of glossy hair and doe eyes and delicate bare feet with hot-pink toenails. But in a gentle way. She wondered if Leo was thinking that her mother was pretty and if that was why he was acting all puffed-up.

There was a kind of fuzzy, floaty, clubby music playing in the background and the room was all lit up with candles, little clusters of votives in interesting pots and bigger candles in glass jars. The French doors opened on to the patio where more candles flickered and danced. Voices came from outside then and Tyler appeared in the doorway with a woman who could only be Tyler's mum because she was virtually identical to her.

Pip's breath stopped. She sat up straighter. This was Cecelia. Sister of Phoebe — a character from a story come to life.

"Hello! Hello!" Tyler and her mum edged into the living room. Cecelia was holding a bottle of wine wrapped in white tissue.

Leo leaped to his feet. "Cece! You came!" He kissed her firmly on both cheeks, her arms held tightly within his hands. "Adele said she'd asked you but I told her you wouldn't come. I'm very pleased you proved me wrong!"

Cece was very tall with long, dead-straight, blonde hair worn with a fringe. Her face was fine-boned and pointy with the same hard-edged planes as her daughter's. She didn't smile or reciprocate Leo's effusive greeting in any way, just seemed to kind of tolerate it. "Hi, Leo," she drawled in a rough-edged London accent. "Long time no see."

"Well, you know where to find us, Cece."

Cece rolled her eyes as though she'd heard it all before.

She didn't look like Pip's imaginings of a neglectful mother. She was graceful and nicely dressed in a dark blue Lycra dress to the knee and matching flip-flops, her blonde hair in a tight ponytail, a small tattoo of a bluebird on a twig on her delicate forearm and another of a daisy chain around her ankle. Her face was tanned and scrubbed. She looked like the type of woman who went on holiday alone to dangerous places.

"Martini?" asked Catkin.

"God yeah." Cece sighed and flopped down on the sofa next to Pip on the other side of the dog. She had that air about her of someone who was always at the tail end of a very bad day.

Cece turned and glanced at Pip. "And who are you? One of the new girls, yes?"

"I'm Pip."

"And which one is Grace?"

Pip pointed in the direction of her sister.

"Hi, Grace," she drawled. "Good to meet you."

Grace nodded and said, "Nice to meet you too."

Cece's gaze lingered on Grace a little longer than was entirely normal and Pip wished she had a pair of magic glasses that would let her see beneath all the strange expressions and half-meaningless words.

"Hi." Cece held out a long-boned hand to Clare. "I'm Cece. Tyler's mum."

Clare took the hand and squeezed it. "I'm Clare," she said. "Grace and Pip's mum."

"Gosh," said Cece, "how did you get those two strapping girls out of that tiny little body? You're mini!"

"Ah, well, they were a lot smaller then." Clare laughed and Cece laughed and Leo laughed and Pip was really happy to see her mum being sharp and funny.

"You all right over there?" Leo called over to Grace, who was standing by the patio doors looking edgy. "Come and sit down." He patted the sofa next to him and Grace smiled and accepted the offer.

"Here," said Leo, passing her a bowl of nuts, "have some nuts."

Pip saw a bolt of colour pass through Grace's cheeks as she pinched some nuts with her fingertips. "Thanks," she said.

Pip thought again of Tyler sitting on the bed in Willow's room with her head on Leo's shoulder. Now it seemed that Leo had cast some kind of spell over Grace too. She didn't get it. Leo was an old man. He was nice but he was old. She thought of stories she'd read in the papers about men like Leo, nice men, trusted men, men with children of their own. Men who found vulnerable children and groomed them into submission. And Grace was vulnerable. Even Pip could see that.

Adele came in then, wafting patterned chiffon and spicy cooking smells behind her. "Cece! How wonderful! I didn't think you'd come."

"Well, this one insisted." She gestured at her daughter. "Said she wanted me to meet her new friends."

Pip felt surprised. She wasn't aware of being Tyler's friend. As far as she could tell, Tyler merely tolerated them.

"Well," said Adele. "Dinner is served, when you're all ready."

They sat in the kitchen at a long wooden table, battered and worn, covered in graffiti. Leo spent some time selecting the right background music. The sisters laid extra places for Tyler and Cece and lit yet more candles. Adele hefted huge pans from the hob direct to the table and threw serving spoons on the table. A big wad of paper napkins was passed from person to person like notes at a meeting; Catkin filled glasses with wine; Leo dressed a salad in a bright red bamboo bowl. Beyond the kitchen windows the day was fading away; Pip saw a sky bruised violet and grey, the lights coming on in the distant windows of other houses. Her mum was laughing along with all the grown-ups at something funny Leo had just said; for the first time ever, Pip saw Fern laugh out loud and even Grace, sitting between Fern and Catkin, was starting to relax. Pip let her misgivings fade away. This was a happy house. These were happy people. Leo was a good man.

Adele stirred the biggest of the pans with a large spoon. "It's chicken curry. No lentils. No beans. No coconut. Just chicken. Hope that's OK, Pip?" Adele winked at her and Pip smiled said, and said, "That's good. Thank you."

"Lentil curry here." She pulled a lid off another pan. "And sag aloo in here. Get stuck in!"

After dinner Adele told the girls to "get your instruments and play us something". Pip watched in amazement as all three girls filed from the living room and then filed back in again clutching various musical instruments: Catkin a flute, Fern an acoustic guitar, Willow a fiddle. Pip had never seen children playing instruments in their own actual homes before and was mesmerised by the spectacle. The three girls played an offbeat version of "Get Lucky" by Daft Punk which made all the grown-ups laugh and then as an encore they played "Blurred Lines" and Leo got up and did the "Blurred Lines" dancing and then so did Adele, and Pip felt that excruciating stab of embarrassment and discomfort that she always felt when she saw adults behaving like that. She turned her head away slightly so that she wouldn't have to look and sought out her sister to share the pain of the moment, but her sister did not look embarrassed. She looked enraptured, suspended in wonder and delight.

After the music, Pip touched her mum's arm and whispered, "Can we go now?"

Five minutes later they were being hugged and squeezed at the kitchen door by Leo and Adele. *We must do this again. It's been wonderful. Thank you. No. Thank YOU.*

Grace, as planned, stayed behind. *We'll walk her back at eleven? Er, maybe ten? How about ten thirty? OK. Ten thirty. Are you sure you don't want to stay, Pip? Sure? OK!*

As they left via the patio, Pip turned, just once, and peered through the living-room window. She saw

Grace, sitting between Leo and Fern on the sofa. She was holding Fern's guitar and Leo was showing her how to place her fingers on the strings. She saw a look pass across her sister's face as Leo leaned into her, unpicked her fingers from the strings and gently rearranged them. It was a look of what Pip could only describe as sheer bliss.

She turned desperately to her mother, hoping she'd seen it too, but her mother was already on the path, waiting for her. "Come on, angel."

She turned again. She saw Grace look into Leo's eyes and smile.

She almost said something to her mother but she couldn't find any words.

"Coming," she said. "Coming."

Dear Daddy,

I miss you so much. I'm lying in bed writing this to you and Grace is not here. She's at their house, the sisters'. We just had dinner there and it was nice but I wished you were there so much. The you from before, when you used to put me and Grace on your knees and bump us up and down so our voices went all wobbly. Or when you'd open up that big brown coat you used to have and we'd both hide inside it and pretend we were camping inside daddy ☺. And I wish you were here now, lying on the floor like you used to do with your knees up and your hands clasped over your tummy, listening to me read to you. But the hardest thing about you not being there tonight was not even being able to TALK about you. I wanted to say, My daddy makes films! My daddy won awards! My daddy is six foot three! My daddy went to Oxford! My daddy can speak five languages! My daddy is really, really clever and really, really interesting! But I couldn't say anything, I just had to sit there and watch everyone make a big fuss over *their* daddy, who's not as great as he thinks he is but everyone acts like he's just, oh, the greatest man out there.

And Grace was being all weird. You know, she wore loads of make-up and tight jeans and she was acting all cool like she didn't want to be there even though it was HER who really wanted to go. And then the minute Leo started paying her some attention she was fine. I feel a bit strange about it all. I don't know if Leo is a bad person or a good person, I just think Grace is desperate for a dad. She's over there right now. It's nearly ten thirty. Mum's waiting up for her but I needed to come to bed and cry and write this letter to you. This letter that you'll probably never read. Tyler's mum came tonight, you know, the one whose sister died in the garden when she was fifteen, and I wanted so badly to ask her about what happened. But obviously I couldn't.

When are you going to get better and come home?

xxxxxxxxxxxxxxxxxxxxxxxxxxxxxxxxxxxxxxxxx

CHAPTER
TEN

Adele appraised Leo over the top of her reading glasses. "What took you so long?"

He pulled off his T-shirt and draped it across the back of a chair.

"I wasn't long," he said.

"Yes you were," said Adele. "You've been gone for twenty minutes. I even called you, but you left your phone behind."

"I just had a cigarette," he said. "On the terrace."

"I looked on the terrace. About five minutes ago."

"Look, I took Grace home. I chatted to her mum for a few minutes . . ."

"Did you go in?" This came out more inquisitorially than she'd meant it to.

"No, I did not go in. We just chatted at the door."

"And then?"

"I came back. I had a cigarette on the terrace. I took some things through to the kitchen. I went for a pee. I checked on the girls. I came into my bedroom to be verbally abused by my wife."

Adele frowned at him and then smiled. "Sorry," she said. "I just didn't understand where you could be. I looked everywhere."

"Well, clearly not, my dear."

Adele gazed at Leo for a moment. She watched him unbutton the fly on his trousers, wriggle them down his hips, pull off his cotton boxer shorts, drop them in the linen basket. He was naked now, pulling clean pyjama bottoms from a drawer and talking about his father, how he was going to visit him in the morning and maybe one of the girls might like to come with him, it would make the old git happy, but Adele wasn't really listening. She was reading and rereading a paragraph in Rhea's memoir. The words were swimming about in front of her eyes; in part because she'd drunk an awful lot of wine tonight, but also because she didn't quite believe what she was reading.

"Leo," she said. "Is it possible that you used to go out with Cecelia and you never told me?"

He stopped, one leg in his pyjamas, one leg out. "What?"

"Listen." She pushed her reading glasses back up her nose and began:

It is the hottest day of the summer and there is more flesh on view in the garden than grass. The Howes boys are all topless, flaunting their skinny boy bodies with their griddle chests and hairless stomachs; they tuck their hands down their waistbands and swagger about; they smoke behind trees and listen to loud music on their oversized stereos as though they are fresh from the Bronx. But they are fooling nobody apart perhaps from the Rednough girls, tiny blonde things with

backcombed hair and hoop earrings who have
been hanging about like lost puppies all summer,
hoping for some fuss. The younger one, Cecelia,
has in recent days been seen wearing a heavy gold
chain that apparently belongs to Leo. And earlier
today I watched her climb into his lap and hang
herself around his neck and he did not seem
surprised. And now they are walking together,
hand in hand across the lawn, and she looks like
the puppy that got the bone and he looks like he's
wondering which girl he'll go for next.

She lowered her glasses and stared up at her
husband, questioningly.

"My God," he said. "I'd forgotten about that. Ha!"

"What do you mean you'd forgotten about it? How
could you forget going out with someone who you're
still friends with?"

"Oh, God I mean, it wasn't really *going out*. It was
kid stuff."

"But she wrote this in 1992. You were eighteen! And
she was only thirteen!"

"Well, actually I was still only seventeen."

"Only just, Leo!"

"Del. Nothing happened between us. I just sort of let
her hang about with me. She was cute."

Adele's heart hammered in her chest. She'd been
expecting Leo to say that Rhea was mistaken: that
there'd been nothing going on between him and
Cecelia all those years ago. She already knew about his
fling with Phoebe that summer, she knew that his

younger brother had been going out with her and that at some point, after a row with Patrick, Phoebe had made a beeline for Leo. She knew they'd done some clandestine things in the dark of night. She knew that Leo and Patrick had fallen out about it for a long time after, especially in the wake of Phoebe's death. She'd always found the whole scenario quite bizarre, something far from her own youthful experiences. But Phoebe had been fifteen. Only a few months short of the age of consent. She'd already slept with Patrick, and she hadn't, apparently, been a virgin when she slept with him. It was wrong, certainly, for an eighteen-year-old to sleep with his little brother's girlfriend, but it wasn't *weird*.

"We didn't *do* anything. We just cuddled and stuff."

"*Cuddled?*"

"Yes. And kissed."

"You kissed a thirteen-year-old?"

"Once or twice."

"But that would be like an eighteen-year-old kissing Fern. Do you not see how weird that is?"

Leo shrugged and pulled on a T-shirt. "Never really thought about it. It was summer. I was young. She was pretty."

"Did anyone know?" she asked. "Did anyone know about the two of you?"

"There was no two of us. It was a week, maybe less, a bit of hand-holding, a snog or two. There was no 'us'."

"She was wearing your chain!"

"Oh, my God." He groaned. "She asked. I think she'd watched too many American high-school movies. So I said yes."

"Who else knew about this? Apart from Rhea?"

Leo pulled back the duvet on his side of the futon and lay down. "My brothers. Obviously. Phoebe. That's about it. It really wasn't that interesting."

"Did your parents know?"

"I doubt it."

"Her parents?"

"Jeez, Del! Can we drop this now?"

But Adele was suddenly filled with adrenaline. "What did she do when you broke it off?"

"Cece?"

"Yes! Cece! Was she upset?"

"I guess. For about five minutes. And then her sister died, so, you know . . ."

Adele had met Leo when he was twenty-two. Hard to believe that a mere four years earlier he had been snogging a thirteen-year-old girl. She rolled on to her side, so she wouldn't have to look at him. "It's made me feel all discombobulated," she said.

Leo groaned. "Oh, come on. You're not going to sulk about something that happened over twenty years ago, are you?"

Adele breathed out. She put the manuscript on the floor by the bed. She couldn't process any of this right now. For a few moments she and Leo lay silently side by side. She listened to the sound of blood pulsing through her eardrums. She felt the warmth of Leo's skin. She heard cars slowing at the speed bump outside the flat, then quickening again. She heard the dishwasher in the kitchen click and rumble as it neared the end of its cycle. She saw her husband kissing Cecelia.

"You OK?" said Leo, reaching to touch her arm.

"Yes," she said. "I'm fine."

"Good."

He reached behind him to turn on the bedside lights and turn off the overhead light. Then he picked up his Kindle and began to read.

Adele lay wakefully, watching shadows move across the walls.

Clare lay wakefully, watching shadows move across the walls. Leo had brought Grace home half an hour ago. The girls had all had a wonderful time, he'd said. Fern had taught Grace some basic chords. Willow had made some fudge. They'd had quite a bit. He hoped she didn't mind. A little bit of sugar's fine from time to time, isn't it?

He'd stood at her back door in the glare of a security light, his face soft and animated, his body relaxed and springy. He was a ball of energy. Like a teenager. She couldn't help but feel good around him.

She'd wanted to ask him in, but wasn't sure if that was a strange thing to do. So instead they'd continued their conversation at the back door until the security light had gone off and they were in sudden darkness and he'd said, "Well, better get back. Adele will be wondering where I got to."

110

She'd locked the door behind him. Drawn the curtains. But his energy had remained, like soft embers in a grate. She'd held it within her, wrapped her own arms around her body to preserve it. It had been a pleasant evening. She felt better about the choices Grace was making, having spent some time with her "alternative family". Adele was wonderful: warm and vibrant and grounded. Her children were unusual and unconventional. Their flat was lovely. The informal style of the evening had been natural and unforced. But it was Leo who had made the evening for her.

She heard Grace in the en-suite bathroom, brushing her teeth. She appeared a moment later, scrubbed and fresh. All the make-up was gone. Her hair was tied up into a neat bun. She was wearing loose pink pyjamas. She looked at Clare and for a moment Clare couldn't predict in which direction her mood was blowing. But then Grace smiled and climbed on to Clare's bed, curled herself up next to her, tucked her face into Clare's shoulder, minty breath and young scalp. She hooked one leg over Clare's body and nestled even closer. Clare grasped the arm that Grace had flung across her chest and kissed the crown of her head.

"Did you have a good time?"

Grace nodded.

"So did I."

"Good," said Grace.

"Not sure what to make of Tyler and her mum, though."

She felt Grace's head move up and down in the crook of her neck. "They're strange."

111

"Yes," said Clare. "They are. Edgy."

"I know."

"Like they're hiding something."

"Exactly."

They lay in silence for a moment or two. Then Grace stretched herself away from Clare and leaned down to kiss her on the cheek. "Night, Mumsy." She rolled herself off the bed and stood in the doorway.

"Night, baby."

"Thank you for coming tonight."

"My pleasure," said Clare, thinking once more of Leo's dark eyes, his slow smile, his easy manner. "My pleasure."

CHAPTER
ELEVEN

Chris had been released from the psychiatric hospital two weeks ago. The discharge meeting had unanimously decided that he was fit to face the world again and discharged him into the care of an unnamed person. Clare had asked who it was but the hospital told her that Chris had requested that she not be told. She'd spoken to people from their past, the small handful of friends they'd had back in the days when things were normal, but none of them had heard anything from Chris. She'd spoken to his mother in Switzerland, who said she had had a call from him and wired him a large sum of money but that he had not told her where he was staying or with whom.

Over the days Clare had pictured him in a variety of scenarios: homeless under a bridge; hiding in the flat across the road, watching their every move through a crack in the curtains that twitched occasionally when she walked past it. She pictured him on a ferry, trying to get to his mum and brother in Switzerland. Or living in the basement under the house in Willoughby Road, still staking out alien rats. Sometimes she even pictured him normal, sitting sad and alone in a rented room in a house somewhere, trying to remember who he was and where he belonged. She scanned the small news stories in the papers with opening lines like: "A 42-year-old man has been arrested after a . . ." Or, "Police are looking for a man in his forties in connection with . . ." All those funny little reports about people behaving strangely were suddenly thrown into relief. Her husband was out there. He might be mad. He might be sane. He might be ill. He might be well. He could, in theory, be doing absolutely anything. But as the days went by and the ether yielded no information whatsoever about his whereabouts, Clare had become more and more certain that he was dead.

He'd tried to kill himself before. When the girls were tiny. It was a side effect, apparently, of the medication he'd been on at the time. He'd made a very poor job of over-medicating himself and been rushed to the hospital to have his stomach pumped out. After which, the doctors changed his medication.

Clare had never told the girls about it. It was bad enough, she'd reasoned, that they had to live with a man who frequently heard voices in his head telling him to do ridiculous things, let alone to know that their father had once tried to remove himself from their lives completely.

So now when she scanned the papers she looked for the small sad stories about anonymous male bodies being plucked from the Thames, pulled out of abandoned buildings, scraped off railway tracks. If she saw more than one ambulance outside a tube station she would stop and wait, her breath held, to see if a man with brown curly hair and size-twelve feet came out on a stretcher.

Chris being dead made much more sense than Chris being alive.

Until today.

It was the middle of June, the day before Pip's twelfth birthday and she'd just found a carrier bag on the doorstep. She peered inside and a cold dread crept from her gut, up her spine and down her arms: a flash of glossy red wrapping paper and a fat pink rosette and a card with Pip's name written on it in Chris's small scratchy handwriting.

She ran to the pavement; she looked left and right. She even looked at the window over the street with the twitching curtains, the one she'd convinced herself several days ago was a figment of her imagination. Nothing. But of course. If he'd wanted Clare to see him he'd have waited with the bag, not left it on the doorstep.

She brought the bag indoors and placed it on the kitchen counter. She stared at it warily for a moment. That she could be concerned that the man she'd fallen in love with when she was nineteen years old, the man who'd given her everything and asked for nothing, who'd carried their babies on his chest in slings and sung them German lullabies at night, might potentially have wrapped up a bomb or a pile of dead rodents or a box of faeces or a severed finger, stuck a pink bow on it and left it on her doorstep for his youngest daughter to open was beyond any definition of sad.

Gingerly she peeled back the Sellotape strips. She breathed a sigh of relief when she saw what was inside: a pad of cartridge paper, a box of Caran d'Ache pencils, a packet of technical drawing pens, a family-sized bar of Milka Noisette and the new Jacqueline Wilson. She smiled. She almost laughed. For a moment she felt herself transported back to another time, when Chris was a good husband and a good father, when life had been relatively normal. But the moment quickly passed. How had he wrapped it so nicely? Chris had never been able to wrap a gift properly. She'd been picturing him on his own. But maybe he wasn't. Maybe he was living under someone's roof with access to food, clothes, money, the internet — with access to *wrapping paper.*

Chris had friends. He had family. But they'd all turned their backs on him after the house fire. Shaken their heads sadly and said, "Let's hope they can help him in there. However long it takes." Even his own mother had virtually disowned him. "He put his babies into danger," she'd gasped in her strong German accent. "He set a match to their home when they might have been in it. That is not brain chemistry. That's a hair's breadth from evil."

Clare couldn't think of one person from their old life who might have taken Chris into their home.

Except — Clare paused, her hand on the birthday card, her eyes wide with realisation — there'd been that girl, back in 2011. The one who'd worked with him on his last documentary. She'd been *in love* with him. He'd come home after the wrap party, tipsy and giggling, and told her about this girl, *virtually a child*, who'd accosted him at the bar and told him that she wanted him. That she would do anything for him. When he'd laughed her off with a: "Well, I am flattered of course but I am a married man and you are young enough to be my daughter," her eyes had filled with tears and she'd said: "But, Chris, you don't understand. I love you!"

Oh, how they had laughed that night.

"What was her name?" she'd asked.

"Roxy."

"Ha!" she'd said. "*Roxy*. Yes. Of course!"

They'd never talked of her again. All sorts of bizarre things happened to Chris when he was working on a documentary. Lovestruck Roxy was just another bizarre thing. But now Clare was thinking about Lovestruck Roxy in a whole new light. She peeled open the envelope of Pip's card, took it out and looked cautiously inside. Maybe Lovestruck Roxy had shopped for the gifts and wrapped them, but she could not have written in the card.

On the front was a photo of a fat Labrador puppy in a mug. Inside was a fifty-pound note and the words:

To my darling Pipsqueak,

I hope your twelfth birthday is full of joy and chocolate. I wish I could be there but, as you know, I'm not allowed. But I will be thinking about you all day long. Every moment, every second. I promise you.

I got all your letters and I loved them all. Your new home sounds really nice and so does your new school. It sounds like you are making lots of new friends. Look after your mummy and your sister.

Love and bear hugs,
Your Daddy xx

Clare read it twice and then three times, trying to find some germ of Chris's state of mind within. But there was nothing. Pleasant, sane, almost bland. Anyone could have written it. Maybe Lovestruck Roxy had dictated and he'd merely transcribed her words.

She pushed the card back into the envelope and attempted to stick the flap back down. Then she put the gift and the card back into the carrier bag. And as she did so, her hand felt paper. A till receipt. She pulled it out and smoothed out the creases. Tesco Metro. Walthamstow. Two days earlier. One pint of skimmed milk. Bananas. Chocolate granola. *Grazia*. Tin foil. Greek yogurt. Kitchen roll. Large Milka Noisette.

She put the receipt in a drawer and took the bag of gifts to her bedroom where she buried it at the back of her wardrobe.

Rhea was on the bench. She had the cat again, in its plastic box, and Fergus was sitting on her lap eating something from her fingertips.

"Good afternoon!" said Rhea. She was wearing a shiny red polo neck with gold chains at her throat, with ribbed black leggings and Ugg boots. Her lipstick was randomly applied and not quite the same shade of red as her polo neck, but she still looked nicer than most old ladies.

"Hi," Pip replied, sliding on to the bench next to her and putting her fingers towards Fergus's nose.

"And how are you today?"

Pip smiled. "It's my birthday!"

"Ah!" The old lady beamed at her. "Happy birthday to you! And you are twelve, yes?"

"Yes!"

"And did you get some nice presents?"

Pip nodded. "Lots of nice things. And my grandma gave me a hundred pounds!"

"A hundred pounds! My goodness! A whole family could have lived lavishly off that for a month when I was young. What are you going to do with it?"

Pip shrugged. "I'm not sure yet. We haven't got much money any more so I might just save it in case there's an emergency."

Rhea nodded slowly. "Very very sensible. Although maybe you could take just twenty pounds and have some fun with it?"

"Yes," said Pip. "Maybe."

"You want to take Fergus for a walk?"

Pip smiled and nodded. Rhea handed her the lead and let Fergus jump down on to the grass. "What made you decide to get a big rabbit like Fergus?" she asked.

Rhea smiled. She had a dimple in her left cheek that was so deep it looked as though it went all the way through to the inside of her mouth. "Well," she said. "Before Fergus, I had a dog. A little Pekingese called

Daphne. And she lived for twenty-one years. *Twenty-one years!* Do you know how old that is for a dog? So when she died I was too nervous to get another dog in case it too lived for twenty-one years and then I would have to leave it behind. So I worked out that I needed a pet that would last about five years. But I wanted a proper pet, not something that shivers in the palm of your hand or lives in a cage. So I found out about these! And now Fergus is four and I am eighty-four and hopefully we will both pass away together. Maybe next year. Yes, next year would be good." She laughed and Pip laughed, although she couldn't quite see what was so funny about looking forward to dying.

Fergus was full of energy and she let him run up the hill with her sprinting behind. The benches at the top of the hill were deserted today. No sign of Tyler, Dylan and the gang. Maybe they were all at after-school clubs. But as she rounded the top of the hill and headed towards the Rose Garden she stopped in her tracks. Sitting on the bench around the corner was a big man in a wheelchair. His face was red and hot-looking, his hair was a disturbing shade of dark brown and he was wearing pyjamas and a blanket.

"Hello, curly!" he said, grimacing at her. "Jesus Christ! What the holy blazes is that you've got there?" He pointed at Fergus.

She smiled uncertainly and called across, "It's a rabbit," before turning round sharply and dragging Fergus back down the hill. It was only as she reached the bottom of the hill that she registered the fact that the man's foot had been wrapped in bandages and she realised that she'd just encountered the sisters' grandfather, the man they called Puppy.

She ran back to Rhea, breathless with excitement. "I just saw him!" she said. "Leo's dad. He's over there." She gestured towards the Rose Garden with her head. "And he's in a wheelchair!"

"Good," said Rhea. "Where he belongs. Keep the old goat out of trouble."

"Trouble?"

"Oh, you know, some old men, they don't understand boundaries. Do you know what I mean by boundaries, Pip?"

"You mean, like, no means no."

"Yes!" Rhea looked delighted by this response. "That is exactly what I mean. A person's right not to be touched. A person's right not to be ogled. A person's right not to be insulted or abused. You know, Pip, I lost a lot of people when I was young. In the camps. You know?"

"The Holocaust, you mean?"

"Yes. My goodness, you are clearly a girl who listens in class! Yes, in the Holocaust. And then I came here when I was a young girl, not much older than you, and I was so grateful to be alive, to be free, that I vowed that I would not accept even the tiniest infringements of my liberties. Not a careless comment about my religion. Or a sweaty finger rubbing against my leg on a crowded train. And certainly, *certainly* not a man talking about my daughter as though she were a doll for his pleasure. And this man" — her nostrils flared — "in his day!

Well, let me say that I once slapped him. Very hard. Across his big fat face. Like *this*!" She demonstrated a very hard slap, and her eyes shone. "And after that he left my daughter alone. But as for the other girls on this garden." She raised her brow and whistled. "Well, he was popularly known as Gordon the octopus." She laughed and the deep dimple reappeared. "Let us all just be grateful that he's in a wheelchair." They both turned then and watched as Adele strode across the lawn from her apartment towards the hill, her arms folded tightly around her body. She disappeared behind the brow of the hill and then reappeared a moment later pushing Gordon in his chair. Rhea shook her head slightly from side to side and tutted quietly.

"So, Pip," she said, "are you having a wonderful party tonight?"

Pip shrugged. "We're going to Pizza Express. With my granny."

"And your mummy and daddy?"

"Just my mum."

Rhea raised a brow.

"Our dad's in hospital."

"Ah, I see. Nothing too serious, I hope?"

"No. Not really. Just . . ." she tailed off. She couldn't quite find the words.

Rhea nodded and smiled. Pip knew she didn't expect her to explain. "You're not going to take any of your new friends then? To your party at Pizza Express?"

"It's not really a party. It's just a meal. My grandma's paying so I can't really invite anyone else."

122

"Ah. Well." She reached into the small leather bag she wore diagonally across her chest and rifled about for a moment before pulling out a tiny purse with a golden clasp. She clicked it open and peered inside, prodding the contents with a finger before pulling out a two-pound coin, holding it to the light, turning it over, turning it over again and then passing it to Pip. "There," she said. "For spending. Not for putting towards your emergency funds. Happy birthday!"

Pip stared at the coin in her hand. She wasn't sure about the etiquette of the situation. Should she accept the coin? Did the lady need it for paying her heating bills? Or was she very rich? The golden chains told her one thing, the tiny purse with no room for any money told her another.

"Take it!" Rhea folded Pip's fingers over the coin. "Please."

Pip smiled. "Thank you."

"You are welcome. You really are."

Dear Daddy,

Mummy told me you've moved to a different hospital and she doesn't know where it is and that you probably won't get my letters any more. But I still want to write them to you anyway. I'll keep them and give them to you when you come home. Thank you for sending me the card and the present and the money. I cried when Mummy gave them to me. Everything was so perfect. And Granny gave me a hundred pounds and the old lady in the garden gave me two pounds so now

I've got a hundred and fifty-two pounds. It's the most money I've ever had in my life. But I don't care about the money. Or even the presents. The card was my favourite thing. Seeing your handwriting. It was amazing! Thank you!

We had dinner at Pizza Express. It was nice. Mummy seemed to be in a good mood and Granny was just Granny. Even Grace seemed quite happy and it was one of those nights where it felt like maybe everything might be normal again one day. Then a quite strange thing happened after school today. Instead of walking home with me or getting the bus, I saw Grace heading off in the wrong direction and I ran after her and said, Where are you going? And she said, None of your business. So I followed her until I realised where she was going — to Dylan's school. And he was waiting outside for her and they just kind of hooked up like it had all been pre-planned. I followed them all the way back down to the crescent and they went in through the garden gate but I didn't follow them, I just went home and in through the front door. And Mum was freaking out! Where've you been! I've been calling you and calling you! God. I told her my phone had been on silent and I'd been for a walk and I was only twenty minutes late. But honestly, she was, like, hysterical.

And then I went out in the garden to see what Grace and Dylan were doing and they were on the benches OF COURSE and Tyler was there and

Fern. But Willow wasn't there so I didn't go over. I wasn't in the mood and it was a bit cold. Sometimes I feel like they don't really want me in their gang. They only want Grace. I think it's because they know she needs them. Whereas I don't need them at all. So I just went back indoors and decided to write to you instead. Oh! And I forgot to tell you! The sisters' granddad is out of hospital and is in a wheelchair. I couldn't really see if they'd cut his foot off or not, there was so much bandaging. But I saw him out in the garden yesterday and he called me CURLY. I didn't like it very much.

So, so far being twelve has been interesting. But not exciting.

Love you, Daddy! And thank you again for remembering my birthday and getting me such cool stuff,

Your Pipsqueak

xxxxxxxxxxxxxxx

CHAPTER
TWELVE

"You know," said a man, standing very close, his hand passing across her and towards the bread display, "this stuff is absolutely amazing. Best supermarket bread you can get."

Clare looked round sharply. It was Leo. She exhaled and smiled, then turned her attention to the bread in question. "Is it?"

"Absolutely. Particularly the white one. It's the only white bread Adele will let me buy."

Clare glanced at the price tag. It was nearly a pound more than the brand she normally bought. She'd worked hard to lose her habit of heedlessly putting things in her shopping basket without looking at the labels. Choosing food for her family based on cost before healthsomeness and taste had been one of the hardest adjustments she'd had to make to being suddenly without any income. But there was something hypnotic about Leo's enthusiasm, his keen presence by her side. "Excellent," she said, taking the loaf from the display and putting it in her basket. "Thank you for the tip."

He was wearing running clothes. Not the shiny, form-fitting stuff favoured by some men his age, but loose things in soft cotton: pale grey shorts, an azure marl T-shirt, faded navy hoodie. Clothes for an eight-year-old. Or even an eighteen-year-old. But they added to his overgrown-boy-next-door appeal. His hair was damp from a recent shower and he smelled of shampoo.

He regarded her warmly and said, "How are you? Haven't seen you since you were over for dinner."

"Oh, I'm fine."

"The girls?"

"Well, you probably know better than me! Grace seems to have virtually moved in with you all." She'd meant this as a throwaway comment but it had come out sounding slightly pointed.

"Ah, yes, our apartment does sometimes feel like a repository for every bored tweenager in the vicinity." He smiled and then he frowned. "Not", he added apologetically, "that Grace could possibly be bored at home. With you. I'm sure."

Clare smiled. "Yes she can."

Leo returned her smile and Clare subconsciously clocked the contents of his shopping trolley. Packets of fresh herbs, chicken stock, chillies, a lime, organic chicken breasts, weird mushrooms, four bottles of wine, fat Japanese noodles, powdered flaxseed, miso soup paste, almond milk, a papaya, a mango, a pineapple, organic dog biscuits and three bunches of white tulips.

She looked at her own: white bread, Shreddies, a six-pack of orange Kit-Kats, a bag of Granny Smiths, a tub of Bolognese sauce, a toothbrush, a tub of spreadable butter and a pint of full-fat milk.

"We don't see much of Pip, though? She's clearly more of a homebody?"

Clare nodded. "I think she finds the whole garden scene a bit . . ."

"Cliquey?"

"Well, yes, I suppose. And the fact that they've taken Grace into their inner sanctum. She feels a bit left out. Not that she'd ever say as much. She's very sparky, Pip, very positive. She'd probably prefer to see it that she's got better things to do."

"Shame though," said Leo, adding a loaf of sunflower and linseed bread to his trolley, "Willow could do with a friend who's closer to her in age. Worries me sometimes that she spends all her time with older girls. Maybe we should try to engineer them together somehow."

Clare smiled in agreement whilst thinking that Pip could not be "engineered" into anything she hadn't thought of first.

"How's your father?" she asked. "I saw him the other day, out in the garden?"

"God! Dad! Thank you! I'd totally forgotten to shop for him!" Leo slapped his forehead. "He's had the op, and now of course he's supposed to be watching what he eats and I keep trying to get healthy stuff into him. But he's like a toddler, he'll only eat his greens if there's reward in it for him. So we have to have constant supplies of cheap biscuits and microwave sponge puddings. Oh, and Jersey gold-top milk."

"You'd think losing a foot would be enough of an incentive to stop eating crap," said Clare.

"You know what," said Leo, leaning against the bread display, "I don't actually think he cares very much. I don't think he — Oh, sorry." He straightened himself sharply as a woman attempted to reach a loaf of bread he was obstructing. He shifted along a little. "Yes, I really think he's happy to be chopped up, bit by bit, so long as — Oh, sorry." He shifted again so that another customer could get to the loaves. He smiled defeatedly at Clare. "Tell you what, shall we continue this conversation over a coffee next door?"

"Oh," said Clare. It was 10a.m. She'd assumed he'd be rushing off to work. She considered her own plans for the day. She had none. "Sure," she said. "Shall I meet you on the other side of the checkout?"

"Perfect."

Clare wasn't sure how to feel about sitting in a café with a man who wasn't her husband, a man who wasn't her friend, a man she barely knew. Despite its location hugging the dual carriageway of the A41, this community was small and incestuous. It was virtually impossible to go ten metres from home without seeing someone you knew or knew of. And they were sitting right in the window.

"Don't ever go the place next to the station," he was saying, "not if you care about your coffee."

Clare didn't really care about her coffee. She didn't have the kind of palate that could distinguish between good coffee and bad coffee — or good wines and bad wines come to that. But she nodded anyway. "You're full of good advice. I take it you know something about food."

"I should hope so," he said. "It's my job, after all."

"You're a chef?"

"Not quite. But almost. I'm a restaurant consultant. I dole out advice for a living."

"Wow," she said. "Sounds like a great job."

"It absolutely is." He made way for the waitress to put down their coffee cups and a small jug of frothed milk. "And what about you? Do you work?"

Clare laughed, wryly. "No. No. I've been a stay-at-home mum for thirteen years."

"And before that?"

"Before that I was a student. Oh, except for when I worked in a posh shoe shop for about six months, until I got too pregnant to lean down any more."

"Was it deliberate?" he asked. "Having a baby so young?"

"Totally. All I ever wanted. And my husband was ten years older than me and ready to go for it, so . . ." She drifted away from the end of the sentence, suddenly aware that they were heading towards awkward territory.

She looked up and saw him gazing at her curiously. She should have guessed he wasn't the kind of man to miss cues, to avoid the meat of a conversation. "And your husband is . . .?"

"Chris," she said. "Christian Wild. He's a documentary maker. You might have heard of him?"

She saw Leo's face brighten with realisation. "Oh, God, of course. Yeah. He did that documentary about the Polish skinheads, the neo-Nazi thing?"

Clare nodded.

"Didn't he get an Oscar for that?"

Clare smiled proudly. "He was nominated."

"So did you get to walk the red carpet then?"

"Sadly not. Pip was eight months old and Grace was nineteen months and it was just too much to contemplate."

"Bet you regret that now?"

"God, yeah. He always said, Don't worry, you'll be able to come to the next one, and then there never was a next one. But I don't mind really. It was just so exciting. Just being on the peripheries of it all was enough." It was so nice to talk about her husband in these terms. For so long all she'd talked about had been his madness, then his crime, then his hospitalisation. He'd come to feel like a fictional character who'd wandered randomly into her life story.

"So where is he now? Is he filming a documentary?"

Clare caught her breath. She could lie. She could say: *Yes, he's filming undercover on a psychiatric ward!* That would solve a lot of problems. But there was something about Leo, about the softness behind his eyes that made her decide to talk honestly. "Look," she said, "I really don't want this to be public knowledge, for the sake of the girls. And I think Grace might actually have told at least one of your daughters that Chris is dead." She looked at him to gauge his response. He looked back at her impassively and sympathetically. If he was hiding anything he was doing so inscrutably. "But no, he's not dead and he's not away filming. He's been on a psychiatric ward since

November. He had a severe paranoid schizophrenic episode and burned down our house." She paused, waited for Leo's response. It came as a widening of his eyes and a sharp intake of breath. "Which is bad, but not, believe it or not, the worst thing. The worst thing is that he's been discharged into God-knows-who's care and has been roaming the streets of London unchecked for more than a fortnight and the other day he left Pip a package for her birthday on our front doorstep. So he knows where we live. And I genuinely have no idea what to do."

She stopped abruptly and became suddenly aware that she'd been squeezing her own arms so hard she'd left red marks on her skin. She smiled apologetically. "Sorry," she said. "I hadn't really planned to say any of that. I've barely told anyone. Not even my own mother. And certainly not the girls. Please" — she looked beseechingly into Leo's eyes — "please promise me you won't say anything. Not to anyone. Oh God, I really shouldn't have said anything. If the girls found out . . ."

Leo was looking at her curiously. "Don't you think they should know?" he asked softly.

She shook her head. "God. No. Especially not Grace. She's only just stopped having nightmares every night. And Pip — God, if she thought he was out there, she'd probably demand I bring him back into the fold immediately. She's totally, blindly devoted to him and I don't think she ever really put the two things together — you know: her daddy and the burned-down house. She's compartmentalised the whole thing."

"But, Clare . . ." Leo leaned across the table towards her, so close she could see the blond roots of his eyelashes. ". . . is he dangerous? I mean, if he's dangerous, they should know. They should be on their guard. Shouldn't they?"

Clare sighed. "I don't know. I honestly don't. He never did anything to hurt the girls before. Never raised his voice. Never raised a hand. Before that night, I genuinely thought he'd never do anything to put any of us in danger. He had his moments — we had to give him a lot of leeway — but even this last episode, it seemed so harmless at first. An obsession with the idea that there was a rat in the wainscoting. Seemed normal enough; you know, everyone thinks there might be a mouse or a rat in their house from time to time. But it became more and more overwhelming; he was laying traps and researching stuff on the internet. He started getting up in the middle of the night, convinced he was about to catch it in the act. Then gradually there were more rats, and more traps; he started getting really angry, like these rats had some personal vendetta against him. Then he went away for two weeks' filming and I got Rentokil in and they said there was nothing there. No droppings, no evidence of any kind of rodent and I'd really hoped that by the time he came home he'd be better and that there'd be no more talk of rats. But if anything he was worse. He kept saying we needed to get the girls out of the house, that it was dangerous for them to live in a rat-infested environment, that they could get bitten. I mean" — she looked up at Leo — "I know this all sounds like it must

133

have been nightmarish, but it really wasn't. We were so used to living with these weird episodes. There was always some fantastical object of his obsession. Traffic wardens. Gas leaks. They came and went; he'd either just stop or I'd get him to the doctors and he'd go on medication and then everything would be normal again for months at a time. Sometimes even a year or two. But this one . . ." She sighed. "Well, events escalated, blah blah blah, he burned down the house."

She paused for a moment, waiting to see if Leo was going to say anything but he didn't, just sat and gazed at her with a look of unmasked fascination.

"That night was the maddest I'd ever seen him. Beyond, you know, the craziness of his natural personality, he always had those intense eyes, full of fire. But this was different. He wasn't seeing me. He wasn't seeing the girls. He genuinely thought he'd saved the planet from an alien rat invasion. He was euphoric."

"And how has he been since? When you've seen him?"

"I haven't."

Leo looked at her in surprise. "Seriously?"

"No."

"Wow. Why not?"

"I couldn't." Her voice cracked slightly. "Just couldn't. Even when they said he was doing really well. Even when they said it would do him good to see me and the girls. It didn't matter what anyone said. All I could see was his face that night."

"But what about the girls? Don't they want to see him?"

"Grace definitely not. She feels the same as me. Scared. You know. But Pip — she's never stopped asking. She's even been writing to him. I probably shouldn't have let her. That's probably how he tracked us down. But I felt so bad. I felt so sorry for her." She shrugged.

"I wonder where he is?"

"I have a theory." She told him about Lovestruck Roxy and the till receipt from a Tesco in Walthamstow.

"Can you remember her surname?" he said. "You could Google her. Find out where she's working?"

"No. No idea."

"Well, what about IMDb? She'll be on the credit list for the documentary she made with your husband."

"Yeah," she said. "But why would I want to find her?"

"Because if you find her, you'll know where he is. And surely you'll feel better if you know that?"

"I don't think anything will make me feel better. Not any more. I'm beyond feeling better. I just wish . . ." she began, but then drew herself back from the words that had been on the tip of her tongue. "I just wish none of it had ever happened."

"Was it a nice house?" he asked.

"It was a lovely house." She gulped. It still made her want to cry whenever she thought about her old home. "It was his aunt's. She left it to him. We never changed a thing. Not even her funny old pine kitchen. Or the brown carpets. We kept talking about it and we never got round to it. Because it was so comfortable. And we were so happy there. And now . . ." She pulled herself up straight. "But, seriously. Promise me," she said, "swear you won't say anything. Not even to Adele. Please."

"I swear," he said. "Solemnly. But, Clare, I'm glad you told me. I can keep an eye out for you. And I will. If you need anything. Or if you're scared. I'm just on the other side of the garden."

She looked at his soft, sincere face, felt the very male kinetic strength of him. And then she realised why she'd told him, a virtual stranger. He was just the man you'd want around in an emergency. He would get things done, keep everything together, save the day. For her whole adult life she'd had Chris there to protect her when there'd been nothing really to protect her from. Now she needed someone to protect her from her protector.

"Thank you," she said. "I'm sure it won't come to that. But thank you. I really really appreciate it."

He smiled. "It's a pleasure, Clare. It really is." He placed a hand on her upper arm and squeezed it.

Clare's body twitched at his touch. Her face flushed pink.

CHAPTER
THIRTEEN

It was the middle of June. Spring had turned to summer. The garden was technicolour bright and full of people that Pip had never seen before.

Tyler was sitting on the grass just outside Pip's garden. Pip looked at her in surprise. Tyler never really came down this end of the garden, and certainly not on her own.

"Hi," said Pip airily, preparing to walk past her.

"Hi," said Tyler, jumping to her feet. "Where are you going?"

"Just up there," said Pip.

"You going to see Fergus?"

Pip looked at Tyler oddly. How did she know about her and Fergus? She shrugged.

"Rhea's up there. I just saw her. I'll come with you."

Pip nodded. She wasn't sure what was going on. Tyler never talked to her unless there was a big gang of them. They walked in silence at first. "Where's Grace?" said Tyler as they neared the brow of the hill.

"Don't know," said Pip. "Probably with the sisters. She's there all the time these days."

"Yeah, I'd noticed. How come you don't hang out there too?" Tyler scratched her scalp with some relish, as though she had nits. Pip noticed that she looked a bit shabby. Her normally glossy blonde hair was lank and dusty-looking and her once-pristine white Converse were grey and dilapidated. There were deep scratches on her arms as though she'd been dragged through a field of gorse and a patch of dry red skin around her left nostril.

"Don't know. No reason."

"Don't you like them?" she carried on. "The sisters?"

"Yes. I like them."

"They think you don't like them."

Pip stopped and turned to face Tyler. "They've been talking about me?"

"Not really. Someone just said something about you and they said, 'Oh, no, Pip doesn't like us.' Or something like that."

"What, just because I don't want to go and hang about in their house all the time?"

"They said you'd rather hang about with a freak-out giant rabbit and an old lady than hang out with them."

"That's crap. I've only seen Fergus like about three times."

"Yeah, well, that's just what they said. It doesn't mean it's what I think. And anyway, your sister doesn't spend all her time at their apartment, you know. She does other things."

"I know," she said. "She hangs out with Dylan too."

"Yeah. Like, *in his bedroom*."

"No she doesn't."

"Er, yes she does."

"She doesn't even know where he lives."

Tyler snorted. "Of course she does. She's there right now. Probably."

Pip looked up sharply at the attic windows that Rhea had pointed out to her. The curtains were drawn on all three windows. But then they always were. Rhea had told her that Dylan's mum was sensitive to light. Then she glanced down again to the tall windows of the Howeses' apartment.

"How would she even get in there?" she asked, knowing even before the words had left her mouth that it was a cretinous thing to say.

Tyler looked incredulously at her and used two of her fingers to mime a person walking up some stairs.

Rhea wasn't at the top of the hill when they got there.

"I've got some money," Tyler said. "Shall we go and get ice creams?"

"I haven't got any money though."

"That's OK," said Tyler. "I can treat you."

Pip didn't have her phone with her. She glanced behind her towards the garden gates. She thought of her nervy mother, who seemed to freak out every five seconds when she was out of her sight, and she thought of Grace doing whatever Grace was doing, and even though Tyler was suggesting a ten-minute round trip it seemed rash somehow and liable to cause problems. But her curiosity overrode her instinctive misgivings and she said, "OK. Thank you. If you're sure?"

They set off up the Finchley Road together. It was five thirty. The tube station was belching out creased commuters, most of whom walked straight into the supermarket to buy their dinner. Tyler and Pip peered through the plate glass. The queue for the basket-only checkout was thirty people long. "Let's not bother with that." Tyler turned in the other direction. "There's a corner shop down this way with a cabinet. Come on."

The ten-minute round trip now seemed to have extended itself into a fifteen-minute round trip. Her mum would be doing tea about now. If Pip wasn't there when she'd finished cooking, she'd try calling her. If she didn't answer her phone, she'd come out into the garden to look for her. If she wasn't in the garden she'd go to the sisters' apartment. And if Grace wasn't there and she wasn't there her mum would go completely mental. Pip picked up her pace and said, "OK. Come on, though. I need to get back."

Tyler looked at her pityingly. "What for?"

"Tea," she said.

Tyler just tutted and flicked her hair as if she'd never heard of such a silly thing.

The pavement was dusty and hot, the sun a burning ochre reflection in the shop windows opposite. A swarm of girls from the private school further up the road were walking towards them, St Trinian's scruffy in short navy and sunshine-yellow skirts, skinny legs, uncombed hair, as loud and territorial as the mums from the halfway house. Pip saw Tyler's lip curl with distaste as they passed.

"Posh bitches," she said under her breath. "They're all anorexic, you know. I could have got a scholarship, because of my gran being the headmistress there for so long, but my mum wouldn't let me."

140

They passed the corner shop that Pip had thought Tyler meant.

"I can't go in there," said Tyler, nodding at the shop. "They know me in there."

Pip looked at her, wondering what that meant.

Buses stormed down the bus lane to their right. Tyler stepped off the kerb to overtake a woman with a buggy and almost got run down by one. It sounded its horn, long and hard, and Tyler tried to pretend she wasn't shaken. "Yeah yeah," she said to the back end of the bus. "Get over yourself."

"Shit. You could have died," said Pip, holding her hammering heart.

"Whatevs."

Pip's discomfiture increased. She should have said no. She didn't even like ice cream very much. Finally they stopped at a shop. Tyler held the door for Pip and for a moment they hung over the sides of a chest freezer, gazing into upturned cardboard boxes, evaluating and critiquing the various types of ice cream on offer, like two normal girls. Tyler chose a Magnum and Pip chose a lime Calippo. The time above the cash desk said 5.41p.m.

"How did you scratch your arms?" she asked a moment later, as they headed back towards the garden.

Tyler glanced at the injuries. "On my mum's dress."

"What?"

"Long story. It was sequinned. You know, one of those dresses that's got sequins all over it. And I tried to get it off her because she was asleep in it and it

141

scratched me right up." Tyler shrugged as if to say: *Hey, you know, just one of those things.*

Pip's skin prickled with the dark glamour of the imagery. It was like something out of one her Jacqueline Wilson books: the feisty neglected daughter and the beautiful broken mother.

"Why did your sister lie about your dad?"

Pip almost stopped in her tracks. "What do you mean?

"You know, she said your dad was dead and he isn't."

Pip shrugged. "Dunno." There was a profound lack of doubt in the tone of the question. She felt it would be futile to try to deny that Grace had been lying. Instead she turned the question round on to Tyler. "What about you?" she said. "Where's your dad?"

"Don't ask," she said.

"Have you met him?"

"Thought I had," she said. "Turns out I hadn't. Turns out everyone's been lying about everything."

They were nearing the tube station. A few more steps and Pip would be able to see the mushroom-shaped turret of Rhea's apartment block.

"Does your mum ever talk about Phoebe?"

Tyler scowled at her. "What do you know about Phoebe?"

"Just that she died. In the garden. Rhea told me."

"Yeah, we talk about it sometimes."

"What do you think happened?"

"I think it was Gordon. The sisters' granddad."

"What! Seriously?"

"Yeah, well, just look at him. He's a filthy old pervert. And Mum says when he was younger he was virtually a rapist. He was always leering over the young girls and making inappropriate comments."

"But that doesn't mean he'd kill someone, does it?"

"Course it does. Maybe he'd been raping her or something and he needed to shut her up. Or, I don't know, maybe she tried to fight him off and he did it by accident or something."

"Is that what your mum thinks too?"

"No. She just thinks Phoebe overdosed."

"She was on drugs?"

"Yeah. Apparently. I don't know. Phoebe was quite wild."

"Rhea told me Phoebe was going out with Leo when she died."

"Yeah. I think they had this on-off thing going on. She was going out with his brother too."

They'd reached the gates to the garden. Tyler pulled a key out of the pocket of her hoodie and let them in. "Oh, wait up." Her phone had made a noise and she pulled it from her other pocket and switched it on. "There you go." She turned the phone to face Pip. "I told you so."

She wasn't sure what she was seeing at first. It was a photograph on Instagram, of a boy and girl. He had his arm around her shoulder and their cheeks were pressed together and there was a cartoon heart drawn around them and the words "Me and the gorgeous G".

It was Grace and Dylan.

"That", said Tyler, pointing at the wall behind them in the photo, "is Dylan's wallpaper. In his bedroom. And that photo was posted two minutes ago. So." She pointed at the attic windows opposite. "Believe me now?"

Dear Daddy,

Grace and Dylan are going out. It's properly official. I don't even know what that means when you're thirteen years old. Some of the kids in my class say they're going out but they're not really, they're just hanging out, basically. Not even holding hands. It's really stupid. But maybe it's different when you're in year eight. Maybe you do kissing and stuff. They keep putting photos of themselves on Instagram. They have their faces touching sometimes. So, I don't know. It's all just really weird. Grace won't talk to me about it. She's really changed. Like, a few months ago we were virtually the same and now she's got boobs, she's started wearing make-up, she's taller than Mum, she's got really thin and now this. I don't like it. I feel like I've lost her. Like I've lost you. I'm feeling sad today. And angry. Angry with you, for doing that stupid thing and leaving us all behind and making us come to this place. And angry with Mum for not letting us see you. And really, really angry with Grace for just kind of walking away from it all and leaving me behind.

So I'm quite glad you're probably never going to read this letter because it's not a very happy one and given the place you're in right now it's probably not a good idea for you to read sad letters.

Love you, Daddy,
Your Pipsqueak xxxx

CHAPTER
FOURTEEN

Adele bumped into Cece on the Finchley Road on Friday. It was the first time she'd seen her since their dinner party earlier that month and since her discovery about her summer fling with Leo twenty-three years ago. It was a sunny day, with a warm breeze, and Cece was wearing denim hotpants, a loose grey T-shirt, pink trainers and black Ray-Bans, an outfit not dissimilar to those her daughter wore. Her long blonde hair was tied up in a ponytail. Men turned and stared as she walked past them. She smiled when she saw Adele approaching and stopped, signifying that she'd be happy to chat for a while. "Hello, gorgeous." She leaned in and kissed Adele's cheek. She smelled of coconut and stale alcohol. "I keep meaning to drop you a note or something to thank you for that lovely dinner the other week. I'm so hopeless."

"Oh, God, honestly, don't worry about it. It was nothing. Just some curry."

"But it was nice. No one ever seems to do that kind of thing any more. It's lovely when someone makes the effort. And I *promise* I'll try and return the favour, but you know, work is crazy, and space is limited. It's so hard to find the time."

"I know. I know." Adele nodded understandingly. Cece was a social worker. In other words she had a real job, a proper job. And she was a single mother. Adele could never hope to compete in a who's-got-the-least-free-time battle with her. And neither would she want to.

"How are the girls?"

"They're fine," she said. "Great in fact. Although we've still got the dreaded Gordon staying with us. Making inappropriate comments left, right and centre."

"Urgh. Gordon. Christ, I forgot he was here. How's his rancid foot?"

"Gone. We're just waiting for the prosthetic. Could be a while."

Cece winced. "And you're playing nurse, I suppose?"

"To a certain extent. He has people coming in to deal with the foot itself."

"Or the remains of the foot?"

Adele couldn't help but laugh. "Yes. The remains of the foot. And Leo's been taking as much time off work as he can. But yes, essentially I'm caring for him."

"And teaching your three girls."

"Yes, and teaching the girls."

"God." Cece shook her head wonderingly. "I don't know how you do it." There was no irony in her tone and Adele was struck by how often women undervalued their own efforts whilst being endlessly impressed by those of their peers.

"Oh, by the way . . ." Adele laughed nervously. "Such a funny thing. You know I've been editing Rhea's memoirs and — ha — she mentions something that happened that summer, the summer you lost your sister. Something between you and Leo. *Ha!* And I honestly had no idea that you and he had . . ."

"Oh God. *That.*" Cece put her hand to her mouth. "How embarrassing. You know, I think I've actually edited that out of my psyche. I made such a total tit of myself."

Adele laughed as though she were in on the joke.

"Poor Leo," Cece continued. "I decided that he was *it*. You know. The sun and the moon and the universe. And I basically stalked the poor guy until he caved. And, God, you know nothing happened, right? He just let me hang out with him. Let me be his pretend girlfriend. I mean — I was only thirteen or something ridiculous. There was no way anything untoward was going to happen. I mean, *obviously*." She stopped and put her face to the air as if feeling for the direction of the wind then turned back to Adele. "Did you talk about it with Leo?"

Adele nodded.

"What did he say? Did he even remember it?"

"Yes. He remembered it. And he said what you said. That it was just a bit of fun. A bit of harmless snogging."

"Oh. *God*." Cece dropped her face into her hands. "Did he tell you that? I didn't think . . . I'm surprised. It was a bit weird, really, when you think about it. I was so young. He was virtually a man. But at the time — I mean, you know what that garden's like. Things happen in that garden differently to how they happen in the real world. Different rules apply. And when you're

148

thirteen, I don't know, you just can't wait for it all, can you? You want it all to start *now*."

Adele smiled tightly. She thought of thirteen-year-old Fern, thirteen-year-old Tyler, almost-thirteen-year-old Grace. With their breasts and their waists and their attitudes. Did they want it all to start *now?*

"Did your mother know?" she asked.

"God no. She was up in arms enough about Phoebe. Thought Phoebe was out of control and I was the least of her worries. Not" — she clasped Adele's forearm — "that there was technically anything to worry about. Five minutes of nothing. That's all it was. But I don't think she'd have liked it. I don't suppose *I'd* like it, if it was Tyler." She smiled wanly. "Anyway" — she glanced beyond Adele at the shops ahead — "I'd better get on. But, I meant to ask: what did you make of the new neighbour? What was her name? Clare."

"She seems perfectly nice, I suppose. A bit quiet. A bit cagey."

"Did you find out about the dad thing? Was I right? Christ, I was burning to ask her." She stopped as the inappropriateness of her choice of words dawned upon her. Then she laughed. "Excuse the pun. But I so wanted to ask her. Did anything come out that I missed?"

"No. Nothing at all. She didn't mention the father. Nobody asked. And according to the girls, Grace said he's dead. I don't suppose she'd say that unless it was either true or more palatable than the truth."

"Poor girls," said Cece vaguely. "If it *was* their dad who did that to their house, they must be so fucked up."

They both shook their heads sadly and then Cece straightened and said, "Right, really must get on. I've got a date tonight. Have to get my eyebrows done. And a wax. But, look, I know you've got a lot on your plate right now, what with Gordon the octopus and everything, but would it be OK if I sent Tyler down to yours? Just until I get home? I won't be late. Elevenish?"

Adele smiled and swallowed a sigh. "Sure," she said. "No problem." And there it was. Classic Cece. No doubt if she hadn't bumped into Adele in the street she'd just have sent Tyler down anyway, on some kind of flimsy pretext. Either that or left Tyler alone for the evening. Phoebe's unexplained death had left so many bruises and scars on her family and as the younger sister she'd had to carry most of her hurt in the small soft core of herself. Tyler had been the result of some kind of mistake, never quite explained, and she'd never really worked out how to mother her properly. Thought parenting was something you could opt in and out of, depending on your mood.

"Are you sure?"

"Of course," she said. "Absolutely. In fact" — a thought occurred to her — "our new tent arrived this week. Maybe I'll put it up and let the kids muck around out there this evening. Invite some of the other children. The weather's meant to be good. What do you think?"

Cece shrugged. "Sounds good to me," she said, as, of course, she would. And then she squeezed Adele to her, told her she was a star and disappeared up the Finchley Road leaving behind her a backdraught of unhappiness.

Tyler arrived at seven o'clock with Dylan in tow. Grace arrived shortly afterwards. Gordon sat in his wheelchair in the living room tutting at each arrival.

"Mrs H.," he called to her in the kitchen, "can't you put a lock on this door? This house is filling up with waifs and strays."

"I invited them, Gordon," she called back, "we're doing a campfire."

"Oh good Christ. What on earth for?" He appeared at her side a moment later. "Hook me up to Skype, will you? I want to talk to my wife. And get away from all those bloody teenagers."

Adele looked up at him from the laptop. She'd been researching something for a project she and the girls were working on for their history module. She thought about protesting but couldn't find the resolve. "Fine," she said, bringing up Skype and clicking on Affie's number. She pushed her chair out of the way and helped Gordon negotiate his wheelchair into the space.

"Any chance of a glass of red?" he asked, tapping his fingertips impatiently against the tabletop as he waited for Affie to answer. "And maybe a square or two of that posh chocolate you've been hiding from me."

Adele rolled her eyes. The posh chocolate was an attempt to control Gordon's appetite for cheap sugar. Leo had bought it for him and was rationing it out, square by square. "If he's going to insist on eating sugar, at least let it be good-quality sugar," he'd said.

She snapped off two squares, poured him a small glass of Pinot Noir and set both in front of him. He growled at her by way of thanks and then Affie's face appeared on the screen. She looked tired. And displeased.

"Gordon, you look thin."

Gordon turned from the screen and beamed at Adele. "There" — he laughed, pointing at Affie on the screen — "did you hear that, Mrs H.? *Affie*," he yelled at the screen, "look at this!" He showed his wife the two squares of chocolate. "Look what they give me here. They call this a 'snack'. They keep telling me I'm too fat! And trying to starve me!"

Adele groaned, took some bowls from a low cupboard and filled them with crisps she'd bought specially. Then she took them into the living room and laid them in front of the children.

It alarmed her slightly, the sheer size of all these children. It felt like only yesterday that her flat had been filled with small, muddy-footed children, running in and out, leaving a trail of toys and leaves and crumbs in their wake. Now those small children were static, adult-sized, seething with unspoken thoughts and warped emotions. They pounced on the crisps, as though they'd not been fed in days, *thank you, Adele, thank you very much*. So polite; all those years of being reminded and cajoled into please-and-thank-yous by their parents finally paying dividends.

152

Adele sat at a remove, not wanting to be in the kitchen with Gordon yet not feeling quite like she belonged in here either. There was something heavy and peculiar in the atmosphere. Tyler was sitting, as she usually did, curled into Dylan on the sofa. Catkin sat cross-legged on the floor, a piece of schoolwork on the floor at her feet, a pen in her hand, her ears plugged with buds attached to an iPod. Fern and Grace sat side by side, slightly awkwardly, as though they didn't know each other. Willow sat on the window ledge, feet kicking back and forth against the radiator, *bangbangbang*, chatting stream-of-consciousness style to Tyler and Dylan about something someone had said about someone else that someone else had said to her that was just so *shocking*, her mouth falling open, her eyes widening every few words to better communicate the horror of the thing.

"What happened to your arms, Tyler?" asked Adele, noticing a pattern of fine red scratches over both her forearms.

Tyler touched her arms, protectively. "Oh. God. Nothing. Just did it getting a football out of the blackberry bushes for some kid." She shrugged and smiled.

"Looks sore," said Adele.

"It's fine. It's healing."

Adele nodded but kept her gaze on Tyler. She didn't look quite right. Despite being something of a tomboy, she'd always been strangely meticulous about her appearance — couldn't bear to have a rip in her jeans or a tangle in her hair. Adele had put this down to the

153

influence of her mother, who despite — in her opinion — being a high-functioning alcoholic and heavy recreational drug-user, always looked immaculate. But Tyler looked slightly dog-eared today: her hair needed a wash; her Converse were grey with a frayed hole on one side. Her skin looked dry. And then there were those scratches on her arms.

There was a slam as Leo arrived at the front door. The dog scrambled to his feet, Willow darted to the hallway, everyone turned expectantly to look towards the door and then he walked in and the whole atmosphere lifted. Tyler's face lit up as it always did when she saw Leo. She'd adopted Leo as her surrogate father from a young age and because she didn't have to live with him, she still saw him with a golden, childish lack of objectivity.

Within moments of his arrival all the children were out in the garden loudly collaborating to get the tent up. Max wandered across and joined in. Smaller children, curious and wide-eyed, stood and watched from the sidelines. Neighbours came over to chat. Catkin wheeled Gordon out and he sat, his half-empty wine glass clutched in his fist, passing a running commentary on the foolhardiness of all involved. It was a day short of the equinox, and the sun sat high in the evening sky. It would not grow dark for hours. Leo brought out chilled wine in a thermal sleeve and a stack of plastic cups, offering it round to all the adults. Up above, Rhea sat on her balcony, her rabbit on her lap, a glass of wine in her own hand, large sunglasses obscuring her small-featured face, the sun glinting off her golden chains and oversized earrings. She held her glass aloft to Adele's and called something down that Adele couldn't hear above the din of conversation. Adele raised her glass up to Rhea and smiled and felt that swell of joy she always felt at this time of the year when the garden came back to life. She hadn't eaten since midday and the icy wine hit her senses like an intravenous shot of pleasure. If, quite against all of Adele's naturally held beliefs, it turned out that there was an afterlife, she strongly suspected that in heaven it would always be a Friday night. Any Friday night would do, even a grey wet one at the fag-end of January, but this Friday night in particular, with the prospect of another three hours of daylight, a low night-time temperature of eighteen degrees, the weekend lying ahead of them, her children engaged and happy with their friends and the early softening effects of a good white wine, *this* Friday night would be a good one to live over and over again, in perpetuity.

Adele cupped her eyes against the sun as a figure approached. She'd thought at first that it was a child. Then realised it was Clare, in a summer dress, her short hair held off her face with a thin black band. She held up a welcoming hand and Clare walked towards her.

"Hi!" she said. "Clare!"

"Hi," Clare said.

Adele tipped her glass towards the tent. "What do you think of our monster tent?"

Clare appraised it. "Very nice," she said.

Leo got to his feet as she approached. "Clare," he said, "hi. Can I interest you in glass of wine?"

155

"Yes. Thank you. Just a small one."

"There you go." He handed her a cup. "Cheers."

Clare sat down on the grass next to Adele and sipped her wine. "Can never get used to how different it looks from over here," she said, surveying the sweep of garden.

"I know," said Leo. "That's the magic of the garden, the way it was laid out to give so many different aspects. Your side was designed to feel like a country hamlet, you know, all the little paths and nooks and crannies. Whereas this side was meant to be sweeping and grandiose."

"Looking down on the little people?" Clare suggested drily.

"Well, yes, I suppose. Like the old estates with the big house at the crown and the workers somewhere at the bottom. Except of course this is central London and we're all equal now." He laughed.

They all turned to look at the tent, which was currently bulging with outlined parts of children's bodies; shrieks of mirth and over-excitement emanating from within. "So nice to see them all actually playing," said Adele. "Instead of just sitting about."

"I know," said Clare. "I miss the playing."

"Such a funny age, isn't it?" said Adele. "Thirteen?"

"Bittersweet," said Leo.

"Animals," Gordon growled from the terrace. "Animals when they're born, animals when they're grown. That's all there is to it. And you lot, you modern parents, you sit and you talk and you talk and you talk, like you can make any difference to any of it." He snapped his left hand open and shut. "Well, you can't. Keep them clean. Keep them fed. Tell them what the rules are. Give them a good hard nip if they break the rules. Let them know who's boss. Then, when they're not animals any more, let them go. That's all there is to it. I fear for this generation of children, I really do. Can't take a fucking crap without Mummy and Daddy standing over them and analysing it all. Making fucking *notes*." He mimed scribbling into a notepad and snarled.

Adele and Leo groaned.

"Gordon, for Christ's sake," said Adele. "Every generation does things differently. And it's all about getting the balance right. I personally think all these kids are amazing. They're confident and focused and sociable."

"Call that middle one of yours confident, Mrs H.? Really? What sort of thirteen-year-old still needs a comfort blanket?"

"It's not a comfort blanket, Gordon, it's a sensory thing. She just likes the feel of it."

"Bullshit. It's a comfort blanket. Poor child probably can't get over the fact that she's not a baby any more. Wants to crawl back up your front passage and into the womb."

Adele, Clare and Leo all exchanged outraged looks. Then they shook their heads and laughed. It got to a certain point with Gordon when there was no suitable response. When you just needed to shake your head and change the subject.

As the sky glowered and the sun slid behind the terrace beyond, Leo lit a match and set his campfire alight. The children emerged from the tent, tousled and eager. Adele passed around the special toasting marshmallows she'd found in a local deli: big, fat ones, the size of muffins, speared on to extra-long wooden stakes. Clare finished her wine and said she was going in. "I want you in when it's dark, girls," she said to Grace and Pip. "I mean it. I don't care what everyone else is doing. Ten o'clock and no later." Adele watched her walking back across the lawn, tiny and unsteady on her feet. She'd only had two cups of wine but seemed slightly unstitched. The campfire crackled red and amber, sending tiny sparkles of gold into the grey night sky. The children were peaceful and contemplative, their faces patterned with coppery shadows.

Adele let her soul fill up with it all and poured herself another glass of wine.

CHAPTER
FIFTEEN

Clare sat in her own back garden. It was ten o'clock and the sun had finally gone down leaving behind a sky that was a curious, reddish shade of black. But the garden was still bustling and alive, filled with the echoing whoop and holler of children roaming freely, the sounds of wine glasses and raised voices.

The flat seemed eerily quiet without the girls in it. Every moment or two Clare would stretch her neck just a little, looking out through the trees for the shadowy outlines of her girls, silently hoping for one of them to appear at the back gate moaning about something or maybe even crying a bit, at which juncture Clare would be able to stride across the garden bristling with annoyance, call the other one in, lock the back door on all three of them and go peacefully to bed.

Her thoughts returned to her drinks earlier with Leo and Adele. She'd only stayed an hour. Just long enough for two glasses of wine. She was a feeble drinker, more than a glass or two and her eyes would cross, her legs turn to jelly, people would have to help her home or tuck her into a spare bed. More than three or four drinks and in all likelihood she would throw up. Possibly endearing as a young girl, but now in her early thirties, with two children the same height as her, horribly unseemly.

A breeze blew across from the trees and ruffled the pages of that morning's edition of *Metro* on the chair next to her. She'd picked it up at the tube station earlier even though she wasn't getting on a tube. She liked the commuter papers. They were written for people who inhabited a different world to hers. She'd never been a commuter. She'd been a student. Then she'd been a wife. Then she'd been a mother. All before she was twenty-one. And she liked to live vicariously in this world of stolen glances across carriages and texted quick-fire observations, of delayed trains from Orpington and people looking after fainting strangers on the underground. It made her feel like a part of it all. It made her feel normal.

There was no response from Grace's phone so she called Pip's. No response from there either. She sighed and went inside to fetch a torch.

The air was still so warm, even with the light breeze that had begun to pick up. As she reached the brow of the hill she looked up and saw the old woman still sitting on her balcony. The sweeping curve of the stucco terrace on the other side was patterned with rectangular cut-outs, each a different shade of gold, each framing a different life, a different set of secrets and problems. It reminded Clare of one of those old-fashioned nativity calendars, with a beautiful vignette behind each door instead of a chocolate.

Leo sat out on his terrace, his laptop open on the table in front of him, a bottle of beer at his elbow, the dog by his feet. He smiled as she approached. "Hello, again," he said. She could see the lines in his handsome face in the harsh up-light from his screen. His heavy eyebrows threw dark shadows up on to his brow and he looked vaguely ghoulish.

"Hi," she said. "Just looking for the girls. Have you seen them?"

He cupped his hand around his ear. "I can certainly hear them," he said. "But I can't say I've seen any of them for a while."

"Oh," said Clare, her heart rate picking up. It was bright here in the light of the big houses, but in other corners of the garden it was dark. She turned and looked over her shoulder. "Do you think . . .?"

"They're fine," he said. "Don't worry about them. They're all together." Then he turned and looked over his shoulder, through the doors behind him. He beckoned her over. He patted the other side of the bench he was sitting on. She sat next to him, conscious of the warmth emanating from him, his square-tipped fingers wrapped around the beer bottle, his bare feet close to hers beneath the table. She breathed in the smell of him and briefly allowed herself a moment's imagining of another world, a parallel world, where she had met a man like Leo, married a man like Leo, had her children with a man like Leo. A world where, she woke up next to this fragrant, sane man every day. Where she got to keep him and her daughters got to keep him and every day was blissful in its simplicity and predictability. Did Adele have any idea how lucky she was? she wondered.

"Look," he said, checking over his shoulder again that there was no one standing behind them, and then angling the screen of his laptop towards her. "Roxy Hancock. 13 Basildon Gardens, E11. And there's her mobile phone number."

Clare widened her eyes at him. "How did you —?"

"Easy," he said. "I told you. Found her name on IMDb, Googled her name with the Walthamstow postcode. It came up on a movie freelancers' site. Took less than a minute."

"Right," she said, staring at the information on the screen. "God."

Leo leaned back and stretched himself out. His T-shirt rode up slightly, revealing a strip of soft, hairy stomach. Clare pulled her gaze from it.

"So, now you know where he's living."

"Yes, I do, thank you. But, God, I'm not sure I . . ."

"You could call her?" he said, leaning forward again, closing the gap between his T-shirt and the waistband of his shorts. "Send her a text? Whatever. It's up to you. But I think it's important you know. Just in case. Here." He passed her a piece of paper. "I wrote it all down for you. Keep it somewhere safe. And now" — he turned his attention back to the screen — "I am going to delete my search history. Because in a house full of people like this you really don't know who might stumble across things they shouldn't."

He did this and then turned to smile at her. "There you go. All safe and hidden away."

She wanted to touch him in some way. Place the palm of her hand against his cheek. Squeeze his knee.

Kiss his hand. She wanted, in some way, to claim him. Instead she said, "Thank you. That's really kind of you." And he smiled at her in that soft-eyed, attentive way of his and said, "You are very welcome."

The garden felt terrifyingly alive. Bushes rustled and crackled. Things darted across the lawns. Shadows grew and shrank and grew again.

Pip jumped.

"It's just cats," Tyler said. "You know they're nocturnal, right?"

They were sitting on the grass on the brow of the hill, hiding in the shadows of a full-grown chestnut tree. It was just the two of them. Pip wasn't sure why. It had been a really strange evening. She hadn't wanted to come out in the first place and then Willow had come to the back door and basically bullied her into coming to the campfire. And then it had been fun for a while; they'd mucked about in the tent and toasted giant marshmallows and her mum had been there for a while too and Pip had been having a really nice time. And then, when the campfire had burned itself down and her mum had gone home, things had changed. The older ones had disappeared into the shadows by the benches and Pip and Willow had hung out in the playground. Then a few minutes later Tyler had joined them.

That had been OK for a while too. It was still light then and Willow had been there and Tyler had been happy playing along with their slightly weird, hyper game where they were pretending to be orphans who'd run away to the circus (this was Willow's game, of course. Willow was totally mad and, like Pip, a big fan of Jacqueline Wilson). And then Willow had gone inside and Tyler had said, "Let's go and sit over there." And that was about an hour ago and they were still sitting here.

Every now and then Tyler would jump to her feet and peer around the chestnut tree at the other kids on the benches at the top.

"What are they doing?" asked Pip.

"Not a lot," she replied. "Just sort of hanging out."

"Shall we go and sit with them?"

"No. Let's stay here."

Pip's shoulders dropped. She felt manipulated and uncomfortable.

"Have you got a boyfriend?" Tyler asked, suddenly and unexpectedly.

"What? No! Of course not. I'm only twelve. Have you?"

Tyler grimaced. "No fucking way," she said. "Boys my age are all losers."

"Apart from Dylan?"

"Yeah. Well. I used to think that. Now I'm not so sure." She picked at the skin around her fingernails and threw a fleeting glance in the direction of the others. Then she turned abruptly to look at Pip. "Has Grace said anything?" she asked. "About her and Dylan?"

"No. Not really. I did ask her about that photo on Instagram. The one you showed me. And she said there were other people in the room. Like, some friend of Dylan's from school or something."

"Yeah, right."

"Well, that's what she said."

"Dylan never invites friends home. He's too embarrassed. You know his mum's like virtually a hoarder and their flat is really tiny and dirty and his mum's really weird and unfriendly. No," she said conclusively, "they were on their own up there. And your sister is a liar."

The accusation rankled. Pip felt she should be able to tell Tyler that she was wrong. That Grace would never lie to her. But she didn't believe that to be the case any more.

"Well, even if she was lying about that, what does it matter?" she countered. "She's twelve years old. He's thirteen. It's not like they'd be having sex or anything."

Tyler looked at her pityingly. "Shit," she said, "really? Do you really believe that?"

"What time is it?" Pip asked, desperate now to get away from Tyler, to go home to her mother. She'd left her phone in the tent and she was too scared to go and get it in the dark on her own.

Tyler pulled out her own phone, looked at it and said, "Five past ten."

"Shit," said Pip, "I need to go. I told my mum I'd be home at ten."

"Five minutes isn't going to make any difference," Tyler snapped. Then she put a finger to her lips and shushed her. "*Listen*," she whispered.

"What?"

"It's gone really quiet up there. Come on."

"What?" She scrambled to her feet after Tyler. "Where are we going?"

Tyler shushed her again. "Just come."

They tiptoed together through the darkness towards the benches at the top of the hill.

"Stop!" Tyler put a hand against Pip's chest, her gaze straight ahead of them, like a hunter with their prey in view. "Get down!"

Pip dropped to her knees. They were a few feet from the benches. "Look!" Tyler said, turning to Pip, her eyes burning with triumph and hurt. "Just look!"

It was darker here; no light from the houses reached this part of the garden and it took Pip's eyes a second or two to work out what she was seeing. And then she knew. Lying side by side on the grass, staring into the starless sky, were Fern and Catkin. They were passing a lit cigarette between them, a tiny nub of glowing gold that shone hot red every time one of them inhaled. And there, on the bench, a kind of two-headed animal which, as Pip's eyes made sense of things, slowly revealed itself to be her sister astride Dylan, her legs wrapped fully around his torso, her face planted entirely on his, his hands in her hair, their twinned bodies rolling together like a dance.

Pip felt her stomach lurch, a huge surge of molten marshmallows rising through her gut towards her mouth. And then a terrible pang of something else. Something wrong and bad. Almost like excitement. She turned away.

"Where are you going?" Tyler hissed.

"Home."

"Aren't you going to say anything?"

"Like what?"

"Like that you saw her? Like that she's a slag?"

"She's not a slag!"

"Er . . ." Tyler directed Pip's gaze back to the benches.

"It's nothing to do with me," she said. "I don't even care."

Tyler grabbed her shoulder and turned her round to face her. "This", she snarled, "is disgusting. Someone needs to know about this. They are *children*," she said, her fingertips digging into Pip's bones. "They are fucking *children*."

And then she stormed away from her, her eyes filled with tears, her hands held in small pointed fists at her sides.

Now it was Pip's turn to call out: "Where are *you* going?"

"I don't know," she shouted back. "Nowhere!"

Pip watched her stamping across the lawn towards the garden gates, her thin ponytail swinging back and forth with each step. She saw her kick the trunk of a tree as she passed it, then she saw her disappear into the shadows briefly before slamming the garden gate shut behind her.

Pip glanced back at the figures behind her. Someone was passing the cigarette to Dylan, although Pip was beginning to suspect it wasn't a cigarette. She watched Dylan inhale on it, then offer it to Grace. Grace shook her head and climbed off Dylan's lap.

Then Pip saw a circle of light swinging back and forth on the grass.

"Pip? Is that you?" Her mother's voice.

Pip looked at the teenagers on the hill to see if they'd heard. She saw someone stub out the cigarette, heard loud whispers, a quick rearrangement of bodies.

"What are you doing out here all on your own?"

"I'm not," she said. "I was with Tyler. She just went inside. Literally."

Her mother was by her side now. Pip pulled her to her, absorbing the familiarity of her body and her smell.

"Where's Grace?"

"Somewhere up there, I think." She pointed up the hill.

Clare called for her and Grace appeared almost immediately, wide-eyed and smiling. "Hi, Mum! Sorry. I lost track of the time."

"I tried calling you both," she said. "Neither of you answered."

"I left my phone in the tent," said Grace.

"So did I," said Pip.

Clare tutted and touched their hair. "If you're going to disobey me at least have your phones with you."

They collected their phones from the tent and then they walked, the three of them, arms linked, across the garden, back to their flat.

In bed that night, Pip stared at Grace across the bedroom.

"Don't you think you're a bit young?" she began.

Grace stared at her darkly, as if daring her to say what she thought she might be about to say. "For what?"

"For what you were doing with Dylan?"

"I wasn't *doing* anything with Dylan."

"You were. I saw you."

"You mean you were watching?"

"No. I wasn't *watching*. I was with Tyler and she said, 'Look at this.' And it was you and Dylan. And then I stopped looking. I'm not a pervert."

Grace groaned. "Fucking Tyler," she hissed under her breath. "What is her fucking problem?"

"Well, it's kind of obvious, isn't it? She's jealous."

"Fuck's sake. What of? It's not like Dylan is her boyfriend or anything."

"No," said Pip, "but he's her best friend."

"And what have I got to do with that? They can still be best friends. I'm not stopping them."

Pip didn't say what she wanted to say, that how could Tyler be best friends with Dylan when he was with Grace all the time. Instead she opened her book and pretended to read.

"You won't tell Mum, will you?" said Grace, her voice soft and scared.

"Of course I won't." Pip had always kept Grace's secrets, from when they were tiny, always proud to be entrusted with them.

"Or about the other stuff?"

"What other stuff?"

"You know, what the others were doing?"

"The drugs, you mean?" Pip felt weird even saying the word.

"Yes. And that was nothing to do with me. I don't do that kind of stuff. I never would. You know", she said, turning on her side to face Pip, "cannabis can give you paranoid schizophrenia?"

Pip looked at her questioningly.

"Seriously, Pip, this is important. Mental illness can be hereditary. Which means that you or I might have it in our DNA already. And if we smoke cannabis, it could bring it out. And we could end up with it." Her eyes were wide and imploring. "We must never take drugs. Never."

"'K," said Pip. "Whatevs."

"Promise me."

"I promise, OK?"

"No, *really* promise me."

Pip rolled her eyes, but deep down she felt touched by her sister's concern. "I really promise. I promise. Promise. Promise. PROMISE!"

She smiled and Grace smiled.

"My best girl," said Grace.

"And mine," said Pip.

Pip fell asleep that night with a lightness in her heart that she hadn't felt for a long time.

CHAPTER
SIXTEEN

"Look at this, Mrs H.!"

Adele turned at the sound of Gordon's booming voice behind her. She looked down, expecting to see him in his chair, and then had to raise it when she realised that he was standing.

"Gordon!" she exclaimed. "You're up!"

"Yes," he said. "Whatsername, physio woman, she noticed how much weight I'd lost, told me I should give the crutches a try. I mean, Christ, look at this." He pulled out the waistband of his old-man jeans to display the looseness. "I'm fading away!"

But for once he didn't sound cross about it. He sounded triumphant. And Adele noticed he'd lost some of the disturbing redness to his face, the look he'd had for so long of a boil that was about to pop. It was possible, for the first time in years, to see the handsome man he'd once been.

"That's amazing, Gordon," she said, "so good to see you on your feet again! I mean your, well, your foot."

He laughed out loud at her faux pas. "Good to be upright," he said, "and pain-free. But listen, Mrs H., bit of a favour to ask you. Are you going to the shops at all today?"

"I certainly am."

"Well, there's something I need you to get for me."

"Right," she said to Gordon a few hours later, unloading shopping on to the table. "They didn't have the one you asked for, so I got you this." She held it towards him.

"Is it brown?" he asked.

"Yes," she said. "It's brown. Slightly lighter than the one you're used to. But I think it will suit you better."

"As long as it's brown, I don't give a shit."

"Good," she said, "right, well, shall we do it now?"

"No time like the present, Mrs H."

She fetched an old towel from the airing cupboard, sat Gordon on a kitchen chair and pinned the towel around his shoulders. Then she opened the package of hair dye and read the instructions. It hadn't been strictly true that they didn't have his shade of brown in stock. They'd had plenty of choice in the "unnaturally creepily dark brown for a seventy-year-old man" department. But she'd chosen something lighter, hopefully less alarming.

The girls were in the garden and in their rooms, their lessons over for the day. Leo was still at work. Scout lay under the table at Gordon's feet. The kitchen radio was tuned into Radio 6. Adele mixed the ingredients of the hair dye together, put on some clear plastic gloves and then, using a plastic comb, parted Gordon's silky hair and began squeezing the cream into his snowy white roots.

"Does Affie do this for you at home?"

"Of course she does. Or one of her daughters."

"Her daughters? But they're only young, aren't they?"

"They're eleven."

Affie's first husband had died when she was pregnant with twin girls. They'd been a year old when Gordon had met her through an Anglo-African dating website ten years ago.

"Gosh," she said, "and you've got them doing your hair!"

"It's different there," he said. "Children aren't put on bloody pedestals. They're brought up to take responsibility for their homes, to respect old people. They wouldn't see it as an imposition to do my hair. They'd see it as part of their role as a member of a family. None of this fucking eye-rolling and tutting that western children do. You know, those girls of yours, yes, they're all very polite with their hello-how-are-yous and their offering around the drinks to guests, but they treat you like a fucking slave, Mrs H. That middle one . . ."

"Fern."

"Yes, yes, Fern. The other day I watched her peel a satsuma and then just leave the peel. Pile it all up in a neat little mound and leave it there. For her *slave* to dispose of. Christ, if one of Affie's girls did that she'd beat them black and blue. Or I would."

Adele stopped in her tracks, the bottle of dye suspended above Gordon's head. "What?"

"Well, not back and blue. But a clip here and there. Of course."

"But, Gordon, they're not even your children. How could you bear to lay a finger . . .?"

"They *are* my children," he said. "I've raised them from babies. I pay for their schooling, their clothing, their food. They call me Papa. Of course they're my children."

"Doesn't Affie mind?"

"Mind? No. Why would she mind? She expects me to discipline them. She'd think I was spoiling them if I didn't. And if there's one thing you don't find very often in central Africa, it's spoiled children. Leo's mother, my first wife — Christ, she spoiled our boys. Spoiled all three of them. I tried to keep discipline in this house but she wouldn't let me. If I so much as laid a hand on one of her precious sons she wouldn't talk to me for days." He sighed, sadly, as though his troubles were deep and endless.

"But they've all turned out OK, haven't they? You know, Gordon, with parenting there's a long game and a short game. The aim of the short game is to make your children bearable to live with. Easy to transport. Well behaved in public places. In other words, to make your own life easier. And, yes, you can achieve that with punishments, with discipline, with a *clip here and there*. But the aim of the long game is to produce a good human being. And personally, I don't believe that you need to play the short game in order to win the long game. I genuinely believe you can skip it. That it's optional."

There was a beat of weighty and ominous silence before Gordon spoke.

"That is utter, utter, *utter* bullshit. Dear Christ, Mrs H., it's in the middle of your so-called *short game* that the worst things can happen. Your dear, oh-so-*innocent* children are running wild out there, just like my boys did, and look what happened there."

Adele drew a breath. "What happened?"

"Well, you know, the business with the girl. Phoebe. The one who died."

"But that had nothing to do with your sons, with Leo."

"Didn't it?"

"No! Of course it didn't!"

"If you say so."

"Of course I say so! Jesus, Gordon. What *are* you going on about?" She shook her head crossly.

"I'm talking about kids, Mrs H. Terrible, dreadful, blasted awful kids. They've all got a darkness inside them. They've all got the capacity for evil. Give them free range over a piece of territory, like that out there, and you've got *Lord of the Flies*. You cannot afford to take your eye off the ball for a second. Not for even a second. You know, you think you're keeping your girls all pure and unsullied in this gilded cage of yours. But what you don't seem to realise is that you can protect children from the world, but you can't protect children from themselves."

Adele's thoughts raced horribly to the strange passage in Rhea's memoir: the Howes boys hanging around with no tops on, acting like gangsters and hoodlums with their gold chains and their ghetto blaster. And the girls, the young, young girls, being passed from brother to brother. Until one of them died.

She shook her head to dislodge the image and slowly she roused herself back to the present. She combed the dye through Gordon's thick hair, allowing the sharp chemical tang to seep into the membranes inside her nose. Then she covered his head with a clear plastic cap and said, "There you go, Gordon, twenty minutes and you'll be a vision."

Still shaken by Gordon's words, Adele watched the girls from the terrace later that evening. Ever since Catkin had been young enough to toddle across the garden on her own and find her way back home again, Adele had used it as an unpaid babysitter. Her children were safe out there. She could concentrate on other things. Cook a meal. Tidy a room. Make a phone call. And as the years had gone by and her girls had got bigger and made friends, spending hours out there instead of minutes, she'd become more and more dependent on the space it gave her. As far as she was concerned the garden was an extension of her home. There were other people out there, but they had her children's best interests at heart, just as she had their children's best interests at heart. Phoebe's death, all those summers before, had been just one of those things. Nothing to do with the community or with the children. Just a wild child come to a sticky end.

But it was a fragile alchemy too, she realised, and the arrival of the two new girls had disordered things. Dylan and Tyler didn't seem as close any more. Catkin was pulling away from the gang. There was a fragility between them all that had never been there before. Was it possible, she thought, that something sinister was going on? That the "playing" that had evolved over the years into "hanging out" had now begun to evolve into something darker?

Willow was indoors with another friend of hers from the garden called Sophie, playing with her chinchilla. Catkin lay in the sun at the top of the hill, her head rested on a rolled-up jumper, reading a book that she was holding above her head. Fern was on the swings, her long legs bent beneath her into acute triangles, listening to music. At the other end of the garden were Pip and Grace, sitting under one of the willow trees, cross-legged, talking in that intense way of theirs.

The scene was as she'd expected it to be: innocent, gentle, an unruffled oasis. She stretched out a hand to pull the dog to her and ran her hands over his powder-puff ears. Then she heard the garden gate slam and loud laughter and the whizz and whirr of bicycle wheels. A moment later Tyler and Dylan streaked past Adele's terrace, engaged in some kind of high-octane race. Tyler stood astride her bike, majestically. Dylan crouched forward, his jaw jutting out determinedly.

"Hi, you two!" Adele called after them, but they didn't hear her. She saw them do a full circuit of the garden and then come to a breathless halt near Catkin. They stopped there for a while. Catkin put down her book and brought herself up to a sitting position, shielding her eyes from the sun with her forearm while she talked to them. Fern wandered over in that slouchy, nothing-interests-me-in-the-slightest way of hers and they all sat together for a while chatting. Adele watched with interest to see what Grace and Pip would do. She saw them look over and discuss the situation. She saw Pip shake her head. Then Grace shrugged, got to her feet and wandered towards the group while Pip went home.

Adele saw Tyler staring as Grace approached, then look her up and down slowly in that awful, forensic way that girls do. Then she saw Dylan take Grace's hand briefly in his before letting it go. Tyler clocked the gesture, picked up her bike, then turned and strode across the garden towards the gates.

"Where are you going?" Fern called out.

"Home," she replied.

The four children on the hill stared after her for a while, then turned and looked at Dylan. Dylan shrugged. Then they all went and sat on the benches.

So, thought Adele, that's all it was. Grace and Dylan were an item. Tyler was jealous, Pip felt alienated by all the drama. Just normal, teenage shenanigans. Nothing darker than that.

She pulled Scout on to her lap and held him upside down, like a baby. She stared into his eyes for a moment and he stared back into hers. She felt moved suddenly by the innocence of him, the complete lack of guile. It was the same look she'd seen in the eyes of her children when they were babies, and it was heart-breaking.

178

She glanced up at the sound of Leo's voice. She carried the dog to her back gate, where she peered around the corner. She saw him by the entrance to the communal gardens. He had a Waitrose carrier bag in each hand and was talking to Tyler. He was leaning down, watching her intently as she talked. Then he put down the carrier bags and encircled her in his arms. She buried her face deep into the space between his pectorals, her hands squeezed together against his chest. He kissed the crown of her head and rubbed his hands down her hair. Then they pulled away from each other and he tipped her face up with a thumb under her chin and wiped a tear from her cheek and she smiled, sadly, and he smiled and then they said a few more words to each other before Tyler reached up on her tiptoes and kissed him on the cheek, righted her bike and disappeared up the passageway towards the gates.

Leo collected his shopping bags and greeted Adele with a smile when he saw her waiting for him on their terrace. "Hello, lover."

She smiled thinly. Tyler had always had an affectionate relationship with Leo. She'd been one of those children who climbed on to people's laps without invitation, fiddled with people's hair, insisted on games of peekaboo with strangers, who instinctively sought to beguile and ensnare. And Leo had long been a favoured object of her widespread affections.

But Tyler was thirteen now. Was it still appropriate for him to maintain that kind of physical relationship with her?

"What's going on with Tyler?" she asked, following Leo into the kitchen, helping him to unload his shopping bags.

"Boy trouble, I think. She didn't really want to talk about it."

She watched her husband as he unpacked his shopping and started assembling things for making a soup. As she watched something vile hit the back of her throat. A sluice of something spicy she'd eaten earlier mixed up with the large glass of white wine she'd poured for herself half an hour ago.

"Poor little Tyler," she said.

"Yes," said Leo. "Poor lost soul."

CHAPTER
SEVENTEEN

Adele loved the entrance to Rhea's mansion block: double doors, wood panelling, claret carpets, the smell of beeswax and the click and whirr of the ancient elevator with its concertina doors polished to a high shine. She took the stairs to the second floor and Rhea greeted her at her front door.

"You'll have to excuse me," Rhea said, gesturing at her outfit of pilled orange polo neck, baggy grey leggings and ancient sheepskin slippers. "I'm not in my Sunday best."

"You look lovely, Rhea. You always look lovely."

She clutched at her throat and her earlobes. "I feel naked without my bling," she said, laughing. "Give me a minute!"

She ushered Adele into her living room, where she'd already laid out gilt-rimmed teacups and saucers and plates of chocolate-topped biscuits, cheese puffs and sugared almonds.

Her giant rabbit sat in a fleece-lined bed staring at Adele impassively, his nose twitching. And all around were the trophies of Rhea's life: framed family photos filled every inch of every wall, at least half a dozen different graduation photographs from three different decades, formal portraits and collaged arrangements of sun-faded snaps. Every surface was covered with some kind of lace topping, including the backs of her block-cut velour sofas. Upon her carpeted floor lay a patchwork of extraneous rugs of varying shapes and textures. French doors on to her balcony framed the most exquisite view of the gardens. From here you could see virtually the entire sweep. Adele stepped on to the balcony and looked down.

A group of young mothers with their toddlers and babies was sitting just there, in the very spot where Phoebe's body had been found twenty-three years earlier.

Rhea returned, a huge gilt-rimmed teapot in one hand, another packet of biscuits in the other, her neck adorned once more with ropes of gold.

"This weather!" said Rhea. "It can't last! Surely!"

"Apparently we're set for a long hot summer," said Adele.

"Well, that would be nice for a change." She laid the pot on the table, her hand shaking slightly, then sat down next to Adele and appraised her warmly. "How are your family?"

"They're fine, thank you," Adele replied.

"Your beautiful girls?"

"They're doing great."

"And your handsome husband?"

"Still handsome."

"And what about your father-in-law? I hear he is your guest for now?"

"Yes." Adele sighed. "For my sins."

"Ah, that man. You know, Adele, it may not be my place to say this, but I would not be happy to have that man in my house. With my daughters."

Adele raised her brow. "Oh, Rhea. He's not *that* bad. He's always had a wandering eye but he's not about to commit incest."

"Well, still, you should keep an eye on him. Once a dog, *always* a dog. A leopard cannot change his spots."

"Thank you, Rhea. I'm sure it's fine. But thank you."

"Here, have some cheesy puffs. These are the best ones. Waitrose own brand. Have you tried them?"

"No, I haven't tried them. But I won't, thank you."

Rhea put the bowl down with a shrug that said: *Your loss.*

"Listen, Rhea, I've had something playing on my mind for a few weeks. Since I read your memoir."

The deep dimple in Rhea's cheek disappeared and she looked momentarily distraught. "Oh, no! Please, what is it?"

"It's just, well, I hadn't realised until I read your book that Leo and Cecelia had had a fling together, that summer."

"The summer of Phoebe?"

"Yes, the summer of Phoebe. And it took me a bit by surprise because, of course, she was only thirteen and Leo was almost eighteen — you know, virtually an adult."

"Well, look, I don't know if it was a fling. I don't know what it was, Adele." Rhea shrugged apologetically, as though she felt bad for bringing it up at all.

"It *was* a fling. I asked Leo about it and he told me. I just wondered . . . did you ever think — I mean, even just as a crazy theory — that Phoebe's death might have had something to do with Leo and his brothers?"

Rhea's dark eyes widened. She clutched her gold chains with her fingertips. "Adele! What a question!"

"I know, it's just . . . I was talking to Gordon yesterday and he said something weird, about how his boys were to blame for her death, how children turn into animals in that garden."

"Well, there he might have a point. Children left to their own devices can be wild. But your Leo? Killing that girl?"

"Well, that's not quite what Gordon was implying. The implication was more that Leo had somehow caused it. He and his brothers."

"Crazy!" Rhea said. "That man is absolutely crazy!"

Adele nodded. "I know. He really is. But, still, when you think about it, Phoebe had to have died for some reason. Maybe it did have something to do with Leo and his brothers? In an indirect way? To do with all the romantic complications? You know, kids, they feel things so strongly. Everything is magnified at that age."

"Adele." Rhea put a hand over hers and squeezed it. "Phoebe was not your average fifteen-year-old. Phoebe was like a time bomb waiting to go off. It was just a matter of time, and there was nothing anyone could have done about it."

"But in what way? The world is full of messed-up teenagers drinking and taking drugs and having sex and they don't all end up dead at fifteen."

"Indeed. This is true. But there was something else about that girl. Behind the good-time girl, behind the fun and the frivolity. This sadness in her eyes. Like she'd seen all the bad things in the world and given up all hope for mankind. For herself. And you know, that is a look I know better than most."

"Yes. I know." Adele moved her hand on to Rhea's and stroked it. "Why do you think she was like that?"

"Her mother. Oh, *her mother*." Rhea rolled her eyes heavenwards.

Adele had heard about Phoebe and Cecelia's mother many times over the years, through Leo, through Gordon, through anyone who'd lived on the garden at the time. Her name was Marian and she'd been the headmistress of the private girls' school up the road for twenty years. Her husband had been Frank, a milkman who'd retired due to ill health in his thirties and then died at forty of a heart attack when the girls were still small. Marian had quickly remarried, leaving the garden community fairly certain that the relationship had begun long before Frank's early demise. The new husband was not interested in children. Marian was only interested in the children at her school and Cecelia and Phoebe were left roaming the garden all day and all night. And then, as Rhea reminded her now, "When Marian *was* at home, the screaming and the crying and the banging and the smashing would start and he'd be there" — she pointed to the other side of the garden — "smoking a cigarette out of the window, until it had all blown over. Then, slam, you'd hear the window go down, and it would be quiet again. An unhappy

185

woman. Unhappy husband. Unhappy children. And now . . ." She sighed. ". . . that Cecelia. She is repeating all the patterns. All the mistakes of her own mother. And I look at her daughter and I see the same thing in her eye that Phoebe had. The same look of hopelessness."

"Tyler?"

"Yes. Tyler."

Adele thought of the odd, brittle, affectionate, energetic, stroppy and fun-loving girl she'd known since she was a baby.

"You don't think . . .? I mean, she won't go the same way as Phoebe, will she?"

"I hope not, Adele. I really do hope not."

Adele thought of Leo's thumb lifting Tyler's chin yesterday and of Gordon's bizarre declaration. Then she thought of thirteen-year-old Cecelia sitting on Leo's lap, wearing his chain, his adult lips on her childish ones. Her head spun. Her stomach lurched.

Clare turned left outside the tube and brought up Google Maps on her smartphone. She was dressed strangely for the warm summer weather, in jeans and a loose-fitting black cotton jacket that belonged to one of the girls, her blonde hair covered by a baseball cap. She was in Walthamstow, with Lovestruck Roxy's address programmed into her mobile. She didn't really know why. It was probably a stupid thing to do. But it had been nagging and nagging at her. And in a strange way she felt she owed it to Leo, for his kindness and his concern.

186

Roxy's flat formed part of a small terraced Victorian house on a nondescript, distinctly ungentrified street. The front garden was cemented over and filled with weeds, used to house numerous bins and recycling containers. There were three bells by the front door. Clare walked past the house four times. She'd been hoping she might be able to find a spot to stand and observe for a while, but on a quiet street like this she'd have stood out conspicuously. It was eleven o'clock in the morning. Roxy would be at work. And if Chris was here, he'd no doubt be lying low. She was about to pass for a fifth time when she heard an internal door slam shut. Then she saw a shadow pass across the opaque glass panels of the front door. She inhaled and pulled herself back slightly, pretending to be looking for something in her handbag. She saw a young woman appear in the doorway of the house. She was very small and slim with her hair cut into a sharp black bob. She was wearing a black asymmetric dress with calf-height leather strappy boots and her arms were heavily tattooed. She was talking to someone standing in the hallway; Clare could see a large hand grasping the doorframe, a male knee in faded black trousers, a huge, socked foot. She heard a male cough.

Moving slightly closer, she heard the young woman say, "I'll be back in a couple of hours. Maybe three if they keep me back for the second session."

Then, as each hair on her arms stood up in turn, she heard her husband's voice, loud as an actor upon a stage, saying, "OK, Rox. And good luck. Not that you'll need it."

She watched Roxy lean in to her husband and accept a brief hug. She saw a flash of his hair, shorter than it had ever been before, a wildly bearded chin, a grey hoodie. And then Roxy turned to go and her husband closed the door and Clare stood, her feet rooted to the pavement as though set in concrete, watching Roxy walk away from her and thinking, *My husband is in that house my husband is in that house my husband is in that house. And he's wearing socks.* For a whole minute she did nothing. And then, finally, she straightened herself, and walked, circumspectly, back to the tube station.

"Mum?" Pip was sitting at the kitchen counter on a bar stool. She'd been doing her homework, but now she'd put down her pen and closed her exercise book. "When are they going to tell us where Dad is?"

Clare jumped slightly. Pip hadn't mentioned Chris for a few days. It seemed strange that she should do so on the very same day on which Clare had seen him, alive and kicking, with short hair and a beard, living with a tattooed lady called Roxy in the dog end of London E11.

"I don't know."

"Can you ask them?"

"Why?"

"I've got things to send him."

"What things?"

"Just letters. It feels weird writing to him and not sending them anywhere. It's like he's disappeared off the face of the earth. Like he doesn't exist any more."

Clare thought of the large hand clutching the doorframe, the booming voice. "Well, I can assure you, he does exist and he's still trying to get better."

"But, Mum, it's been more than six months. I mean, what are they doing? What are they actually doing in there? Why isn't he better yet? I don't understand."

"No. I don't understand either."

"Can you call them? Please? Call them and find out what's happening? Can you do it now?"

"Pip, it's late. All the office people will have gone home now."

"Well, will you call tomorrow?"

"I'll try."

"Why 'try'? Why can't you just do it? It's not fair. He's my dad and I know you're still really cross with him and scared of him and everything but I love him and I haven't see him for so long and I don't understand why I can't!"

Clare sighed and pulled her hair back off her face with the palm of her hand. "You're right. You're absolutely right. It isn't fair. And I will call them tomorrow and see what I can do. But I can't promise anything, OK?"

Pip's face softened and she smiled a small smile. "OK."

Clare checked the time on the oven. Fifteen minutes until the lasagne was ready. She stood behind Pip and squeezed her middle-section, savouring the substance of her, the yielding softness around her belly, the solid warmth of her.

"What would I do without you?" she said.

"You'd probably just die," said Pip, drily.

"Yes," said Clare, "I probably would."

"I love you," said Pip.

"I love you too." She pulled away and smiled. "Right, I'd better go and find your sister."

"Can't you just call her?"

"Well, I could, but I fancy some fresh air. And it's so lovely out there. Will you lock the door behind me?"

Pip rolled her eyes. "Seriously, Mum, what do you think is going to happen?"

"I don't know," she said, "but I wouldn't leave you here with the front door unlocked, so why would I leave you with the back door unlocked?"

Pip rolled her eyes again and followed Clare to the back door to lock it after her.

Clare breathed in deeply as she started across the lawn. Coming out to find Grace was something of a pretext. She was really hoping to run into Leo, to tell him about seeing Chris at Roxy's place, to ask his advice about what to do next. There was no sign of the gang at the top of the hill so she took the path around the perimeter of the garden towards the Howeses' apartment. There she found them all hanging out on their terrace: Tyler, Max, the sisters, Leo and — somewhat unexpectedly and in a way that made her stomach tense and contract — Grace, sitting on Dylan's lap, his arms around her waist. She sat up and looked startled when she saw her mother standing there. Clare saw her quickly unthread Dylan's fingers and slide off his lap.

"Hi!" said Clare, feeling exposed and strangely foolish.

"Clare!" said Leo. "Hi! Come in. Come in."

"Oh . . ." She shook her head. "No. Thank you. I just came to let Grace know that dinner's ready." She smiled broadly.

"You could have just phoned," Grace countered.

"Yes," she said lightly, "I know, but I fancied some fresh air." She looked at Dylan from the sides of her eyes, at this boy she'd noticed from the very beginning because of his green eyes and his perfect skin and his way about him that seemed far beyond that of an average thirteen-year-old boy. She'd noticed him and her daughters had noticed him and yet it had never occurred to Clare that one of her daughters would end up sitting on his lap. *Who are you?* she wanted to say. *Who are you and are you now a part of my life?*

He saw her looking at him and quickly averted his gaze in a way that Clare could not quite judge; was it dodgy, guilty, shy, dismissive? Was it *knowing?*

"Anyway," she said, "it's ready. You can come and eat it now or have it later when it's cold. It's up to you."

"OK." Grace sighed heavily. "I'll come soon."

"Good." Clare turned and headed home, her cheeks flaming. Were they kissing? Were they touching each other's bodies? She thought of the things she'd read in the papers about how young boys expected blowjobs at the drop of a hat these days. Had she? Had her baby, not yet thirteen, had she done that? She pictured Dylan, his green eyes averted from hers, those broad shoulders and sculpted cheekbones. What kind of a boy was he? She had no idea.

"Whoa, slow down!"

She turned to see Leo striding up behind her. "You OK?" His hand resting on her arm again, bringing that same surge of relief followed by fear she felt whenever he touched her.

"Yes. Sorry. Just, you know, *teenagers*."

He smiled wryly. "I certainly do know teenagers."

"And I had no idea, you know, Grace and Dylan . . ."

"Ah." He nodded, realisation dawning. "I assumed you . . ."

"No." She shook her head. "No. Definitely not. She's only twelve."

"God, is she? Really? I thought she was older."

"No, she looks older — they both do, my girls — but no, she is still only twelve. And I'm not sure she's ready and I know for a fact that *I'm* not ready and . . . agh." She shuddered. "I am feeling very strange right now."

He moved his hand back to her arm. "Listen," he said, his eyes firmly upon hers, "if it's any comfort, I've known Dylan since he was a baby and he is a fine, fine boy. Very mature. Very caring. You should see him with his brother . . ."

"He has a brother?"

"Yes. Rob. He's much older, has lots of special needs, lives in a residential home. He's essentially a child but Dylan has always looked out for him, protected him. Rob comes back for holidays and the odd weekend and Dylan includes him in everything.

192

He's a kind boy. I mean, *obviously*" — he moved his hand from her arm to his heart — "I am a very old fart and can only guess what's really going on with *the young people*, but honestly, if I were you, I would let it run its course. These things never last. It'll all be over this time next week."

Clare nodded and sighed. "Have you been through this yet?" she asked. "With your girls?"

"Ah." He dropped his chin. "No. Well, at least, not as far as I'm aware. There was an American boy, a couple of summers back; he and Catkin hung out a fair amount but I don't think it went further than that. And Fern is Fern, living in her own little world. Willow is still a baby. And, you know, they live a fairly sheltered life. So no, I haven't had to deal with this yet. But I hope when I do that I can keep calm about it." He smiled. "So. How are things? Generally?"

She thought of the lasagne in the oven and wondered if Pip would think to take it out when the alarm went off. She decided to risk it. "I went to Walthamstow today," she whispered. "I saw him."

Leo's eyebrows jumped. He let out a puff of air. "Wow. So your hunch was right."

"Yes. Looks that way."

"And how was it? Did you talk to him?"

"No, I just saw him, fleetingly — not even all of him, just bits of him."

"Bits of him?"

"His knee, his hand, the side of his face."

"And?"

She shrugged. "He seemed fine. He seemed normal. She was going somewhere, an interview or something. He wished her luck and gave her a hug. That was it. And now . . ." She looked for the words that would somehow make sense of the mixed feelings she'd been having all day long. "I don't know now . . . His voice." She glanced up into Leo's eyes. His attention was fixed on her, intensely. "His lovely voice. I'd forgotten. So soft and deep. And he was wearing socks."

"Socks?"

She smiled. "Isn't that the silliest thing? Socks. His big feet in socks. And he seemed so normal. When the last time I saw him he was so mad. So mad." She shook her head. "And now I'm not sure. I'm not sure what to do. Am I being irresponsible knowing where he is, when he could be a threat to me and my children, and not doing anything about it? Or am I being compassionate? I mean, he could be building up to another episode right now, and he knows where we live, yet . . ."

"Yet he's a human being."

"Yes! Exactly. And for so long, in my head, he's been a monster."

Leo nodded. "You know," he said, softly, "maybe you should talk to her? To Roxy?"

"You think?"

"Well, she'll have the clearest perspective on him right now. On his state of mind."

"Yes, but she's *in love* with him. And she's not a mother. She'll do anything to protect him. Even lie."

Leo sighed. "You're right," he said. "You are absolutely right. Listen. I've got a friend. He works in mental health, over in Islington. I could talk to him? Ask him anonymously? Would that be helpful?"

"God, yes. That really would."

Leo smiled, touched her arm yet again. This time Clare found herself unthinkingly clasping her hand over his, holding it there tightly. "Good," he said, their hands still held together, "leave it with me."

Slowly, she unpeeled her hand from his, and slowly he let his hand fall from her arm. There followed a tiny, exquisitely awkward silence before Clare pulled herself back into shape and said, "Well, I'd better go and rescue our lasagne from the oven before it's nuked."

Leo simply smiled and nodded and watched her go.

Virginia Gardens Annual Summer Party!

Face-Painting!
Live Jazz!
Tombola!
Beautiful-Pet Competition!
Petting Zoo!
Races & Tug O' War!

Saturday July 5th!
2p.m. till late!
All welcome!

CHAPTER
EIGHTEEN

Through the garden door Clare could see the white peaks of the tents and gazebos that had been assembled by the eager beaver garden committee since early this morning. The sun was high in a cloudless sky. The garden was full of the sounds of industry and expectation. It was the day of the Virginia Gardens Annual Summer Party.

And also the day that her firstborn became a teenager.

She'd thrown Grace a small party in their back garden earlier: non-alcoholic cocktails, helium balloons, a giant red velvet cake with thirteen candles, all her friends from the garden, a round of "Happy Birthday to You", nothing fancy.

Now she stacked sticky paper cups into a tower, gathered up handfuls of brightly coloured straws with concertinaed tissue fruits attached, balled up used paper napkins and shreds of ripped wrapping paper and envelopes and dropped them all into a black bag. She took birthday cards through to the living room and arranged them on the dining table, piled up Grace's gifts neatly: a hoodie from Tyler, just like the hoodies that Tyler herself wore; a John Green novel and a framed arrangement of silk butterflies from the sisters; money and a malodorous celebrity perfume from Clare's mother; clothes from her; a glittering diamanté bracelet from Pip in a suedette box; and from Dylan, well ... Clare didn't know what he'd bought her daughter; Grace had taken it still wrapped into her bedroom after the party, saying she was saving it for later.

They'd gone now, all the children. Grace had changed into the floral camisole top and silky boxer shorts that Clare had bought her for her birthday, applied more make-up to her fresh-skinned face and they'd all headed out into the communal garden.

Clare took the bin bag to the hallway and opened the front door. She stopped when she saw Leo passing by on the street, the familiar loping gait, his hands full of shopping bags.

"Hi," he said, smiling warmly. "Birthday party over?"

"Yes, just clearing up."

"How did it go?"

"It was good. They're fed and watered, ready for the garden party."

Leo nodded and as he did so his sunglasses fell from the top of his head to the pavement. Clare dropped the bin bag on the front path and ran to pick them up for him. "All in one piece," she said, dusting them down and sliding them back on to the top of his head.

"Thank you," said Leo.

The moment had been strangely intimate, her fingers against his hair, and it stretched itself out somehow,

198

beyond real time. Clare found herself flushing and took a step back from him.

He looked towards his carrier bags. "Doing a barbecue later on. Plenty here for you and the girls. You're welcome to come over and join us?"

"Oh," said Clare, slightly thrown by the invitation. "What sort of time?"

"Whenever you like. We'll be on the terrace all day. Whenever you like."

Clare nodded. "Lovely," she said. "Thank you. Can I bring anything?"

Leo smiled. "Just your lovely self," he said. "Just your lovely self."

Adele was halfway through transforming an angelic toddler into a horrible ghoul when her daughters appeared with Grace and Dylan. Since Grace's party had finished they'd all been wandering about aimlessly, territorially, pretending that they weren't having fun.

"Happy birthday, Grace!" she said. "Did you have a nice party?"

"Yes, thank you," said Grace, smiling her inscrutable smile. "Thank you for the presents."

"Oh, you are welcome. It wasn't much, but I'm glad you liked them."

"Can we help? said Catkin, smiling in amusement at the sombre child in the chair.

Catkin unfolded another chair and picked up a handful of brushes. Adele looked up from her little skeleton girl and smiled at her daughter. Fern flipped open a third chair and called over a little girl who wanted to be painted as a rabbit. Willow acted as assistant, cleaning brushes, passing colours.

Adele picked up a damp sponge wedge and smudged out the dark sockets around the toddler's eyes. Then she lifted her head from the child's face to see if she could spot her parents anywhere. As she looked around, her eye was caught by the sight of Grace and Dylan, heads together over her little shoulder bag, looking at something inside it, smiling at one another, closing the little bag and then leaving the garden through the communal gates, Grace looking back just once, over her shoulder, as though checking that they hadn't been seen.

CHAPTER
NINETEEN

Clare felt a flutter of anxiety as she approached the Howeses' terrace later that afternoon. There seemed to be an awful lot of people clustered around the table.

"Clare! Pip! You're here! Excellent." Leo got to his feet and pulled chairs out for them. "Clare," he said, "this is my sister-in-law, Zoe." He gestured at an attractive dark-haired woman who was unmistakably Adele's sister. "And this is John, Zoe's husband." A nice-looking man with a blond beard and thick-framed glasses stood up to shake her hand. "And these little cuties are my niece and nephew, George and Darcy. Everyone, this is Clare, our neighbour from across the way. And this is Pip, her daughter."

"One of my daughters," she replied. "I'm not quite sure where the other one is."

"I saw her just a few minutes ago," said Leo. "With the gang."

Clare exhaled. "Oh. Good. What are they up to?"

"No idea," he replied breezily. "Hanging out. Talking crap. *Stuff.*" He waved a bottle of wine and said, "Red? Or white? Or, in fact, Pimm's? Is there any Pimm's left?" He swept his gaze across the table. "No, we must have drunk it all. Sorry about that."

Leo poured her out a glass of white wine and passed Pip a beaker of cordial. "Where's Adele?" she asked, feeling slightly out of place without the mother figure here to bind them together.

"Just putting away the face-painting stall. She left the girls to run it for an hour and apparently the stall got hijacked by a bunch of younger children who completely trashed it." He laughed, rubbing his hand across his stomach. "Apparently there is a small naked boy running about out there painted head to toe in sludge brown. Apart from around his private parts. He's supposed to be a poo."

"Leo," Gordon called from the French doors. "Pass me a foldy chair, will you? I'm going to stake my place for the jazz."

Leo rolled his eyes good-naturedly. "I'll do it, Dad. You stay here." He pulled a stripy retro deckchair from a small wooden shed and smiled conspiratorially at the others.

"No," said Gordon, "not much in the mood for socialising. Think I'll just take a walk." He nodded towards the stripy chair. "Put me front row centre."

Clare watched Gordon leaving. Huge pile of a man. His movements so forced and peculiar. The dyed brown hair. The violently patterned shirt. She watched him stand for a moment in the heart of the garden, turning his big head this way and that, looking both lost and imperious. Like a deposed king, she thought.

"Pip," she said quietly in her daughter's ear. "Do me a favour, will you? Can you have a look for Grace for me? Just find out where she is? You don't need to say anything to her."

Pip sighed. "OK, then."

"How old is she?" asked Adele's sister, watching Pip's retreating figure.

"Twelve," said Clare. "Just."

"Gosh, she's very tall."

"Yes," said Clare. "Her dad is six foot three."

"Wow. And you're so tiny!"

Clare regarded her wine glass. She had drunk half already. There was going to be a lot of small talk ahead. She would need more than her usual small glass to get through it.

Pip returned a moment later and slid back on to her chair, her hand reaching automatically for the crisps in front of her.

"Well?" Clare asked quietly. "Did you see her?"

Pip nodded and put a crisp in her mouth.

"What's she doing?"

"I don't know. She's with Dylan and Tyler and they're all just kind of talking."

Clare peered curiously at Pip, who appeared to be processing crisps down her throat as a form of distraction rather than for pleasure.

"Are they all OK?"

Pip nodded and took another crisp. Clare put her hand out to Pip's to stop the process. "Are you sure?" she asked. "Do I need to go over?"

"No," Pip snapped under her breath. "Don't go over. They're fine. Just leave them."

Clare looked at her in surprise. She saw Leo staring at her meaningfully.

"Everything OK?"

She nodded, then picked up her freshly filled glass and knocked back a third in two gulps.

Adele was back. She'd said she was filthy and needed a shower and had appeared on the terrace five minutes ago all fresh and pretty in a floral dress and a black shawl, wearing red lipstick and earrings that glittered. The air was still golden and filling up now with the sounds of the jazz band warming up: stray squawks of saxophone, sonorous vibrations of double bass, hoots of trumpet. High-pitched feedback from the sound system. *Testing testing.* The crowds of people in the garden had moved across to the spot just outside the next-door house. They arranged themselves afresh on their blankets, opened new bottles of wine, adjusted their sunglasses to the lowering golden sun. Zoe and John had taken their two small children out and sat now with a child on each of their laps just outside Leo and Adele's back gate.

"You not going to watch?" Adele asked her.

Clare shook her head. "Not really a fan of jazz," she said.

Adele laughed. "Me neither," she said. "I like music with proper tunes."

Leo had gone indoors to start getting the food ready for the barbecue. Adele and Pip were sitting side by side, drawing.

They're really good with kids.

She remembered one of her girls saying that to her a while ago.

Clare sighed and collected her wine glass from the windowsill, taking it through with her to the kitchen.

Leo was slicing open film-topped packets of sausages and chicken pieces, arranging them on to a huge platter. He looked up at her and smiled.

"Came in for some water," she said. "Think I need to sober up a bit."

He grimaced at her and laughed. "Why on earth would you need to sober up? It's Saturday! It's summer! It's a party!"

"I know, I know. But I'm a single parent. Sole responsibility and all that. It's not good . . ."

"Oh, come on now. Your girls are virtually adults. I think you can afford to let your hair down from time to time. Not that you have much hair to let down."

Clare smiled anxiously and put her hand up to her boyish crop. She thought of Adele's lustrous mahogany mane, imagined her pulling out that elastic band at the end of the day, it falling in waves over her bare shoulders, down her olivey back.

He looked at her curiously, as though he'd been watching her thoughts. Then he poured her a glass of water and passed it to her. "What you need", he said, turning back to his pile of meat, "is something to eat. You will stay, won't you? I have, as ever, royally over-catered."

Clare nodded. Then she looked behind her and said, in an urgent whisper, "He's been again."

Leo glanced up at her. "Chris?"

"Yes. This afternoon. Another carrier bag. Gifts for Grace." She shivered at the memory of her mother standing in the hallway with the bag in her hand saying, "Clare. I found this on your doorstep."

She'd lied to her mother. Said it was from a schoolfriend of Grace's, that her mum had promised she'd drop it off. Then she'd put it on the table in front of her, violently resisting the urge to open it until her mother had left.

A gigantic make-up kit in a smart metal-cased box. Expensive shampoo and conditioner: *For the Coolest Curls Around*. A book by a famous (according to the bio) beauty vlogger. A tasteful card, the numbers 1 and 3 decorated with glitter and paper lace, a fifty-pound note slipped inside.

Darling Grace,

The day you were born was the happiest day of my life. It is hard to believe that today you are a teenager and even harder to believe that I can't be there to celebrate with you. But I hope you understand why that is. And I hope one day I can be a part of your amazing, beautiful, extraordinary life once more.

I love you and am thinking about you today and every day,

Lots of love,

Your Daddy

How did he know, she wondered, that the big, almost chubby, fresh-faced girl he'd last seen when she was twelve and a bit was now a leggy, Amazonian thirteen-year-old in skimpy shorts and full make-up? How did he know that everything had changed?

"Did you see him?" Leo asked now.

"No. I mean, assuming it even *was* him. It could be he sent Roxy."

"And was it OK?" he said, washing his hands at the sink. "The gift?"

"It was more than OK," she said. "It was perfect. She'll love it."

"And a card?"

"Yes. A beautiful card. Full of beautiful sentiments." She sighed.

Leo pulled a bag of courgettes out of the vegetable drawer in the fridge and looked at Clare thoughtfully. "You know," he said, "he's handling this really well. Do you think it's possible he might be better?"

Clare frowned. "Better?"

"Yes. You know. Not ill any more?"

"Well, obviously he's not ill any more. They wouldn't have discharged him if he was still ill. It's not about whether or not he's ill. It's about the way I feel about what happened. And I am not over it. I mean, *totally* not over it. He broke something inside me the night he did what he did, something that I'm not sure can ever be fixed."

"Your trust?"

"Yes! My trust! My faith that whatever happened, however ill he became, he would never ever do anything to hurt his family. And I know that wasn't him that night. I know it was an imbalance of chemicals. But, you know, we're all just a cocktail of chemicals when it comes down to it. There's not much else to us, so maybe that was the real him? And maybe this one" — she pointed across the garden towards her flat — "the one sending the thoughtful gifts to his daughter on her thirteenth birthday, the one taking medicine every day, is the fake? And if that's the case, then did I marry a monster?"

She'd begun to cry towards the end of this outburst. It was the wine. It was the emotion of the day. It was him. He crossed the kitchen and came towards her with his arms outstretched. He took her into his arms and she put her face against his T-shirt. She could hear the beating of his heart. She could smell the warmth of his skin. She could feel the depth of his soul. And she wanted, more than anything, to kiss him. And she knew, more than anything, that she must not. That he was married to a good woman. That she was a disaster.

He pulled back from her and for a terrible, remarkable moment she thought he would, that he was going to kiss her, and she tried to decide what she would do and she really didn't know, because she'd had two huge glasses of wine and she was a mess and he was so good and so handsome and she felt hot blood fill her head and sheer panic course through her and then suddenly he was walking away from her, back to his courgettes, and she felt limp and broken.

"No," he said coolly, picking up a courgette and slicing it into rounds, as if nothing had just happened. "You didn't marry a monster. Of course you didn't. And of course your trust feels broken and maybe that will never mend. But the really important thing here is the girls."

She nodded, fervently, as though the girls had been the only thing on her mind all along.

"Maybe it's time to think about letting them see him. Or at least, to give them the option?"

She nodded again. She would agree with anything he said, just so long as he kept talking to her in that steady, calming voice, just so long as she had his attention.

"Obviously in a highly regulated environment. You could do it here, if you'd like. Or maybe talk to Cece. I mean, you know she's a social worker? She'll probably know about those sorts of things."

"Is she coming?" she asked, her hand covering the blotches on her throat. "Tonight?"

"Oh." He looked up at her and smiled. "I doubt it. She has an aversion to nice people. She'd much rather hang about with low life and scum."

"Really?"

"Yes. She collects them. I think she thinks it makes her *real*. I think she thinks hanging out with people like us is some kind of bourgeois joke. Tries to avoid it in case some of our niceness rubs off on her and she ends up remembering that she's middle class too . . . *heaven forbid*." He smiled wryly. "So, no. She avoids the garden party like the plague and she certainly won't want to come and sit and eat organic meat and vegetable kebabs with us. You won't be seeing Cece tonight, that's for sure."

As he talked she noticed the blade of his knife catching the light as he hacked at another courgette and the bony, pointed mounds of his knuckles tight and white-skinned. She saw a muscle flicker in his cheek and she felt suddenly as though she should not be here.

"Thank you," she said, putting her empty water glass down on the kitchen table. "Thank you for listening to my woes. And thank you for the water and thank you for the hug."

He snapped back into his normal shape, his eyes bright once more, his grasp on the knife looser. "Any time, Clare. Any time."

She went back to the terrace where Pip and Adele were still busy drawing and she poured herself another glass of wine.

CHAPTER
TWENTY

The terrace was rammed; all the teenagers were here, sitting cross-legged on floor cushions, ketchup-smeared paper plates balanced on their laps. Leo stood at his monstrous American-style gas barbecue turning over the next batch of chicken pieces, filling the air with the aroma of burning herbs and spices. Adele passed Gordon a paper napkin. His jowls were slick with chicken grease and there were clots of mayonnaise in the creases of his mouth. She mimed wiping his face and he rolled his eyes at her but did as he was told.

Beyond the terrace the garden was emptying out. The jazz band had finished their set and the PA system was being dismantled. Voices echoed from the communal garden gate as people corralled their children, called out goodbyes to friends. The garden was being reclaimed for its residents. Small children appeared in their pyjamas, some with teated bottles of warm milk, some with freshly shampooed hair.

It had been a great party. The weather had been gorgeous. And here, on their own terrace, the party still continued. An extraordinary amount of alcohol had been consumed by all the grown-ups and the conversation around the table now was loud and bombastic — probably, Adele suspected, horribly annoying to the more sober people trying to get on with their evenings in the open-windowed flats above.

Clare, in particular, was a revelation. Brought to some kind of unnerving life by white wine, she was being chatty, almost flirty, leaning in towards Leo with exaggerated interest every time he talked, tipping back her head and then reaching across the table to cover his hand with hers every time he made her laugh. Which was disproportionately frequently.

Her words now were beginning to bleed into one another and Gordon was teasing her. "Another vat of wine for you, young lady?" he said, tipping the wine bottle in her direction. "Or could I interest you in a trough?"

The teenagers drifted away into the garden after they'd cleared their plates. But Willow stayed behind, expressing a desire to get into her pyjamas and chill out. She took Pip into her bedroom, in her usual somewhat forceful way, and then, as the sky began to darken and the garden started to empty, it was just the grown-ups left on the terrace.

Clare got to her feet, her hands gripping the table. "Going to the loo," she said, slurring her words. "I will be right back."

Adele jumped to her feet to help her on her way. As they passed into the hallway Clare turned suddenly to Adele, her Bambi eyes wide and sincere, grasped her arms and said, "You are so, so pretty. I mean, I'm not just saying that, you really are. And you're such a good

212

mother." She took her hands from Adele's arms and pressed them against her own heart, wobbling slightly, enough to give Adele cause to hold her upright. "Such a good mother. I wish I could be such a good mother. I'm a shit mother."

"Oh, Clare, no. Of course you're not."

"No. I am. I really am. I married a shit man. A dangerous man. I did that. I did that to them. And now, I'm just useless. I mean, seriously, look at you. You're teaching your children. You're giving them yourself. What do I do for my children? What kind of role model am I?"

"Clare! For goodness' sake! You're a single mother. You're doing everything you can. And your girls adore you. Be kind to yourself."

"I don't deserve them," she said. "I don't deserve my children."

"Oh, Clare. Come on. This is just the wine talking. Let me make you a nice big mug of coffee and we can have a little chat."

"You're so lovely. And Leo's so lovely. You're so lucky to have him. Do you know that? Do you know that?"

Adele smiled. "We're lucky to have each other."

"You know, Adele . . ." Clare swayed gently and grabbed hold of the wall. She squinted into Adele's eyes and then held a pointy finger out towards her. "I am almost jealous of you." She swayed again, this time nearly falling over completely. She righted herself. *"Nearly jealous of you.* But I can't be because you are so *fucking nice."*

Adele took her elbow and began guiding her towards the bathroom. Clare stopped halfway, spun round and said, "I used to be you, Adele. I used to have a big strong handsome husband and a rickety-rackety house full of old things and people. I used to be *you*." She jabbed Adele in the ribs with her pointy finger and then stumbled into the bathroom.

Adele stood for a moment outside the bathroom door, wondering what she should do. Should she oversee Clare's toilet visit, make sure she was OK? But there'd been something in the tone of her voice, something harsh and unpleasant. It had felt, in some bizarre way, as if Clare hated her.

So she left Clare to it, went to the kitchen and made her a big strong coffee instead.

On her way back on to the terrace she passed Pip and Willow.

"Where are you two going?" she asked.

"To the playground," said Willow, pushing her bare feet into filthy, battered trainers. Behind her Pip smiled uncertainly, looking as though she had no desire whatsoever to go into the playground with Willow. "We're going to play the circus game again."

Adele smiled. "That's nice," she said. "But remember, Pip's your guest. Make sure it's what she wants to do too."

"Of course it's what she wants to do," said Willow, grabbing Pip by the hand and yanking her out into the garden.

On the terrace she placed the mug of coffee on the table at Clare's empty place and sat down next to Leo.

214

"A bit of a mess," she whispered into his ear, "you might need to take her home soon."

Leo nodded knowingly, and put his arm around her, squeezed her, loved her. *My man*, thought Adele, weirdly, unexpectedly, violently. *My fucking man*.

Even by Willow's usual levels of hyperactivity, tonight she was entirely crazy. The circus game kept building up layers of surreal detail, going off at alarming tangents and developing increasingly complex rules and sub-rules, all issued by Willow in a breakneck staccato. Pip tried to go along with it, but her head was spinning and she was growing tired of being bossed about.

"No!" snapped Willow. "When the lion tamer takes off his hat you have to jump up like this" — she jumped to demonstrate — "and say *I am Delilah Detroit and I am your daughter* and then you have to jump down again and run towards the fire eaters!"

Pip had reached the end of her capacity for Willow's particular style of play and sat down on the bench. She smiled sadly and said, "I'm quite tired now. I don't think I want to play any more."

Willow's face dropped. "But you have to! Or we won't get to the end of the story!"

"But, Willow, I don't actually think there *is* an end to the story." She smiled again, apologetically. She was a tiny bit scared of Willow.

But before Willow could respond Fern appeared. She looked perturbed and distracted. She didn't say anything, just sat on a different bench to Pip and stared into space.

Willow looked at her curiously. "Fern, will you play with me? We're doing circus orphans and you can be the ringmaster."

Fern glanced at her. "Er, no. Thanks."

"Please, Fern, please!"

Fern didn't reply, got to her feet, stared over the top of the boundary hedge towards the top of the garden and then sat down again.

A moment later Tyler appeared. Her pointy face was extra-pointy, her eyes flashing with some kind of terrifying rage.

"Tyler, will you play with me?" Willow wheedled.

But Tyler didn't even respond. She sat next to Fern and the two girls began talking to each other in hissy whispers, both turning every now and then to look behind them.

"What's going on?" Pip asked Tyler.

"Nothing," said Tyler.

"What's going on?" Willow asked Fern.

"*Nothing*," said Fern. "Go back to your game."

The two older girls started hissing and whispering again. Stray words appeared through the impenetrable fog of their conversation. *Bitch. Slag. Whore.*

"Watch your language in there, young ladies!"

All four girls turned as one at the sound of Gordon's voice.

He stood at the gate to the playground, leaning on his weird wooden stick, smiling alarmingly.

"What are you all up to?" he asked with narrowed eyes. "You all look highly suspicious."

"Nothing, Puppy," said Fern. "Just hanging about."

"Just hanging about, eh? Well, keep yourselves out of trouble, young ladies. Your parents are all pissed as farts and totally useless so you'll need to keep your wits about you." He tapped the side of his swollen nose and continued on his way turning just once to throw them all an amused look, his eye catching Pip's for just a beat too long.

Pip shuddered. She thought of what Tyler had said about thinking that Gordon had killed Phoebe. She thought of Rhea slapping Gordon round the face for being inappropriate with her daughter. Then she watched him limping across the garden, stopping every few feet to mop his brow and take a breath. *Harmless old man*, she thought to herself, shuddering again, *just a harmless old man with a metal foot*.

His interruption had punctured the strange tension hanging about the older girls and as he walked away Tyler turned to Willow, smiled and said, "OK, tell us about this game."

So for a while Pip sat on a bench watching Tyler and Fern play circus orphans with Willow until the game became so twisted and weird — the older girls had somehow managed to persuade Willow that they were child sex traffickers who had infiltrated the circus to steal the orphans and transport them in the back of a truck to be child prostitutes in LA — that she began to feel uncomfortable. Tyler in particular was being very physical with Willow, snarling in her face about how she was going to get what she deserved and twisting her arm up behind her back when pretending to bundle her in the back of the truck.

Nobody noticed Pip leaving the playground and heading back to Leo and Adele's terrace. Nobody said goodbye. And even from here she could hear the sound of her mother's voice, loud and jarring, slurred as though heard through the hull of an upturned boat.

"Pip!" she said when she saw her return. "Listen. We've been talking and it's been decided. Leo is going to be your new daddy." She stretched her arm around the back of Leo's chair and pulled him to her. He smiled awkwardly. "Would you like that, Pip? Would you like him to be your daddy?"

Pip shrugged, stepping from foot to foot.

Leo unpeeled Clare's arm from his shoulder and said, kindly, "Time to take you home, I think."

"I can do it," said Pip. "I'll take her home." She'd never seen her mother drunk before. She'd barely seen her mother have a drink. She wanted to be away from here now, away from eyes and looks and neighbours and people. She held out her hand to her mother. "Come on," she said, "time for bed."

Her mother smiled at her, crookedly, blearily, almost gratefully, and took her hand.

After

CHAPTER
TWENTY-ONE

A watery dawn crawled slowly up the walls of the waiting room, turning them from deathly grey to oyster-shell pink. Clare uncurled herself from a foetal ball and stretched herself straight. She hadn't slept, not really, just skated about that ethereal plane just under the surface of consciousness where fleeting fragments of dreams come and go, where you can believe for a few seconds at a time that everything is OK.

Pip was awake already. She smiled bravely and moved closer, enfolding Clare's hand inside hers. "Did you sleep well?" she asked.

"Not really. No. How about you?"

Pip shook her head. She looked like a ghost, haunted and hollow-eyed. "How's your head?" she asked.

Clare nodded. "It's fine," she said. This wasn't quite true. Her brain felt like a desiccated, throbbing lump of lava rock. Her stomach swirled. Her hands shook. She was clammy, confused. Thinking back to the moments after Pip appeared in her room last night, shaking her bodily, shouting into her face, "Mum! You have to wake up! It's Grace! Something's happened! *Wake up!*" she was having trouble piecing it all together in her mind. She remembered trying to find shoes, failing; she remembered running, barefoot, across the gardens, adrenaline temporarily cancelling out the alcohol, the faces in the windows, the circle of people atop the hill, dark and unsettling, a hand against her arm, *She's still breathing.* As though there'd been a moment when maybe they'd thought she wasn't. Then: *An ambulance is on its way.*

Pushing her way past bodies to get to her. Her baby. Bleeding: from her nose, from her lips, from her mouth. Her skin corpse-white. Her breath hubble-bubbling. Her eyes wide and glassy. Then the blue of the on-off lights, someone standing at the gates, already waiting, *They're here!* through cupped hands. The soft thud of footsteps and fluorescent yellow glow of paramedics, oxygen mask, torchlight. *Please move away.* Kind hands on her shoulders. And then at some point during the ride to hospital in the back of the ambulance the adrenaline had run out. Nausea had encroached. She'd been sick in a paper bowl.

Her greatest shame.

And now she tried to recall events but the memories wouldn't line up in any meaningful order. She knew this much, though: her daughter was in intensive care. She had a possible head trauma. She was in a coma. *We'll let you know when you can see her. Not yet though, I'm afraid. Not yet.*

The police had arrived last night, alongside the ambulance. They'd taken down names and addresses and were due again this morning to talk to Clare and Pip. Clare was dreading it, having to admit to the level of her negligence. When she thought how obsessive

222

she'd been about protecting her girls all this time. Then — the very first time she'd let her guard down, done something for herself, behaved selfishly — look what had happened.

A man appeared in the doorway then. It was Mr Darko, the consultant looking after Grace. He wore a suit and a serious expression. Clare's gut clenched so hard that she had to massage it with her fist.

"Good morning," he said. "Not much change, I'm afraid. Grace is stable, but still in a coma. So as far as Grace is concerned we're still looking at highly intensive care. More of the same. Indefinitely. But . . ."

Clare kneaded at her stomach.

"There have been other developments. And I think, Mrs Wild, that maybe it would be better if we could talk in private?" He looked at Pip, who looked at her. Clare nodded and Pip went outside.

Mr Darko sat down and indicated that Clare should do the same. "Well, we've studied the MRI we took last night and we can't actually see any damage from the head trauma consistent with Grace's comatose state. And about an hour ago we had the results back from our blood tests and, well . . ." He pulled down a pair of reading glasses and studied the notes in his hand. "Would Grace have had access to sleeping pills? At home?"

"No. I don't think so. I mean, I might have some Nytol somewhere, but —"

"I'm talking about prescription sleeping pills. Specifically Ambien — Zolpidem, that genre of drug. Very heavy-duty. In small doses it causes euphoria. In larger doses it can cause unconsciousness. In an overdose situation" — he sucked in his breath — "well . . . it can bring on coma. And that's the situation we find ourselves in, Mrs Wild. Grace has experienced an overdose."

Clare nodded, as if what he'd just said was reasonable. Then the truth of his words hit her consciousness and she shook her head and said, "Are you telling me she tried to kill herself?"

"Well, no, that's unlikely. Possible, but unlikely." He paused; she could see him carefully forming his next words. "Mrs Wild," he said, "as well as its medical uses and recreational uses, Ambien does have another reputation. It's what is commonly, somewhat sensationally, known as a date-rape drug."

Clare brought her hands, balled up into fists, straight to her mouth. Then she whispered one word. "*Rape.*"

"That doesn't of course mean that your daughter has been raped, Mrs Wild. But it does mean that we should consider it as a possibility. So I need your permission to bring in a sexual-assault nurse examiner. A forensic nurse. Who would be able to examine Grace for any signs of assault."

"But" — she held her fisted hands against her chest — "is there any sign of anything? I mean, surely, if there'd been — a rape — there would have been something. Blood. Or something."

"So far we've been focusing on other things. Now that we've got Grace stabilised we can look at further factors. I've been told this happened in your garden. Is

224

it possible that someone could have got into your garden? Someone you don't know?"

"It's a communal garden," she muttered. "There was a party."

He nodded, knowingly. "Ah. Well, in that case it is possible that a sexual assault might have been a motive for the overdose. Would you like me to leave you to think about it? Or I could send someone to talk to you? From the unit? Talk you through what will happen. What it entails? Although . . ." He paused. "I would recommend taking action sooner rather than later. In cases like this time really is of the essence. Forensically speaking."

Clare nodded. Then shook her head. Wished that Chris was here. Not the Chris from outside the burning house, but the Chris on Roxy's doorstep, the one in the socks. What would he do? What would he say? Would whatever it was even have happened if Chris had been around?

There'd been times in the year building up to his breakdown when she'd fantasised about being on her own with the girls, away from his dysfunctional and occasionally alarming presence. And now here she was. A single mother. And she would give anything for Chris to walk into the room with his smell of sleepy man and hug her so hard it almost broke her ribs.

She would say, *Chris, someone hurt Grace.* And his big, open face would crease into a frown and he would say, *Who?* And she would say, *I don't know who. It could be anyone. It could be the boy whose lap I found her sitting on the other day. It could be the boy's*

225

learning-disabled brother. Or the ancient glad-eyed grandfather of her new friends who's just had a prosthetic foot fitted. Or a stranger hiding in bushes all day waiting for their chance.

And Chris would not stop to ask any more questions. He would grab his jacket, stride into the garden and start banging on doors. *What have you done to my daughter?* he would boom in that voice that was so unapologetically posh he'd twice been punched in pubs because of it. *What have you done?*

But that option did not exist. It was all down to her. And Clare had never felt smaller or less capable in her life.

Mr Darko's expression had passed from concern towards impatience. He had other people's lives to save. Other mothers in other rooms. He needed an answer. She nodded. "Fine," she said. "OK. You can do the exam."

He looked relieved. "Good," he said, closing his notebook definitively and smiling. "I think that's the right decision. I'll see if we can get someone to come today, but in reality I think we'll be looking at tomorrow morning. Obviously we won't know what really happened until Grace regains consciousness, but in the meantime at least we can start building up some kind of rough outline."

Until Grace regains consciousness.

She grabbed the consultant's arm as he rose from the seat. "She will?" she said. "She will regain consciousness?"

226

Mr Darko looked glad to be asked a question to which he had a firm and happy answer. "Yes," he said. "She will. It's a matter of when, not if."

She released his arm and sank into the sofa. "Thank you," she said. "Thank you."

CHAPTER
TWENTY-TWO

On Monday morning a pair of police officers in uniform rang on the Howeses' doorbell. A small woman with pale red hair tied back into a bunch and pale blue eyes and a man of average height, slightly balding in spite of youthful features, both around thirty years old.

"Good morning. Mrs Howes? PC David Michaelides." The man gestured at himself. "WPC Tara Cross." He gestured at his colleague. "We're from West Hampstead Police Station, just making some general inquiries in the area after the occurrence on Saturday night. Which I assume you are aware of?"

"Grace?"

"Yes. Grace Wild. A neighbour of yours, I believe. And according to her mother, Clare, a friend of your daughters? Would it be possible to come in and speak to you for a short time? Or we could come back later if it's not convenient right now?"

"Well, my husband's not here right now — I don't know if you'd rather come back when he's at home?"

PC Michaelides checked his notebook, running a fingertip down the lines. "Ah, yes, Leo Howes. Yes, we do need to speak to him. But not necessarily at the same time as you." He shrugged, good-naturedly. "It's up to you."

Adele looked behind her at the hallway. The girls were all engaged in silent study. Gordon was having a nap. "Fine," she said, opening the door wider. "Sure, come in. How is she, by the way? Clare's phone is switched off so I haven't managed to get any news from anyone. Is she OK?"

"She's still in a coma, but stable."

"And do they have any idea yet . . .?"

WPC Cross shook her head. "Not yet. They've done scans, blood tests; I think they'll be getting a fuller picture by now. But our last update was inconclusive."

Adele took them into the kitchen and made them cups of tea under the curious gaze of her three daughters.

"No school today?" the WPC asked them all jauntily.

Willow replied at once. "This is school. We're home-schooled."

"Oh!" WPC Cross looked taken aback. "Lucky you!"

Adele could see them taking in the detail of her home, the expensively thrown-together shambles of it. Mismatched kitchen units, reclaimed shop display cabinets full of vintage kitchenalia, piles of paperwork heaped up all over the place, scuffed wooden floorboards and graffitied dining table. And her girls: Fern still in her oversized fleece pyjamas with her head of asymmetric brown and turquoise hair, rubbing her silk comforter back and forth across her top lip; Willow, rocking hyperactively on her wooden chair, staring at them with undisguised fascination; and Catkin, imperious and disinterested, in her charity shop summer dress, bony white shoulders, knotty hair, grubby, threadbare Scandi slipper-socks.

"Are you here about Grace?" said Willow. So outspoken. So confident. Almost preternaturally so. Adele had wanted to raise her girls to feel unassailable, the equal of anyone they encountered. She herself had been raised to be a good girl, to blend in, to put other people at their ease. When none of her three daughters had shown any early signs of being naturally compliant or sycophantic she'd let them be; pleases and thank yous and sorrys were about as far as her expectations went. She led by example, hoping that if her daughters saw her being polite and charming, at some point on the road to adulthood they would follow suit.

"Yes," said WPC Cross. "That's right."

"We were there," Willow continued. "We were with her all night. You could ask us questions too."

Adele laughed nervously. "I think we can leave the police to do their jobs, Wills."

"Well, actually," said the WPC, "we will probably want to talk to you. We'll be talking to as many people as possible."

"Cool!" said Willow, jumping off her chair and doing a rain dance.

Catkin looked at her in disgust and tutted. "Wills," she hissed, "that's not appropriate."

"Girls," said Adele, handing mugs of tea to the police. "I'll be next door with the police officers. Just carry on as you were. And no eavesdropping . . ." She directed this at Willow with a stern glance.

The police officers stopped at the threshold to the living room and she could feel it in their body language: the impact of the otherness of her home. What was beautiful to her was peculiar to others; what was normal family clutter and dirt was squalor and laziness: the threadbare psychedelic sixties sofa; the high ceilings with the ornate plasterwork and ancient cobwebs, some as old as her children; the mishmash of artwork; the sumptuous chinoiserie wallpaper, exquisite but ripped in places, stained brown in others; the old dusty curls of paper streamers hanging from the seventies chandelier; the handprints on the huge picture windows; the paintwork peeling off in sharp-edged ribbons. And a smell probably, she couldn't be sure, of dog and teenager and damp and dust. She hated seeing her home, her children, her *life* through the fresh eyes of the professionals and tradesmen who occasionally had cause to be here: the awful shock of objectivity.

"Come in," she said, "sit down." She shooed the dog off the sofa, as though he wasn't usually allowed to sit there, although he absolutely was.

WPC Cross looked through the picture windows and out into the garden. "Gosh," she said, "what an amazing space."

Adele nodded, glad for the attention to be turned away from her. "Yes," she said, as she always did. "We're very lucky."

"How big is it?" asked PC Michaelides, standing at the window with his mug of tea.

"Almost three acres."

"Wow," said WPC Cross. "That's massive."

"I know. It's an incredible amount of space to have in central London."

"So," said WPC Cross, consulting her notebook, "Saturday. You had a big party here? In the communal garden?"

"Yes. We have one every year. It's an institution. It's been going on for about thirty years."

"And who organises it?"

"Well, there's a garden committee; my husband is the chair. We have a meeting a few weeks beforehand and divide up the jobs, so it's a group effort. I usually do the face-painting. With my daughters."

"And did you do that this year?"

"Yes. Well, at least, I started off doing it and then the girls, well, they're all so big now, they kind of ended up running it themselves. And we had guests. So I left them to it after a couple of hours. Went back later on to help them clear up."

"And meanwhile you were here?" WPC Cross indicated the flat.

"Well, we were out on the terrace all day."

"We being?"

"Me, Leo my husband, Gordon my father-in-law, my sister Zoe and her husband John. Their two little ones. Then Grace's mother Clare came later, about fiveish, when the jazz started, with her youngest, Pip."

"And all this time, your daughters were on the face-painting stall?"

"Yes. I'd say from two p.m., when the doors opened, to about five thirty, six o'clock."

"And where was Grace during this time?"

"Not on the face-painting stall, no. But around and about. Yes."

"And was there anyone else? That you're aware of? Just generally. Hanging out. Anyone who might have been spending time with Grace?"

"Well, there's the whole gang . . ."

WPC Cross looked up at her with sharp interest.

"The children on this garden," she said, "they've all grown up together. From babies. So when I say gang, I don't mean that in the 'street gang' sense of the word. Just a gang of friends. They're all very close. They spend a lot of time together."

"And this group of friends, who does it consist of, would you say?"

"Well, there's my three, another girl called Tyler who lives in a flat at the other end."

"A girl? Called Tyler . . .?"

"Yes. Tyler Rednough. Her mother is Cecelia Rednough."

"Funny name for a girl, isn't it? And how old is this Tyler?"

"She's thirteen."

"Same age as Grace?"

"Yes. And my middle girl, Fern. And then there's Dylan. He's thirteen too. Nearly fourteen. He lives in the attic flat of this building."

"And his surname?"

"Maxwell-Reid. Dylan Maxwell-Reid. His mother is called Fiona."

"Thank you. Anyone else?"

"Well, there was Robbie on Saturday. Robbie is Dylan's half-brother. He's ten years older. Has quite severe learning difficulties. He usually lives in residential care but he was home on Saturday, for the party. And when he's around, he always hangs out with Dylan. They're kind of inseparable."

"That's great, thank you, Mrs Howes. And if you could give me some sense of the timescale of events on Saturday, from your perspective?"

"From what sort of time? You mean, right from the beginning of the party, or . . .?"

"Well, shall we say from around five thirty when you helped pack up the face-painting stand?"

"Right, well, OK. I told them they could go. I mean, some smaller children had got to the face-paints and the whole thing was chaos, so I said I'd do it. They all headed off to the top of the garden, their normal place for hanging out."

"They being the whole gang?"

"Yes, all of them. Oh, and Max. I forgot Max."

"And Max is . . .?"

"He's younger, about nine. Bit of a loner, but hangs around with them on the off chance of an impromptu game of football. That's all he wants to do, as far as I can tell. I don't know his surname and I'm not sure where he lives, I think on the other side, on the terrace. And I think his parents are American."

"So, at five thirty they all went off on their own?"

"Correct. And I packed up the stall, took the folding table and gazebo to the middle of the garden; that's where we leave everything for the van to collect this morning; they take it to a storage unit. So at about six o'clock I rejoined our guests, here. Leo did a barbecue. The children came back for an hour or so at about seven p.m., to have something to eat. Then they all disappeared again."

"Including Grace?"

"Yes, including Grace. But her little sister Pip stayed on the terrace with us. She's a bit of a mummy's girl, not so keen on being part of the clique."

"Clique?" WPC Cross looked up at her again with those penetratingly clear blue eyes.

"Yes. Gang. You know. Anyway, we all helped clear up after the barbecue. Drank some more. Talked. Then at about nine o'clock it was obvious that Grace's mum Clare had probably had a bit too much to drink. I don't think she's much of a drinker. Small bones, you know?" She laughed nervously. "Anyway, she was a bit wobbly on her feet and Leo offered to get her home but Pip said she could manage."

"And Pip is Grace's sister?"

"Yes. She's twelve. Very sensible girl. Anyway, that was at about nine. Then I made Leo go over and check on them both — I was a bit worried, not sure Pip could handle it by herself. So he took the dog and went over and spoke to Pip . . ."

"And this was roughly what time?"

"I guess, just after nine?"

"OK, thank you."

"Leo came back about twenty minutes later, then my sister and her family left. Her children had fallen asleep on the sofa. In their pyjamas. They got a minicab back to Willesden."

"And then?"

"Leo and I tidied up. Went back on to the terrace. Had another glass of wine."

"And did you see any of the children during this time?"

"Yes, we saw them come down the hill and head into the playground. At about a quarter to ten."

"Did you speak to them?"

"No, I waved, but they didn't see."

"And was Grace with them?"

And there it was. The black spot on Adele's consciousness, the moment she had replayed and replayed until she'd driven herself almost insane the past two nights. She had seen the children as an amorphous mass that had looked roughly the right size and shape. She could not remember who had been in the group. Not specifically.

"I'm afraid I don't know," she said, her face filling with colour, her heart racing with nerves, feeling inexplicably culpable.

"That's OK, Mrs Howes. That's fine. We can put the rest of the picture together talking to other people. You've given us loads. Plenty. We'll go and ring on a few doorbells. And if we wanted to speak to your husband and your children, when would be a good time to come back?"

"Well, Leo normally gets back from work around six, unless he's with clients, in which case it might be a lot later. I can call him now, if you like? See what his plans are?"

"Don't worry about that. We'll just try again after six and if he's not here, we'll maybe get him to come into the station."

"The station?"

"Yes. Just for convenience. But really, whatever's easier." WPC Tara Cross put her barely drunk mug of tea on the coffee table, put her neat leather bag over her shoulder, exchanged a look with PC Michaelides and got up to leave.

In the hallway she popped her head into the kitchen. "Bye, girls, see you later!"

They all looked up from their textbooks and Willow jumped to her feet and ran to the doorway. "Are you coming back to ask us questions?"

"Possibly," said WPC Cross. "We'll see how it goes."

"Please come and ask us questions. It will be so exciting."

Adele tutted. "Willow," she said. "Grace is in hospital. In a coma. Show some respect."

"I *am* being respectful. I want to help the police find out who hurt her. What's disrespectful about that?"

"Just . . ." Adele sighed, threw the police an apologetic look, "maybe try not to be so excited about everything. It's not a time for excitement."

"You know Grace had a boyfriend?" Willow asked, not showing much sign of being any less excited.

The police officers stopped and turned back. "Really?" said WPC Cross. "What kind of boyfriend?"

"Dylan," said Willow, her eyes shining. "He's our friend. We've known him, like, forever."

WPC Cross turned to Adele. "Is this the same Dylan you mentioned earlier?"

"Yes. I suppose it is. Although, boyfriend and girlfriend at that age" — she laughed — "well, you know, it's not exactly a *relationship*, it's —"

Willow cut her off. "It is," she said, her back pressed into the doorframe, climbing up the other side of the frame with her bare feet, until she was suspended halfway up, something she did all the time but that looked decidedly odd in the presence of a pair of police officers. "It is a proper relationship. They *lurve* each other."

Catkin and Fern were both tutting loudly now and looking appalled. Adele pulled Willow gently by the hand to detach her from the inside of the doorframe and as she slid down her T-shirt rose up, revealing two large bruises in the small of her back.

"Nasty bruises you've got there," said WPC Cross.

Adele looked at the bruises in horror. They were violent and fresh, the result of a fall off the swings in the dark on Saturday night. She'd landed backwards on a child's plastic toy and appeared on the terrace crying like a five-year-old. Adele had administered tiger balm and hugs and sent her back on her way a while later.

"Fell off the swing." Willow shrugged and skipped back to her schoolbook. "Didn't hurt."

"You're a brave girl then," said WPC Cross, smiling, her eyes tracing an arc around the interior of the kitchen, over Adele's bruised children, her choices, her lifestyle, before smiling again and saying goodbye.

Adele closed the front door behind the two officers a moment later and leaned heavily against it. She was shaking slightly, feeling horribly incriminated in some deeply irrational way. She'd agreed to them talking to the children later, but only if Leo was present. After Willow's unexpected outburst about Grace and Dylan being in love and the revelation of the awful bruises, which looked like those of a child who'd been kicked in the back with a hobnailed boot whilst lying in a foetal ball on the floor, she couldn't face another interrogation without another grown-up in the room.

Gordon appeared in the hallway then, his prosthetic foot in his hand, leaning heavily on his carved African stick. "What the hell did they want?"

"They're just trying to piece together what happened on Saturday night," she said, trying to sound as though the whole episode had been perfectly pleasant. "Asking around the neighbourhood. They're coming back later to talk to the rest of you."

"Not much point talking to me," he muttered, hopping towards the living-room door. "Don't know diddly." He grimaced and called over his shoulder, "Give me a hand with this blessed contraption, will you, Mrs H.? They keep telling me it's easy and it's not fucking easy. I'd like to see them try."

She followed him into the living room and hoisted his leg up on to the pouffe.

"What time are they coming back?" he said after a moment's silence.

"Six-ish," she said, rolling up his trouser leg, marvelling at the neatness of what remained of his lower leg; where once there had been putrefaction and decay now there was a shiny pink and white knob of flesh and bone.

"Don't know why they're bothering," he said. "No one's going to know anything. And anyone who does isn't going to say anything. If there was foul play involved we'd know by now. Just one of those things," he said, "like that Rednough girl. Stupid little girls get in over their heads. And look what happens. Just look what happens."

He shook his head heavily from side to side and Adele resisted the temptation to whack him over his big fat crown with his prosthetic foot and storm out. Even now, she thought, with a young girl in a hospital bed, wired up to machinery, her mother in the next room, probably unable to eat or form a thought beyond her daughter's welfare, even now this horrible old man could find not a shred of normal human decency within him, not an iota of empathy.

She fitted his prosthetic in icy cold silence and then returned to her daughters in their kitchen classroom, feeling as though every aspect of her perfect life had been taken out of its box, bent out of shape and left in a warped, unappealing heap on the floor.

CHAPTER
TWENTY-THREE

The WPC turned up at the hospital again early on Monday morning. She'd introduced herself the day before but Clare couldn't recall her name.

"So, Grace. How old is she?"

"Well, she's thirteen. It was her birthday. On Saturday. So, only just."

"And what sort of girl would you say she was? Generally?"

"Well, you know. A bit moody. A bit stroppy. Prone to unpredictable outbursts of affection."

The WPC looked at her with arctic-blue eyes. "Mature for her age?"

"Physically, well, yes, I guess so. She's tall. Big-boned. Developed. In, you know, some ways."

"Mm-hm. OK." She wrote this down. Clare couldn't think why. "Lots of friends?"

"A few. Yes. She just started a new school in January, and she hasn't really found her feet socially there yet. But in the communal garden, yes, she's definitely part of the scene out there. She spends a lot of time with a family over the way. They have three daughters, similar ages."

"Ah, yes." The WPC flipped some pages in her notepad. "The Howeses?"

"Yes, that's right. Leo and Adele." Clare blanched at the memory of the way she'd behaved on Saturday night.

"I've just come from theirs. They said you were there on Saturday night. From . . ." She ran her finger along the lines of her handwriting. ". . . five till about nine?"

"Yes, that's right."

"And you had your youngest daughter with you?"

"Yes. For most of the time."

"And Grace was hanging about with the other teenagers?"

"Yes." Clare only knew that because Pip had told her. She had barely given Grace a thought from approximately her third glass of wine.

"So when would you say was the last time you saw Grace before she was found?"

The answer to this question sat painfully on the tip of Clare's tongue. "Well, I saw her for a little while during the barbecue. At the Howeses'. She was there for a few minutes. Not very long. But before that, the last time I saw her properly was around two p.m." Her eyes fell to the floor.

"Two p.m.?"

"Yes. I threw her a little birthday party — well, not even a party really, just a gathering. On our patio. We had non-alcoholic cocktails, presents, cake."

"OK. And who was there?"

"Me and the girls, obviously. The three sisters. Another girl from the garden called Tyler. A boy called Dylan."

The WPC stabbed her notepad triumphantly. "Maxwell-Reid!"

"Who . . .? What . . .?"

"Dylan Maxwell-Reid?"

"Is he?" said Clare, confused. "I don't know. Anyway, he was there. And my mother came too."

"No one else?"

"No."

"Grace's father?"

"No," Clare replied circumspectly. "We're estranged."

"OK. So what happened at two p.m.? Party ended?"

"Yes. The party ended. The older ones disappeared. Pip and I tidied up. Then Pip went out into the communal garden — she was taking part in some pet competition thing. My mother left a few minutes later and I sat in my back garden for a while, reading. Then Pip came back, said she wanted me to come and look at some animals with her, some kind of petting zoo. I don't know. We looked for Grace then. Couldn't find her anywhere. So I called her . . ."

"When was this?"

"I don't know. Fourish, I guess. She was at Tyler's house."

She checked her notes again. "Tyler Rednough?"

"I don't know what her surname is."

"And where does she live, this Tyler?"

"Just over the way from us, the mansion block on the right."

"And does Grace spend a lot of time at Tyler's house?"

Clare shook her head. "No, no — I think this was the first time she'd been there. As far as I know. Her flat doesn't open on to the garden. So you have to leave the garden, walk on the road to get in and out. And I thought she knew she wasn't supposed to do that."

"But clearly she didn't."

"No." Clare cast her eyes down. "No. I told her I wasn't happy about it. But, you know, it was her birthday. I didn't make her come back. Didn't want to cramp her style."

"No." The WPC looked at her sympathetically. "Of course not. And do you have any idea what she was doing between then and seven o'clock when she came to the Howeses' for the barbecue?"

"She was at the face-painting stall, as far as I know. And then I sent Pip to check on her at about six o'clock and Pip said she was up on the hill, their usual spot, with all the others."

"So," said the WPC in a let's-get-this-straight tone. "Two p.m., she left your house. Four p.m. she was at Tyler's flat. Six p.m. she was on top of the hill with her friends. Seven p.m. she was at the Howeses' having her dinner. So really we're looking at a big black hole between seven thirty and ten o'clock when your younger daughter found her. Can you tell me where you were between those times?"

"Well, I was at the Howeses' until about nine o'clock. Then Pip and I walked home and I went to bed."

"At nine p.m.?"

"I was feeling a bit unwell." Clare felt her mouth grow dry. She reached for a plastic cup of water on the table in front of her and spilt some down the front of her top. She wiped it away with the back of her hand. "I was sick." No point lying. The police would be talking to everyone, she assumed. Someone was bound to mention the fact that she'd been paralytic, that her twelve-year-old had had to virtually carry her home.

"Ah, yes. Mrs Howes mentioned you were a bit the worse for wear. And your younger daughter? What was she doing while you were asleep?"

Clare gave up the façade. She didn't have the energy for it any more. She let her head drop into her hands; then she lifted it again and looked at the WPC openly and frankly. "I have no idea," she said, with a wry smile. "I was out cold."

"But she was with you?"

"Yes. I assume. She says she sat with me for a while and then she went to get her phone to try to call Grace, to get her to come in. But apparently Grace's phone was out of charge. Oh, and she said Leo Howes came to check on us both, shortly after we got back. And then at some point she left me and went out to look for Grace." She shrugged, as if to say: *Take me to the stocks, take me to the ducking pond. I am the worst mother in the world.*

"Well, me and my colleague are going back to the Howeses' later to talk to their daughters. They were out with Grace for most of the evening so they might be able to shed some light on that vital couple of hours. And we'll talk to Mr Howes. But just generally, Ms

Wild. Grace — did she have any problems on the garden? Anyone who might have wished her harm? Any complicated relationships with her friends? That kind of thing?"

"God. No. I mean . . . No. They're just children. They're just —"

"Children," she cut in. "Yes, that's true. But children are hard to define sometimes, aren't they?" She gazed at Clare coolly. "My niece goes from playing Barbie dolls with her little sister to screaming at her mum cos she won't let her wear a push-up bra." She blinked and paused, as though she thought Clare was about to laugh and say: *Oh yes, so true, how naïve of me!*

"Well. Of course. It's a difficult age. Neither one thing nor another. But no, they're all just friends."

"Ah, now, that's interesting." The WPC flipped through her notepad again. "Because one of the Howes girls — the little one . . .?"

"Willow."

"Willow. Yes. She told me — and obviously she is very young and who knows how much truth you can get out of a child that age — but she told me that Grace and Dylan Maxwell-Reid were going out together."

Clare sighed. "Oh, for goodness' sake. I mean, yes, I've seen them hanging out together. It does look like they're quite close. But they're thirteen! It's not like they going for candlelit dinners together, you know. It's just, you know, innocent, childish —"

"Willow tells me that they're in love. That it's serious."

246

Clare laughed, a loud bark of a laugh that didn't quite sound like it had come from her.

The WPC laughed too. Put a lid back on her pen. "Kids," she said.

"Have you got children?" asked Clare.

"What. Me? God, no. Not yet. Plenty of time for that."

Clare nodded. The WPC looked about thirty. Barely younger than her.

"So, we're still waiting on the full medical report on Grace. And I hear there's a forensic nurse on her way over right now. So, depending on all the test results, and, well, I'll keep asking around, fill in the blanks, we should have a much clearer idea of what happened. You know. The big picture." She put her notepad into her little leather shoulder bag, hooked it over her shoulder, smiled. "What do you think happened, Ms Wild?" She asked this in a friendly, talking-off-the-record tone.

Clare smiled weakly, unable to find the energy even to lift her head. "I don't know. I should know. But I don't. I'm so sorry."

The WPC looked down at Clare and smiled sympathetically.

"We'll get there. Don't you worry. A thirteen-year-old in a garden full of people in central London? We'll get there."

After she left the room, Clare put her face inside her hands and cried.

CHAPTER
TWENTY-FOUR

Her mum was crying when Pip returned to the waiting room. She was trying to act like she wasn't. She was trying to force a smile but it was really tragic. "Pip," she said, reaching for her hands. "Listen. This is really, really important. Really important. The police have just been and they will probably want to talk to you at some point too. So we really need to talk about what happened out there on Saturday night. We really need to work out the details. Because Mr Darko told me yesterday that the coma isn't actually a head trauma. That the injuries to her face are superficial. That apparently . . ." She paused, smiling shakily. ". . . someone gave her an overdose of drugs."

Pip straightened. Felt her blood fill with adrenaline. She still hadn't told anyone about Grace's top being up, about her shorts being down. She'd covered her sister up before anyone had come up the hill. She'd been too embarrassed to say anything. And then scared that she might get into trouble if she did.

"So what's happening," her mum continued, massaging Pip's hands with hers, "is that the police are sending a special nurse, quite soon, and she is going to examine Grace for any signs of anything bad having happened to her. And then we'll have a better idea about things. But in the meantime, baby, I need you to really, really try and remember anything, everything from Saturday night. Hm?" She smiled a watery smile at Pip and squeezed her hands.

Pip nodded and forced the words through the block inside her throat. "When I found her," she whispered, "her top was up."

Her mum stopped massaging her hands and looked at her sharply. "Up?"

"Yes. Like, you know . . ." She pulled at the hem of her own top and raised it slightly. "But higher."

"Could you see her bra?"

She nodded. Gulped. "It was up, too."

"Could you see her breasts?" her mother asked breathlessly.

"Yes. Her bra was kind of . . . It was like" — she put her hands behind her back to demonstrate — "*twisted*. You know. Like it hadn't been undone. Just sort of *pulled*. And her shorts, too. They were, like, *down*."

Her mother made a pained noise under her breath.

"Not all the way down," she continued. "Just, you know, to here." She pointed to a spot on her upper thigh.

"Pants?"

Pip nodded. Cast her eyes down.

"Pip," said her mother, "baby. Why didn't you say so? Before?"

"I don't know," she said. "I tidied her all up when I found her. I didn't want other people coming from the garden and seeing her like that. I thought she'd be really cross. And then when everyone came and then the police came and nobody asked, and then when we found out she was in a coma . . ." She shrugged. "I thought maybe it didn't matter. I thought maybe it wasn't important." She paused. "I'm sorry," she said. "I am really sorry."

"No," said her mother, opening up her arms. "No. Please, baby. Don't be sorry. You didn't know. How could you know? It was my job to know and I failed."

Pip let her mum hug her, holding her breath against the sour smell of her. Then Clare released her and held her at arms' length. "Was there anything else, though? Anything I missed? You need to tell me, Pip. Tell me every last thing."

Pip thought back through the day. Then she thought back through the preceding days and weeks. She thought of all the moments over the past six months when things hadn't felt quite right and she looked at her mother and didn't know where to start. Then one memory came to the fore. The wild-eyed boy on the hill; the way he'd looked at her.

"Someone needs to talk to Max," she said.

"Max?"

"Yes. You know, the boy with red hair. The one who's always playing football. He was there."

"Where?"

"On the hill. When I was looking for Grace. He came down the hill and he looked really weird."

"How old is he, this Max?"

"Nine," said Pip.

"Too young to have had anything to do with it then?"

"Yes. But he might have seen someone. He might have seen something happening. And someone needs to talk to Rhea. The old lady. Fergus's owner. She lives in the flats at the top of the hill; her balcony overlooks the place where I found Grace. And Gordon. Willow's granddad. He was out there, when I was in the playground with Tyler and Willow and Fern. He was wandering about in the garden. He might have seen something. And Dylan. They really, really need to talk to Dylan. He was with her nearly all day and night." Memories and fragments of memories spun round her head, and then came another, suddenly, hard and fast.

"Leo," she said. "They have to talk to Leo. I think . . ." She felt her whole body fill with ice as she talked, with the frozen enormity of what she was saying. "I think Leo had something to do with it."

"What?"

"He was out there. Remember? Before it happened. And . . ." She was sure now. So sure. "There's something not right about him."

Her mother stared at her with her jaw left open. "Leo?" she said. "*Our* Leo?"

"He's not *our* Leo." Pip tutted. "And that's exactly what I mean. Everyone thinks he's so great. *He* thinks he's so great. Grace thinks he's so great. But he's not. He's weird. Do you know . . ." She was gabbling. ". . . once, ages ago, like the first or second time I went to their house, I walked past Willow's bedroom and Leo was in there, on Willow's bed. Holding Tyler in his arms. Holding hands with her." She left a pause for her words to sink in. "Seriously," she said. "That seriously happened."

Clare rested a hand on her thigh, pushing a lock of hair from her face with her other hand. "Pip," she said, "there were dozens of people in the garden on Saturday night and if it turns out that there *was* some kind of sexual assault on Grace then the police will be launching a full-blown investigation and if that's the case then you really, really can't go around casting aspersions on our neighbours. Leo is a good, good man . . ."

"But what about Phoebe?" she cried. "Phoebe Rednough. Leo was her *boyfriend* when she died. *Of a drug overdose.* In the same garden. In virtually the same exact place! Isn't it obvious? Can't you see? History repeating itself? Can't you see?"

"Who is Phoebe Rednough?"

"She was Tyler's mum's sister. You know, the one who was found dead in the garden when she was fifteen."

Clare nodded, thinking of the bench in the garden with the girl's name on it and then suddenly remembering something her mother had said the first time she'd come to see them in their new flat, something about a girl dying in a communal garden years earlier. Could it have been their garden she was remembering?

As she thought this the door opened and a nurse appeared with another woman, middle-aged, slightly overweight, wearing a cotton jacket over a blue tunic. The nurse pointed out Clare to the other woman and then left the room. "Hello," the woman said, "Mrs Wild? My name's Jo Mackie. I'm a forensic nurse examiner. I think your daughter's consultant told you to expect me?"

Clare sat up straight and nodded. "I wasn't expecting you so early."

"Pure luck," she said in a gentle Scots accent. "Good timing. I was just over Islington way. And, obviously, it's been a while now since the incident?"

"Thirty-six hours," said Clare.

"Yes. Quite a while. So there's no time to waste." She looked at Pip and smiled. "Is that your sister in there?" she asked pleasantly.

Pip nodded.

"Well, I've spoken to Mr Darko and he says she's stable enough for us to start straight away. So." She gestured at Clare to get to her feet. "Shall we go?"

Pip got to her feet too and Jo Mackie smiled and said, "I think just Mum, for now. OK?"

Pip sat down again. She didn't know what a forensic nurse examiner was exactly, but she knew what forensics were and she knew what a nurse was and she knew what an examination was and she could take an educated guess.

She thought again of the bunched-up top, the yanked-down shorts and she thought of Leo on Willow's bed looking up at her with those darkly hooded eyes and she prayed to herself: *Please, Jo Mackie, don't find anything on my sister. Please. Jo Mackie, find nothing at all.*

253

CHAPTER
TWENTY-FIVE

The doorbell rang again about two hours after the police constables had left. Since their visit Adele hadn't been able to concentrate on the girls' lesson at all. She'd set them a reading objective, left them all curled up in various spots around the flat reading their set pieces while she sat at the kitchen table staring through the window at the gardens beyond. Gordon was out there with his physiotherapist. She could just see them in the distance. There were other people too, sitting in the sun, making the most of another glorious summer's day. It felt as though summer was happening now only to other people, no longer anything to do with her. She got heavily to her feet and went to the hall to answer the door.

"Hello again!" It was PC Michaelides, alone this time. "Sorry to bother you again, Mrs Howes, but I've just had a call from WPC Cross; she's been up at the hospital talking to Mrs Wild, and there's been a further development. Regarding Grace. I wonder if I could just have a short word with you about it. Won't take more than five minutes."

"She is OK, isn't she?"

"Well, no change as far as we know." He wiped his feet on the doormat, despite days of dry, sunny weather, and followed Adele into the kitchen.

He turned down her offer of a hot drink, said he'd had enough tea and coffee this morning to wire himself up to the National Grid. Then, once they were both seated at the table, he ran his finger absentmindedly over the etched-in grooves of the wooden surface and said, "They've had the test results back, for Grace. The MRI and the bloods and apparently there is no evidence of any kind of head trauma or injury commensurate with her current condition. But . . ." He looked up at her with his chocolate eyes and said, "They found drugs in her system. And alcohol."

"What!"

"Well, yes. Quite a surprise. I mean, obviously. She's very young. Although, according to your daughter earlier, maybe mature for her age?"

She nodded, then shook her head. "What sort of drugs . . . ?"

"Er, sleeping pills. Apparently. Prescription ones. Heavy-duty."

She shook her head before he'd even asked her the question. "We don't have anything like that. Not in our house. I'm anti- all those kind of non-essential drugs. You know, the painkillers and muscle relaxants and decongestants, that kind of thing. I treat those sorts of smaller problems homeopathically. Or naturally."

"Herbs and stuff, you mean?"

"Yes. Sort of. If anyone has trouble sleeping in this family it's camomile and essential oils and half an hour of meditation before bed." She laughed, over-loud, over-insistent.

"I see." He smiled. "So they're unlikely to have originated from here then?"

"Highly," she said. "Definitely, in fact."

"Great," he said. "But maybe you could ask them to think about who else might have had access to that type of thing. Older teenagers, maybe? And the alcohol. Did they see anyone giving Grace a drink? That kind of thing."

"I did see something," Adele said, a memory suddenly opening up in her consciousness. "When I was face-painting. Around two p.m. I saw Grace and Dylan leave the garden together. They looked like they were up to something. She had a shoulder bag with her and they were looking inside it and at the time I thought they were going to the shops to get sweets or something. It's possible they were going to get alcohol, I suppose. Or something worse?"

PC Michaelides rippled his fingertips over the tabletop as though it was a piano keyboard and then jumped nimbly to his feet. "Right, well, that'll do for now. I've got some more calls to make and we'll be back later to speak to your husband and to your daughters, and in the —" He stopped and looked up as a cacophony of sound came from the direction of the terrace and Gordon and his physiotherapist appeared in the kitchen doorway.

"Oy oy," said Gordon, heaving his bad leg over the step and eyeing the PC unpleasantly, "back so soon?"

Adele saw the PC take in the unusual form of Gordon: the improbable hair, the garish shirt, the swollen girth and then, last of all, the prosthetic foot. "Good morning, sir," he said. "I'm PC Michaelides. That's a fine-looking foot you've got there."

"Yes," agreed Gordon. "Fucking marvellous. Taking some getting used to, but fuck me, the things they can do these days. You know, if I'd lost a foot even fifteen years ago I'd have been stuck with a fucking peg and a crutch."

"Recent addition then?"

"Yes, yes." Gordon hobbled to the table and flopped down heavily on the bench. "Blasted diabetes. Had to have it chopped off. They were going to do it in the CAR, that's where I live, but I thought, Fuck me, I love this country but you're not sawing me up with a knife. Straight back here to the good old NHS. They took it off last month ago. Biggest relief of my life. Christ, the pain of that foot by the end. It was unspeakable."

"So, do you live here, sir?"

"Live here? Well, yes and no. It's my flat. I own it —"

"You own half of it, Gordon."

"OK, OK. Half of it. Yes. But currently I am *residing* here with my son and his family while I recover from my operation and get used to this thing."

"Talking of which, Gordon," said his physio, "we've still got another ten minutes." She tapped her watch.

Gordon sighed and pulled himself heavily to his feet. "Love you and leave you," he muttered before hobbling to the kitchen door.

"Were you here, sir?" said the PC. "On Saturday night?"

"Yes, I most certainly was."

"In which case, sir, I wonder if it would be possible to speak to you later on, when we come back to talk to the rest of the family?"

"Nothing to hide, be delighted to."

"That's great, sir. Thank you. I'll see you this evening."

After he'd gone, PC Michaelides turned to Adele and smiled. "Quite a character," he said.

"You could say that."

"Anyway. I've taken up way too much of your time already today. Forgive me. I'll be around the area if you think of anything else. If anything occurs to you. I'm off to see . . ." He leafed through his notebook. ". . . Fiona Maxwell-Reid now. Dylan's mum. She lives upstairs from you, I believe?"

"Yes," said Adele, smoothing down the skirt of her summer dress. "But I'm not sure you'll get much out of her. She's very introverted. Keeps herself to herself. She doesn't get involved in stuff in the garden. Or anywhere else for that matter."

"Well, thank you for the warning. I'll see what I can do." He stood in the doorway, looked upwards at the top floors of the house. Then he looked back at Adele and smiled. "See you later."

"Yes," she said, "see you later."

"Gordon," Adele said, finding him a moment later emerging from the bathroom with a crumpled newspaper in his hand and his fly not quite done up properly. Something had occurred to her while Gordon was chatting with the PC about his foot. Something she'd almost but not quite said, because she'd realised as the words had hovered at the tip of her tongue that once it was said it could not be unsaid.

"Yes, Mrs H. What can I do for you?"

"Just wondering: when you were undergoing surgery — you know, before and after — did you have any trouble sleeping?"

"Dear God, did I ever. You try sleeping with an open wound for a foot."

"And did they give you anything? To help you sleep?"

"Sweeties, you mean?"

"Well, yes. Sleeping pills."

"I should say they did. Jesus Christ."

"And do you have any left?"

"Oh, dear girl" — his face lit up — "don't tell me the old hippy-dippy magic potions aren't working? You'll be telling me you think the children should go to proper school and be taught by proper teachers next. Heh heh." He squeezed her hand conspiratorially. "Leave it with me, Mrs H. I'll be right back."

She watched him hobble down the hallway towards his room.

"Thin end of the wedge!" he shouted joyfully over his shoulder. "It'll be microwave chips for tea next! Heh heh."

She chewed at the inside of her cheek while she waited for him. It seemed to take him a long time and the longer it took him, the more she chewed her cheek, pressing the flesh closer to her teeth with the tip of her index finger. *Come on, Gordon,* she chanted under her breath, *come on.*

Finally he appeared, looking flustered and confused. In the palm of his hand he held out two small blue and white pills. "Mrs H.," he said, solemnly. "We appear to have a problem. Last time I looked I had half a fucking pot of these things. Now I've got two." He paused, jiggling the pills in the palm of his hand. "Someone", he said at last, "has been stealing my sweeties."

"Well," said Jo Mackie, snapping off her rubber gloves a while later. "No sign of any trauma or injury. The hymen is intact."

Clare felt an overwhelming upsurge of relief pass through her. She reached behind her to find the wall.

"No bruising. No scratches. I've taken a swab but I think it's safe to say that Grace has not been raped, vaginally or anally. Also, your younger daughter mentioned that Grace's top had been pulled up. So I've examined the breasts for trauma but there are no signs of anything. And I've taken swabs from that area."

An image passed through Clare's mind so terrible that she needed to blink several times to dislodge it.

"And also from inside her mouth. Now, unfortunately, because of the time that has elapsed since your daughter was attacked, it's possible that any sperm traces in the mouth may have been destroyed by salivary enzymes. But we might get lucky. It's not been quite two days yet and I'll take these swabs myself to the lab and wait with the technician. We'll move everything along superfast."

Clare blinked again. Sperm. On her daughter. In her daughter. No.

"Is that likely?" she said. "I mean — in these cases. Is that what happens?"

Jo Mackie smiled at her. "Anything can happen, Clare. But, hopefully, given the lack of any other signs of sexual assault, it didn't happen in this case. I'm really just going through the tick list."

Clare felt a small hurt of hope inside her heart. A tick list. No sperm. Just a tick list.

"So." Jo Mackie clipped down the lid of a metal case that she'd filled with swabs and samples. "I should have some news for you in a few hours. Or, better still, no news at all. But either way, I'll be back."

"OK. Thank you."

"And in the meantime, off you go." She held open the door of the small office they'd been talking in, a quiet smile on her face.

Clare looked at her questioningly.

"You can see her now."

"I can?"

"Yes. I asked the nurse in charge. She said it's fine now."

"Oh." Clare touched her heart. She hadn't seen her daughter for thirty-six hours. "Can I take my other daughter in? Do you think?"

"Maybe just you for now," she said. "Get used to it. Make yourself strong first. *Right*." She picked up the metal case. "I need to run. I'll see you later."

She watched Jo Mackie leaving with her box full of bits of her child's DNA and then she headed towards the intensive-care ward, her breath held tight inside her lungs.

Grace was beautiful in her repose. The bruises to her face, bruises Clare could barely remember from the night they'd been inflicted, had faded to early evening storm-clouds. Her skin was not broken. Clare wondered where all the blood had come from. A small hump on the bridge of her nose led to her to conclude it had been a simple nosebleed. She remembered the thoughts of brain damage, of internal bleeding, of ineradicable facial scarring that had spun around her head in the back of the ambulance. Before the test results had come through she'd thought, crazily, that Grace had fallen out of a tree.

Out of a tree!

Like a plucky, foolhardy kid!

She'd thought that her daughter was still a little girl.

She looked strangely adult now lying here with her chalky skin, her unmade-up face. Clare thanked the nurse who had silently passed her a cup of water. She rested the cup on the bedside table and reached out for Grace's hand. "Is it OK", she said, "if I touch her?"

"Of course," the nurse said kindly. "And do talk to her. She'll like to hear the sound of your voice."

"Will she?"

She thought of Chris and herself talking to her pregnant bump. Someone had told them to do that. Told them that it meant that when the baby was born it would immediately recognise its parents' voices. That that would be a good thing. It had seemed an abstract concept at the time, pregnant with her first child, no possible notion of what a parent-child bond would feel like in reality as opposed to in theory. And now that person who'd been hidden away inside her body was hidden away inside her own head and once more she was being asked to talk to someone who couldn't hear her, being asked to accept and act upon an abstract notion.

How could it be possible, Clare thought, that she knew so little about a person she'd once grown inside her? A person who had taken milk from her body and slept on her shoulder? Who had, at one stage, given her a bullet-pointed rundown every day of what she'd done at school, missing out not one detail? And now, for all Clare knew, she might have been abused, her body might have been violated.

She took Grace's hand. It was warm and pulsed with life. "Hello, my baby girl," she said. "I'm sorry I haven't seen you for so long. They wouldn't let me. But I've been here the whole time. Me. And your sister. We've both been here. And all the news is good so far. Your head hasn't been hurt. And a nice lady just came to look at some other parts of you and she says those haven't been hurt either. I hope you didn't mind her coming to look at you? Anyway, your face looks fine. No scars. Just some bruises. And we're all just waiting for you to wake up now, baby girl. Wake up and tell us what happened."

She squeezed Grace's hand, tenderly. Rubbed her thumb up and down the back of it. Turned it over and traced a circle on the palm of her hand with her fingertip.

Round and round the garden, like a teddy bear.

How Grace had loved that game.

She tried to think of something else to say. But she couldn't. All she could think, suddenly and fiercely, was: *Chris, I need you.*

CHAPTER
TWENTY-SIX

The flat had the slightly awkward air that homes often have when one returns after some time away: an uncomfortable loss of familiarity.

Clare went straight to her room to pack.

Pip meanwhile wandered from room to room, trying to find her way back into the flat. There were still hints of Grace's party here and there. The balloons tied to the garden chairs bobbed in and out of view through the back window; her cards sat on display on the dining table along with her presents. Pip touched things gently as she passed them, trying to assimilate them into herself. She heard her mum going through the wardrobe in her room, the jangle of her coat hangers knocking together. "Choose yourself a fresh outfit, Pip," her mum called out to her. "And a spare for me to pack. And be quick! Really quick!"

She went into her own room. Here were the loudest suggestions of the hours before Saturday night. Grace's original outfit discarded to the floor where she'd changed into her new clothes. Her make-up piled on the floor around the mirror. The wrapping paper from Dylan's gift to her. The one she'd squirrelled away in here, not wanting to open it in front of the others. Pip went through the room, trying to find the gift, wondering if it contained a clue as to what had happened to her. But there was nothing, just the gift tag upon which he'd written:

13!
xxxxx

Like thirteen was really old or something. Like thirteen meant something.

She went into the kitchen and peered through the window. It half amazed her to see people out there. Just getting on with their lives.

"Pip! Hurry up!"

She could see Catkin out there. She was reading. For a moment Pip was tempted to stride out there and shout into Catkin's face: *How can you sit there reading a book when my sister's in a coma and it was probably your weird father who put her into it?*

She looked away from Catkin and towards the block at the top of the garden, squinting to see if she could make out the form of Rhea sitting on her balcony. But there was no one there. Then she looked up at the tiny pinprick eyes of the attic flat above the Howeses. Was Dylan in there? Had he taken the day off school in the aftermath of his "girlfriend" being in a coma? Or was he at school mucking about with his posh mates as if today was just a normal day? Did he even care?

And then she looked right, towards Tyler's block of flats. Tyler with her scratched-up arms and her hard-girl façade. What did she know about Leo? About Grace?

"Pip! Come on, darling, we need to get back to the hospital. Grace might be waking up!"

Pip was about to turn and join her mother in the hallway when she saw a flash of red hair, a streak of milky leg, a blaze of orange fluorescence as a ball arced across the garden.

Max.

She ran across the lawn, catching him by the walls of the Secret Garden where he was leaning to pick up his ball. He saw her and immediately walked away.

"Max," she said, sharply, because in this new disordered world of hers, sharp was something she was allowed to be.

He pretended not to hear.

"Max," she said, louder. She caught up to him and grabbed his arm.

He shook his arm free of her hold and looked at her crossly. "What?"

"You know what," she said.

"I don't know anything."

"You do. When I saw you on the hill — you'd seen something. You know you had. What was it?"

"Nothing," he said. "I didn't see anything. Just your sister. Like that."

"So," she said, "why didn't you get help? Why didn't you do something?"

"I was going to," he said. "I was going to. And then you came."

Pip narrowed her eyes at him. "Did you see Leo?"

"What?"

"Leo. The girls' dad? Did you see him?"

He looked at her incredulously. "No-oo."

Her shoulders slumped. She believed him. "Then tell me what you did see. My sister's in a coma. In an actual *coma*. Someone gave her a drug overdose. This is so serious. And you saw her. Which means you're a witness, Max. The police are going to talk to you. You may as well tell me."

She saw him hollow out, his thin chest go concave. He was losing his resolve.

He sighed. "I didn't see anything. I just heard stuff."

"What sort of stuff?"

"Fighting. Arguing."

"Whose voices were they?"

"I don't know. Kids' voices."

"And what were they saying?"

"I don't know. I wasn't listening, I was just looking for my ball." He stared down at the ball in his hands, rolling it fondly between his fingertips as if it reminded him of better times.

"How many voices?"

"A few. A lot."

"Boys? Girls?"

"Both. I don't know. And then there were other noises. Footsteps. Running."

"Was she . . .? When you found Grace, was she dressed?"

Max's moon-face flushed pink. He stared resolutely down at his ball. "Kind of."

"What? Kind of what?"

"She was kind of half-dressed, half-undressed. I tried to pull her bra down. I tried pulling up her, you know, her pants and stuff . . . But she was too heavy." He looked up at her, appalled. By himself, or by the situation, Pip didn't know. "I tried talking to her. But she was out cold," He stared into Pip's eyes. "I was coming. When I saw you. I was coming to tell people. Honestly. I was."

"Who do you think it was?" she asked, softer now. "In the Rose Garden? Who was arguing?"

"I don't know," he said. "I swear. I don't remember anything else."

"OK." She patted his arm, reassuringly. "Thank you, Max."

"I hope she's OK," he said, awkwardly.

"Yes," said Pip. "So do I."

"Leo," Adele whispered urgently into her phone. "You need to come home."

"What? Why?"

"Something's happened. The police have been again and apparently they've had the test results back for Grace and she was overdosed."

"What!"

"I know. But listen. They said it was sleeping pills and at first I said, well, we don't *have* any sleeping pills, because we don't. But then Gordon came in and started talking about his foot and I suddenly thought, fuck — *he* had sleeping pills. So I pretended I wanted one and he went to get me one and they were gone."

"Sorry — what were gone?"

"Gordon's sleeping pills!" she replied exasperatedly. "He had half a pot and there were only two left."

"Sorry, Adele. I don't get it. What are you trying to say?"

"I'm saying that someone gave Grace an overdose of sleeping pills on Saturday night. And that nearly all of Gordon's sleeping pills have gone. You have to come home, Leo. You have to come home now. We need to talk to the girls about this, before the police come tonight."

"What — you think one of our girls gave Grace an overdose?"

"No!"

"Then — what?"

"I don't know, Leo. But the police are going to be here in six hours, asking questions, and we need to talk to our children and you need to come home!"

"I can't come home, Del. I'm on my way to a meeting that's been in the diary since May."

"Well, then, come home after. Please, Leo."

"I will. I'll be back as soon as I can. And in the meantime, go and talk to the neighbours. Because, hey, you never know, maybe some of them have got sleeping pills in their houses too."

Adele waited until she heard the communal front door slam shut and then scooted to her bedroom window to see if it was PC Michaelides leaving the building. She saw him stop on the pavement for a while, consult his notebook, and then turn right. Presumably, she thought, to Cece's place. He wouldn't find her at home, though.

"Wills," she said, knocking gently at her daughter's bedroom door, "I'm just popping out for a minute. Catkin's in the garden and Fern and Puppy are in the kitchen. Won't be long."

Willow smiled up at her from her book. "This book is shit," she said in her customary jolly tone. "Do I have to read it?"

Adele sighed. It was *Little Women*. "Seriously?" she said.

"Yes. One hundred per cent seriously. I still don't know why Jacqueline Wilson isn't on the national curriculum. It's just totally ridiculous." She threw *Little Women* down on the bed at her side, folded her arms and huffed.

"Look, whatever. Read something else. Ask Fern to choose something for you. I have to go now. I'll see you in half an hour."

Fiona Maxwell-Reid's tone over the intercom was tired and uneasy.

"It's Adele. From downstairs. Mind if I come up for a word?"

She heard Fiona sigh and say, "Sure, come on up."

Adele was breathless by the time she reached the top floor of the house. Fiona had left her door open and Adele could see her moving about near her kitchenette. "Come in," she said. "Excuse the mess."

Fiona was extraordinarily posh and extraordinarily poor. Robbie's father had left her the flat but no cash.

Her mother had left her a desolate house in Cumbria which she rented out to hikers. She worked part-time in the petrol station on the Finchley Road to pay her household bills and occasionally taught the flute to schoolchildren. And Dylan's school fees were paid for by a partial bursary, the shortfall made up by Fiona's father, who only did so because he was a snob about private schools and it made him feel better about having a mixed-race grandson.

Adele followed Fiona into her tiny living room with its claustrophobic eaved ceilings and piles of boxes and clothes and old newspapers and was surprised to see Dylan sitting on the sofa.

"Oh," she said, "Dylan. Not at school today?"

He shook his head and when Adele looked at him she could see he'd been crying. Fiona looked from Dylan to Adele and gave her a wry look.

"Have you seen Grace?" he asked croakily.

"No, love. I haven't. I can't get through to Clare and I don't like just to turn up. You know."

He nodded, rubbing the side of his hand across the end of his nose.

"I feel really bad," he said, looking at Adele with his startling green eyes. "I should have stayed with her."

"What happened, Dylan?" she asked, trying to find somewhere to sit. Fiona moved a pile of papers from a chair and Adele sat down.

"I don't know," he said. "We'd all been at the top of the hill — you know, hanging out. And then Tyler and Fern went to the playground and it was just me and Grace and Robbie and Catkin, and Robbie said he wanted to come back indoors so I brought him back upstairs and then when I came out again everyone was in the playground except Grace, and her mum wasn't at your house any more so I just thought they'd all gone home. And I texted Grace to say goodnight and she didn't reply and I thought, well, maybe she's already asleep. So I just texted her that I loved her . . ." His face flushed rose pink. ". . . and then the next thing, Pip's looking for her and then . . ." Fresh tears sprang to his eyes and he pressed them with the heels of his hands. Fiona rolled her eyes at Adele and passed her son another tissue.

"So," said Adele, mentally trying to piece it all together. "When you came in with Robbie, you left Grace on the hill, on her own?"

"No. She was with Catkin."

"And when you came back to the garden, Grace was gone. And Catkin was in the playground?"

Dylan nodded, sniffed, rubbed his eyes again.

"So, what . . .?" She pressed her fingertips into her temples. "I mean, how long were you gone for? With Robbie?"

He shrugged. "I'm not really sure."

"You brought Robbie back at nine fifteen," said Fiona. "I'd say you were here for about half an hour before you went back out."

Adele looked questioningly at Dylan for confirmation. He nodded. "That sounds about right."

"And did you go up the hill to look for Grace?" she asked.

"No. I could see everyone else in the playground so I went straight in there. And I asked where Grace was and nobody knew. And then I saw Leo on his terrace and I asked him if he'd seen Grace and he told me she'd been waiting for me by the gate. Said she must have given up and gone home."

Fiona looked at Adele curiously. "They told you about the overdose, did they?" she said, her mottled arms folded across her heavy middle.

Adele nodded.

"And the alcohol?"

Adele nodded again.

"It was just some champagne!" said Dylan plaintively. "It was my present to her. That and a ring."

Adele's eyebrows arched in surprise. "Where did you get champagne from, Dylan?"

"I can't tell you." His head hung almost between his knees.

"Did you tell the police?"

He nodded. Fiona stared at him with pursed lips. "You may as well tell her, Dylan. It's not like it's going to make any difference to anything."

He looked up at her through wet lashes. "I gave Tyler five pounds to get it for me."

"Get it?"

"Yes. Steal it."

"Oh dear God." Adele sat back in her chair.

"I know. I tried buying it myself but everyone asked me for ID. I even asked some of the older boys at school, but none of them would. So Tyler just said,

'Give me a fiver and I'll sort it out.'" He shrugged. "I didn't think she meant she was going to nick it."

Adele pulled herself straight. "Right, so," she said. "You gave the champagne to Grace as a birthday gift. And then, when did you drink it?"

"Well, we took it to Tyler's house. She said we could keep it in her fridge because her mum was out and wouldn't find it. And then she'd bring it down later when it was dark and we could all share it, up on the hill."

"Ah," said Adele, pieces of the puzzle coming together in her head. "So that's where you were going. I saw you both, sneaking off together."

"It was supposed to be a really nice thing. You know. It's not like Grace is the sort of girl to get drunk or whatever. She's not like that. But I just thought, she was thirteen, it would be nice to do something a bit grown-up. And instead it's turned into this really big horrible deal and now Tyler's going to be in the shit and Grace is in a coma and I wish I'd never ever done it. I wish I'd just bought her chocolates instead."

He started crying again. His mother passed him another tissue.

"Champagne," she said drily. "At thirteen. Bloody ridiculous."

"It was supposed to be romantic, Mum!" he shouted at her. "But I wouldn't expect you to understand that."

Fiona sighed and rolled her eyes.

"Who else had the champagne?" Adele asked.

"Just me, Tyler, Grace and Catkin. Fern tasted a bit of Grace's and didn't like it. Willow wasn't interested. Obviously Robbie didn't want any."

"So you had, what, a glass and a half each?"

He nodded. "Tyler probably had a bit more than that because she drank her first glass faster than us."

Adele sighed. Even for such young kids it wasn't all that much. Nothing to get worked up about. Quite sweet really. But then another thought occurred to her.

"What did you drink the champagne out of?"

"Plastic cups. You know, disposable ones."

"Where did they come from?"

"Catkin brought them. From your house."

"And who poured the champagne?"

"Me."

Adele nodded. She'd run out of questions. The champagne, as naughty as it was, appeared to have nothing whatsoever to do with the sleeping pills.

"You know, Dylan, that a tiny amount of alcohol like that wouldn't have done Grace any harm?"

"The policeman said she was in a coma because of alcohol and drugs."

"Well, that's what was found in her system, yes, but you'd have to drink a lot more than a glass of champagne to end up in a coma, Dylan. Don't be too hard on yourself. It *was* romantic. Misguided, yes, but romantic. Wish I'd had a boyfriend like you when I was thirteen."

"No," said Dylan, his eyes suddenly dark. "You don't. Take my word for that. You *don't*."

CHAPTER
TWENTY-SEVEN

Jo Mackie returned to the hospital three hours later. She took Clare back into the same room where they'd spoken before, lined up her paperwork on the table in front of her and then looked at Clare.

Clare knew immediately that something had come up on the swabs. She could see it in the strained kindness of her expression.

"How was Grace?" asked Jo, peeling apart a sheaf of paper, looking for something in particular.

Clare stroked the sides of a paper coffee cup. "She looked better than I expected her to look. Last time I saw her she was covered in blood. I thought she had a brain injury. So, you know, it was kind of a relief."

"Good," said Jo Mackie, looking at her again with that fearsome look of compassion. "So, we rushed these through and, as I suspected, we found nothing untoward in the vaginal or rectal passages."

Clare sat towards the edge of her seat, knowing that she'd heard the good news and that the bad news was on its way.

"Nothing on the breasts either. But . . ."

Clare swallowed, hard.

"We did find traces of semen."

Clare's stomach turned.

"In her mouth."

She lifted her hands from the sides of her chair to her mouth.

"From just one source."

She groaned. Was it her fault, she thought, for buying her daughter those tiny shorts? That skimpy top?

"But no signs of trauma around the mouth itself. No bruising. No tearing."

"But — her nose? The bump . . .?"

Jo Mackie nodded, as though this was a possibility she too had considered and discarded. "No," she said, "the nose injury looks more like it was inflicted by a hard fall."

"So, whoever attacked her did it when she was unconscious. Is that what you're saying?"

"Well, not entirely, no. I mean, Clare, at this stage, we can't rule out the possibility that she wasn't attacked at all."

Clare recoiled from Jo Mackie, regarding her with disgust. "I beg your pardon?"

"I'm not saying that she wasn't attacked. Of course not. I'm just saying that it's not clear-cut. Forensically, I mean. For example, does Grace have a boyfriend?"

"She's twelve!" Clare said, unthinkingly.

Jo glanced at her in confusion. "Oh," she said. "I thought she was thirteen?"

"Sorry, sorry. Yes. She is. Just. It was her birthday."

"Look, Clare. I'm a mum. I have an eight-year-old and a five-year-old. I cannot conceive of them getting any bigger. I cannot imagine a world where my children

278

detach themselves from me and have secrets from me and do things that adults do. But Grace had been drinking that night. Hanging about with teenage friends. You can't rule out the possibility that whatever happened to Grace happened to her consensually."

"But she was *drugged!* Why would anyone drug her if she was giving it away for free?"

"That I don't know, Clare. I can only talk about what I see, forensically. And that is a child with no physical signs of an assault, apart from a broken nose which could have been caused by any number of unrelated mishaps."

"But the drugs! What about the drugs?"

Jo Mackie sighed and sat back into her chair. "Until Grace wakes up, that is something for the police to investigate. And, once they've found out where the drugs came from and how they got into Grace, then they can look into the possibility of assault. But right now, Clare, it might be worth you going home and talking to your daughter's friends. Find out how well you really knew her."

"Rhea," Adele called into the intercom. "It's Adele. Mind if I come up?"

She'd tried Cece's flat but there'd been no one home, as she'd expected.

"Yes. Please do. Please!"

Rhea greeted her at her front door in a floor-length kaftan, her cat staring aggressively at the visitor from the other end of the hallway. "Come in. Please. Sit. Tea?

Coffee?" She reappeared a moment later with a bag of her favourite cheesy puffs and a large bottle of Coke.

"Please," said Adele. "Don't open the crisps on my account. I'm really not hungry."

"No," said Rhea sadly, putting the bag down. "No. I can't say that I am either."

"Have the police been?"

"Yes," she said pensively, sitting down next to Adele, smoothing out the front of her kaftan. "A nice Greek boy. He just left."

"Did he say where he was going?"

"Yes. He said he was going to try Cece again. I told him not to bother. Told him she is a full-time social worker. But . . ." She shrugged. "That's for him to find out."

She began to twist at the lid of the Coke bottle. Adele smiled and took it from her. Poured them a glass each but didn't touch hers. She hadn't drunk Coke since she was about seventeen, since she'd seen that trick where someone left a penny in it overnight and it virtually disintegrated.

"What did they tell you?" she asked.

"They told me about the overdose. My God. I thought she'd knocked herself unconscious. I never thought . . . my God . . ."

"What else did he say?"

"Well, really he wasn't here to talk, he was here to ask questions. And listen, Adele." She reached across and covered Adele's hand with her own. "I have to be honest with you. I saw something on Saturday night. And really, it was nothing. But the nice Greek boy, he seemed to think it was important. He was asking me a lot of questions about it. A *lot* of questions."

Adele waited for Rhea to continue.

"At around nine fifteen I was sitting on my balcony and I saw Leo walking your dog up here, like he does every night. Around the Rose Garden. And then he went into the Rose Garden. And I noticed this because I could see that the dog did not want to go into the Rose Garden. He was pulling against the lead. And Leo had to drag him through the gate."

Adele nodded, her hands clasped together on her lap.

"I told the police boy that Leo and the dog were in there for about five minutes, but I really don't know for sure. It was certainly longer than a minute. Then they came out again and headed down the hill back to your house. At which point I felt the cold a little and came indoors."

Adele nodded again, encouragingly.

"And that is that."

Adele narrowed her eyes. "And the police seemed interested in that?"

"Yes." She nodded. "Very. Wanted the timings to the closest half-second."

"And do you have any idea why?"

"Well, no, apart from the fact that the girl was found outside the Rose Garden forty minutes later. I suppose they need to place everybody."

"And, when Leo was in the Rose Garden, where were the kids? Could you see them?"

"Which kids?"

"Well, at that time it would have been Grace and Catkin, I suppose."

"Yes." Rhea's face brightened with remembrance. "They were in the Rose Garden. I saw them go in, after the boy and his brother left."

"Dylan and Robbie?"

"Yes. Dylan and Robbie."

Adele turned her gaze towards Rhea's balcony. "Would you mind if I . . .?"

"Of course not. Please do!"

Adele stood on Rhea's balcony and looked down. From here she could see the far end of the Rose Garden where the gate was, but not the near end, where the two benches were.

"Could you see them?" she asked, turning to Rhea, who was standing just behind her. "Could you see the girls?"

"No. Not from here. And of course it was beginning to get dark around then, shadowy, you know."

Adele turned back to the view. "And so Grace and Catkin were in the Rose Garden, then Leo came in with Scout, and then he left. And the girls were still there?"

"So far as I know, Adele, yes. And then I came indoors."

Adele frowned. "I can't think why they would be so interested. I mean, if Catkin was there it's not as if anything could have happened, is it?"

"I did find it strange, yes. But you know, Adele, I did tell the police boy another thing. I told him about Phoebe. And I told him about Gordon. And I also told him that I had seen Gordon wandering about the gardens a lot that night. After the jazz. Just wandering about on that new foot of his. He caught my eye at one point; he looked up and you know what he said? He said, 'How's that lovely daughter of yours?' I said, 'Gordon, she is fifty-six years old and has a grandchild.' And he said, 'I've got seven grandchildren and one foot, what's that got to do with anything?'"

Rhea rolled her brown eyes theatrically. "I know you say he has changed, Adele, but I don't see any evidence of it. So, anyway, I don't know. The police boy didn't seem very interested in Gordon. Or in Phoebe for that matter. But" — her eyes watered slightly — "in Leo, he seemed very interested indeed. And of course the idea, the *notion* that your lovely, handsome husband should be in any way involved or have anything to do with . . ." She shook her head. "Preposterous. But I just thought you should know. So it doesn't take you by surprise."

"Thank you, Rhea," said Adele. "I really do appreciate it."

Adele let herself back into the garden through the gates on Virginia Terrace. She lowered her sunglasses from the top of her head and moved fast and stealthily to avoid unwanted conversations with nosy neighbours. She saw Catkin, still on the lawn outside their flat with her book and the dog. She would talk to her in a minute. But first she made her way up the hill, towards the benches and the Rose Garden. She sat for a moment on the benches where Grace and Dylan and her girls had been sitting for a while that night. From here you could see down the hill and towards her terrace and the playground. In front was the entrance to the Rose Garden. Behind was the wall dividing the garden from the backs of the shops on the high street. The wall was ten feet tall, topped with curls of rusty barbed wire and watched over by two cameras. In the whole history of the garden, no one had ever got in over that wall.

She got to her feet and walked to the Rose Garden. She passed the spot where Grace had been found on Saturday night, on the grass just outside the gate. A shiver passed through her and she pushed open the gate.

The Rose Garden had always been her favourite spot in the garden. It was a cliché, of course, but it really was an oasis within an oasis. Before they'd had children she would come here with novels and college work and nail polish and newspapers and sometimes with Leo to sit on the bench and kiss him for a while away from the gaze of his parents and brothers. She'd breastfed Catkin in here, too, at first, but then stopped once Catkin was older and more vocal, feeling that she didn't want to spoil the peace and quiet of the spot for other garden residents.

She was alone in here now. The tall hedges muted the sounds of the garden and cut out the majority of the landscape. She looked up into a cloudless blue sky, watching a jet trace its way lazily from one end of the horizon to the other, leaving a thin hazy thread in its wake. She lowered her gaze to Rhea's balcony and then lower still to the benches on the other side. There was

Phoebe's bench on the right. The bench on the left was dedicated to a dog called Sparrow who had died in 1987. Between the two benches was a waste bin. Adele stared at the bin for a moment, registering its significance.

She stood over the bin and inventoried what she saw. An empty bottle, not of champagne — Dylan had been well and truly duped — but a nasty cheap Cava in a black bottle. A stack of five clear disposable cups, ones she recognised from her own home. She came to a Coke can. She picked that out and sniffed it. No trace of anything untoward. Some screwed-up paper muffin cases, probably from the cake stall earlier in the day. Balled-up nappies in pale yellow bags. Sections from Saturday's *Times*, read and discarded. She was reaching deeper and deeper into the bin now, through the flotsam and jetsam of the day, not sure even what she was looking for.

She pulled out the plastic cups, examined their bottoms for the residue of crushed-up pills. Because surely that was how they had been administered? They could not have been swallowed whole. But there was nothing. There was a rustle in the undergrowth behind the benches and Adele jumped slightly when a large tortoiseshell cat landed on the back of the bench and stared at her blankly. She stared back at the cat and then at the space from where he had arrived. A kind of tunnel in the hedge, a passageway with a dipped-out bottom scratched out of the dry earth by, she assumed, the claws of cats and foxes. It was a big hole; big enough, she mused, for a person to clamber through. If they needed to.

She shook her head, wondering why she was thinking this way. Then she stroked the cat's head, her eyes just flicking over Phoebe's memorial plaque, her thoughts grazing the spot in her consciousness where Gordon had suggested that Leo had something to do with her death, her breath held deep and icy cold inside her.

As soon as she and Pip had got back to the hospital from their brief trip home Clare had plugged in her phone to charge it. She switched it on now and found a phalanx of missed calls, text messages and voicemails. She would go through them later. For now, though, there was something more important she needed to do.

She found a number on her phone, one she'd programmed in a couple of weeks before. For a few moments she stood with her thumb over the call button. What she was about to do was irreversible. But, she now knew, inevitable. She focused on the image of the size-twelve feet in the thick woollen socks and pressed call.

"Hello," said a woman with a small voice and a London accent.

"Hi, is that Roxy?"

"Speaking."

"Hello. My name is Clare Wild. We haven't met, but I believe you know my husband, Chris."

There was a beat of surprised silence. "Yes."

"I believe he may be staying with you at the moment."

"Well, yes, kind of. I mean, you know, on the sofa, it's —"

"I'm not calling to put you on the spot. He needed somewhere to stay and I'm grateful to you. But there's been . . . there's an emergency. Chris's — *our* daughter. She's in the hospital. It's very serious. And I need you to tell me honestly — really, really honestly — how he is."

"He's good."

"No, I need more than good." She'd raised her voice, frustrated by Roxy's immediate retreat into the evasive, inadequate teenage parlance of her own children. "This is so, so important. Really. Before I bring Chris back into the picture, I need to know, properly. Is he well? Is he well enough to be at the side of his child's hospital bed?"

She sensed Roxy on the other end of the line pulling herself up tall, and heard the tone of her voice change. "He's been taking his medication. Every single day. Going to all his outpatient appointments. And counselling."

"Counselling?"

"Yes. Post-traumatic stress counselling. Trying to come to terms with what he did." She paused. "To you. And the children. He cooks me a lovely meal every night. He irons my clothes. Looks after my plants. Looks after me."

Clare felt herself rankle at this last comment. A flash of jealousy passed through her. She embraced it.

"And for the last few weeks he's even been talking to people about another documentary. I mean, honestly, I swear, if you didn't know his history, if you didn't know what happened last year, you would just think he was the sanest, normalest person out there. I mean, he's like a teddy bear."

Now Clare envisaged Chris as a giant teddy bear — in oatmeal socks. And as she did so she felt the residual traces of the image that stained her consciousness for so long, of the wild-eyed man in the wetsuit, begin to fade away.

"Where is he?" she said. "Right now?"

"At home," said Roxy. "Probably."

"Are you with him?"

"No. I'm at work."

"Do you have a landline?"

"Yes."

"Could I have it? To call him?"

"Sure, sure."

Clare wrote it on the back of her hand.

"What's the matter", asked Roxy, "with your daughter? May I ask?"

"She had a . . ." She struggled for the words. "She was . . . There was an accident. We're not sure what happened. And she's in a coma."

She heard Roxy's intake of breath. "Oh, Jesus. Oh God. I'm so sorry."

"Yes," said Clare. "So am I."

She didn't pause before tapping in the number for Roxy's flat, gave herself no time to overthink it or find a reason not to do it. She acted on the ache inside her, the need to hear her husband's voice, to bring him to the bedside of their sick child.

"Hello."

Oh, there it was. The baritone bear growl. The voice that said: *I am here; all is well.*

"Chris."

"Clare?"

"Yes. It's me."

"It's you?"

She found herself laughing. "Yes. Me. Clare Wild."

"Clare Wild? My God. Clare Wild. Hello! Hello!"

"Chris," she said, the name sounding raw and beautiful in her mouth. And then: "Chris. It's Grace. She's in hospital. At the Royal Free. And you have to come now. Right now."

CHAPTER
TWENTY-EIGHT

As soon as Pip walked into the waiting room after a trip to the toilets, she knew something was different. Her mum looked somehow supercharged, as if she'd had too much coffee, or someone had just told her the funniest joke she'd ever heard and she'd only just stopped laughing.

"I've got something to tell you," she said. "Sit down."

Pip blanched; she sat down with a dreadful heaviness in her limbs.

Grace was dead.

"It's Daddy," Clare began.

Her dad was dead.

"He's on his way. Here. To the hospital."

Pip recoiled slightly. "What?"

"He's going to be here in a few minutes."

She felt colour rise through her. The soft heat of joy.

"But, how? Did the hospital give him special permission?"

She saw something pass through her mum's eyes, a flicker of doubt. "Yes," she said. "They said he could come. Because of Grace. And stay as long as he needs to stay. And even maybe not go back if we need him here."

Pip let out a small peal of laughter. "Oh my God!" she said. "Oh my God! I'm going to see my daddy!" And then she felt her stomach twist a bit and lowered her hands and said, "Is he OK? I mean — better?"

"I've spoken to the person who's been looking after him and they told me he's much, much better."

Pip looked at her mother, her eyes wide over the tops of the hands she had clasped across her smiling mouth. For the first time in eight long months, she was about to feel her father's arms around her again.

Adele sat down next to Catkin on the lawn, regarded her for a moment and then gently pulled the too-long tangles of her waist-length hair back from her shoulders. Catkin had refused from a young age either to get her hair cut or to allow her mother to brush it properly. From time to time Adele had been forced to cut chunks of it out, matted locks of hair that could not be saved. Nowadays Catkin chose to keep them; she said she liked them. Adele found them hard to stomach, but she had never laid claim to her children's bodies or their sartorial choices. If Catkin wanted to look like a feral street urchin, that was entirely her decision.

"Hello, beautiful."

Catkin looked at her mum over the top of her paperback. "Hi."

"How are you feeling?"

Catkin shrugged. "A bit weird," she said.

"Yes," said Adele, tucking a few loose, baby-soft hairs behind Catkin's ear. "I'm not surprised. It's all been a bit shocking, hasn't it?"

Catkin shrugged again and pulled the hairs back into their original position.

"I've just been talking to Rhea," Adele said, staring into the middle distance.

She saw Catkin nod.

"She says she saw you and Grace in the Rose Garden on Saturday night. After Dylan left to take Robbie home."

Catkin nodded again.

"So what were you doing, the pair of you?"

"Not much. We just sat there for a while. Talking. Dad came over. With the dog."

"And what did you talk about with Dad?"

"He told Grace that her mum was a bit tipsy. That Pip was on her own in the flat with her. Said she might want to go home. But Grace said she was waiting for Dylan to come back."

"And was there any drinking at this point?"

Catkin threw her an alarmed look.

"It's OK," she said, "I've spoken to Dylan. He told me about the champagne."

"No," she said. "That was all there was."

"And then what happened?"

"Grace said she was going to wait by the garden gates for Dylan to come back. She said she wanted to say goodnight because she needed to go home."

"Did you go with her?"

"No. I went to the playground. To see what the others were doing. She went to the gate."

"Then what?"

Catkin looked at her enquiringly. "Why are you asking me all these questions? Isn't that the police's job?"

"Yes. It is. And they're coming back later to talk to us all and we'd better know exactly what happened. Because . . ." She paused, resisting the temptation to move the loose hair back behind her daughter's ear again. "Apparently Grace was given an overdose. Of sleeping pills. And that's what made her ill. Not a blow to her head."

"What?" Catkin covered her mouth with her hands. "You're kidding? Right?"

"No. I'm not kidding. The policeman came back a couple of hours ago. He told me."

"Oh my God. But that's awful. Who would have done that? I mean, you don't think she did it to herself, do you?"

"Well, that's certainly not a line they're pursuing. But, listen, can you see now why we must be absolutely certain about what happened out here, before the police come back? Can you see?"

Catkin nodded. She grew thoughtful for a moment. "When Dylan came back to the playground," she said quietly, "he had a bottle of water."

"And where was Grace, when Dylan came back?"

"She must have gone home."

"Tell me more about this bottle of water."

"I don't know anything about it. I just noticed he had it."

"So, starting from the beginning: you and Grace were in the Rose Garden. Dad came in and had a little chat. Then Grace left to wait for Dylan. And you went to the playground. Dylan came back, without Grace but with a bottle of water."

Catkin nodded, shrugged, pale bones moving inside the thin skin of her shoulders.

"Then what?"

"Then we just hung out. Until Pip came past asking if we'd seen Grace. And then, well, you know . . ."

"And all this time you were all in the playground: you, Fern, Tyler, Dylan?"

She nodded.

"Anyone else?"

"No."

Adele squeezed the back of her daughter's neck gently and got to her feet. "Thank you."

"Mum?"

She turned. "Yes?"

"There was . . ."

She saw Catkin's bony chest rise and fall, rise and fall. "Something did happen. Earlier." Her mouth sounded dry.

"What?"

"When we'd had the champagne. When we were all a bit tipsy. Tyler was teasing Grace. For not putting out."

"For what?"

"She was calling her a prick-tease. Saying that she was thirteen now and it was time for her to stop mucking about and give Dylan what he wanted. She said —" Catkin stopped abruptly. "Well, that was kind of it really. Grace and Dylan both got really embarrassed. That was it." She trailed off.

"Are you sure?" Adele asked.

"Yeah. I'm sure."

Adele stroked her back one more time and headed back inside, a terrible feeling of gnawing discomfort growing within her by the second. Because, according to Catkin's account of things, the only time that Grace had been alone all afternoon and all evening was during the twenty minutes that her own husband had been walking the dog.

There he was. There, in the doorway. Backlit. Enormous. Clare pulled herself slowly to her feet. He was thinner than she remembered. And there was that beard, the beard he'd never had before but which looked so entirely a part of him that she already couldn't imagine him without it. And the hair, the wild hair that had tumbled about his shoulders and fallen into his eyes, the hair she would badger and badger him about getting cut because it made him look like a mad person: it was gone. His hair now was short and sane. He wore a soft cotton shirt in baby pink, the sleeves bunched up above his elbows, with wash-worn black trousers and giant suede desert boots in a camel colour.

He looked first at Clare, then at his younger daughter and then at his elder. He was torn. Pip made the choice for him; she leaped to her feet and flung herself around his neck. She looked small next to him, Clare noticed. She looked little again.

She had briefed Chris. He knew that the official line for Pip was that he'd come straight from the hospital. There would be no talk of the month he'd spent living four miles away with a 26-year-old girl. No talk of all these weeks that Clare had been protecting her children from their father when all along the real criminal was lurking in their back garden. There would be no talk of the mistakes Clare had made and the lapses in her own judgement. The only talk would be of Grace and how to get her to wake up.

"She's still scared of you," she whispered in Chris's ear as he came towards Grace, his hand outstretched. "I don't know how she'll react to the sound of your voice. Maybe it would be better . . .?"

He smiled at Clare. "I get it," he mouthed silently. He took Grace's hand in his. With his other hand he caressed the bruised contours of her face. Then he turned to Clare again, his face soft with hurt, and said, in the quietest whisper a man of his size could manage: *"Who the hell did this to her?"*

"Did you get my letters?"

"I did get your letters. I loved your letters. I used your letters to work out where you lived. So that I could send birthday presents to you."

"Why didn't you ever reply?"

Her father stopped and regarded the ceiling as though the answer were up there, Sellotaped to the water pipes. "I tried," he said. "I did try. I wrote you loads of letters, but every time I read them back to myself they sounded wrong. Mad. You know. I didn't want you to get a letter from me that would make you worry. So I just screwed them all up. Chucked them in the bin. Decided to wait until I was all better, so that I

296

could do this, instead." He brought his arms around her and squeezed her hard.

"You're thin," she said, pulling back and regarding him.

"I know," he said. "It's the medicine. And missing you all, of course."

"Are you really allowed to stay out now?"

"Yes." He smiled. "I'm free."

"Forever?"

"Hopefully," he said. "But you know, you're twelve now, you're a big girl, you understand that I'm ill. That I will never get better. Not properly. And I might get sick again and have to go back. But the doctors have found a much better way to treat me now, using much better medicine, so hopefully" — he crossed two pairs of huge fingers — "I'll never have to leave you for such a long time again."

Pip stared at him, drinking him in, all of him.

"You know," she said, "Grace told me that she and I could never take drugs because it might give us paranoid schizophrenia. Because that's what happened to you."

"She told you that, did she?"

"Yes. And she said it's genetic so we might already have it and if we take drugs it might unlock it inside us. And now someone's given her drugs. Do you think . . .? I mean, will she . . .?"

Her dad picked her hands up in his and brought them to his beardy chin, kissing the backs of them. "No," he said, softly, "no, sweetheart. She won't. Wrong kind of drugs."

Pip sighed with relief. Then she looked up at her dad, at the new finer contours of his face, the plush beard and the cropped hair and a memory came to her, from left field, fast and vivid. A man on Fitzjohn's Avenue, weeks and weeks ago. She'd been on the bus. He'd been on the pavement. Their eyes had met. "I saw you," she said, throatily. "In Hampstead. A month ago. I was on the bus."

He looked down at her tenderly. "No," he said, "you didn't. It must just have been someone who looked like me." He kissed the crown of her head. "If it had been me," he said, "I'd have waved."

CHAPTER
TWENTY-NINE

Adele and the girls had had a rather subdued lunch around the kitchen table: home-made sandwiches and cold sausages and chicken leftover from Saturday night. The only child with any conversation to her name was, of course, Willow, who hadn't stopped talking about the impending visit from the police, saying things like: *Right, we must all get our stories straight*, and, *Fern, where exactly were you between nine and ten?* The older girls had just tutted and looked away from her disdainfully.

But lunch was now over, the table was cleared and Adele was about to ask Fern just that question.

"Fern, can I have a word?"

Fern looked up from her novel and pulled a bud from her ear, releasing a thin trickle of tinny music. Her eyes were circled with dark rings; she looked as though she hadn't slept for days. "What?"

"We need to talk about Saturday night."

"What about it?"

"Well, the fact that you were one of the last people to be with Grace before something terrible happened to her."

Fern started to pluck at a piece of loose skin on her thumb. It came away leaving a bead of blood, which she sucked off. "None of us know what happened. We've already told you a million times."

"Hm." Adele sat down next to Fern. "Thing is, Fern, I've been talking to other people and there's lots of stuff you and your sisters didn't tell me yesterday. Like that there was champagne involved."

"Hardly," said Fern, finding a new piece of dry skin to tug at. "There was, like, one bottle. We all had, like, a mouthful."

"That's not the point. You should have told me. It's relevant."

"We all said we wouldn't," she said. "So I was just going along with that. It was supposed to be, like, this big secret."

"Catkin also mentioned some teasing going on: Tyler telling Grace that she should be 'giving Dylan what he wants'? I find that quite disturbing."

Fern shrugged. "Well, that's Tyler, isn't it? She *is* quite disturbing."

"Is she?"

Fern shrugged again. "I guess. I mean, she's not your average thirteen-year-old, is she?" She turned her hands palms up and started looking for shreds of skin there amongst the patches of eczema.

Adele put out a gentle stopping hand. "Isn't she?"

"No. Course she's not."

"And what is an average thirteen-year-old?"

Fern considered the question. "I don't think there's any such thing," she said eventually.

Adele stared out of the window for a moment, trying to work out what the essence of this situation actually was. "Now, the police are coming back later and I really don't want weird stuff coming out unexpectedly. So, please, whatever happened, whatever you saw or heard, tell me now. Hm?"

"There's nothing to tell you. I was in the playground with the others. The whole time."

Adele stilled herself for a moment before bringing herself back to life. "Did you see Dad?" she said. "During that hour between nine and ten?"

"I think so," said Fern. "I saw him walking Scout."

"Where did you see him going?"

"I saw him going to Grace's house, then a few minutes later he walked past us and went up the hill."

"Did you see him come back again?"

"No."

"Did you see him with Grace?"

"What? No." Fern looked at her curiously. "Why are you asking me that, Mum?" She began picking again at the eczema on the palms of her hands. "You're acting really weird."

"Am I?" Adele tried for a normal smile but didn't quite get there. "Sorry. It's all just — very unsettling and it's making me feel very weird. You know?"

"Yeah. I guess." Fern looked up suddenly from her hands and into Adele's eyes with those red-rimmed eyes of hers and said, "Do you think it had something to do with Dad?"

"What? Oh, God, no. Of course not."

"It was Tyler," she said abruptly.

Adele stared at Fern, aghast. "What?"

"It was Tyler who pushed Willow off the swings."

Adele exhaled. "Oh," she said. "Right. And why was that?"

Fern shrugged. "I don't know. She just did it. And you know," she said quietly, so quietly that Adele had to strain to hear her, "Tyler said something last night about Puppy. She said that she thought he had something to do with Phoebe dying."

Adele flicked her gaze at Fern. "She said what?"

"I don't know. It didn't make any sense at the time. And everyone was being really crazy. But she said her mum had said that Puppy killed Phoebe. Gave her an overdose."

Adele laughed. "Well, that's the biggest lot of nonsense I've ever heard. And as you know, between Cece and Tyler lies an infinite sea of fantasy and conjecture."

"I know," said Fern. "I know. That's what I said. It was so obvious she was making it up. Just to get attention."

"Exactly," said Adele. "Lovely as Tyler is, she's always been a bit of an attention-seeker."

"I only said it because you were asking all those weird questions."

"I know." Adele stroked the dirty-blue tips of her daughter's hair. "I know."

But as she got to her feet, she felt herself wobble a little. Lurch slightly. Because she really didn't know. She didn't know anything any more.

Adele called Leo at three thirty. "Are you nearly home?" she asked.

"Nowhere near," he said in his "I'm-in-a-meeting" voice.

She tutted and sighed. "I can't do this by myself," she said.

"Do what?"

"Keep asking all these questions," she snapped. "You do know that, according to all the witnesses, you were probably the last person to see Grace before she was attacked."

There was a beat of silence at the end of the line.

"No," he said. "That's not true. It was Dylan."

"Well, that's not what Dylan is saying."

"Of course that's not what he's saying. Like I told you, he's the most likely culprit."

Adele sighed. It didn't matter how far she stretched her own credulity, she could not bring herself to believe that Dylan had anything to do with this. Beautiful Dylan who respected his weird mother and cared for his learning-disabled brother and bought girls champagne for their birthdays to be *romantic*. "Also," she said, "you should probably know that Tyler's been shooting her mouth off about Phoebe's death. Telling your children that Gordon had something to do with it."

"What?"

"She's told your children that Gordon gave Phoebe an overdose."

In the silence that followed she heard the true significance of things filter up through her husband's consciousness. "I'll wrap this up now," he said. "I'll be home within the hour. I promise."

She saw Tyler appear at the top of Virginia Crescent. It was 3.45 p.m. She was in her school uniform, battered rucksack swinging from one shoulder, PE bag from the other. Her hair was pulled back in a half-hearted ponytail. One sock up, one sock down. She looked nothing like the pristine girl of old.

"Tyler," said Adele, stepping into her path. "How are you doing?"

Tyler smiled. "I'm good," she said.

"Listen. The police have been here today. I know they've been looking for you and your mum. There've been some developments regarding Grace."

"Is she OK? Is she . . . ?"

"She's still in a coma. But no change, so . . ."

"Have you seen her?"

"No. No. Not yet."

Tyler nodded, looking around herself.

"Can I have a word, Tyler? Now?"

"Er, yeah? Where?"

"At your flat? Maybe? Or we could go to the café on the corner. I can buy you a muffin or something?"

Tyler's eyes lit up at the mention of a muffin. She rubbed her tummy and said, "I didn't have lunch today. Mum didn't top up my card."

Adele sighed, confused as ever by the fact that Cece spent her days caring for other people's children, yet let her own go without lunch money or company.

"Come on then," she said. "I'll get you a jacket potato if you like?"

"Yeah," said Tyler, eyes shining with gratitude. "I would like that. Thank you."

Adele watched as Tyler fiddled with the cutlery, the salt and pepper pots, the menus, then the paper tubes of sugar in a metal pot. She took them all out, rearranged them by type, put them back again.

She was so like Willow, Adele. thought. So much nervous energy, all channelled into such inane activities. Maybe one day girls like Willow and Tyler would rule the world, but for now they were just compulsively fiddling about with bits of it.

"So, how was school?"

"OK."

"Did you say anything to anyone, about Saturday?"

"No," she said. "No one knows Grace, so it wasn't like anyone would be interested."

"What did your mum say?"

"I don't know. Not much."

Adele pulled the salt and pepper pots from Tyler's hands, set them back on the table, brought her gaze up to meet hers. "Tyler," she said, "I'm hearing a lot of weird things about Saturday night. Things about stolen champagne. About teasing Grace and Dylan. About pushing Willow off the swing. And, kind of most worryingly of all, accusations about Gordon?"

Tyler shook her head and cast her eyes back to the tabletop. "No."

"No?"

"No. I didn't say anything about Gordon. Why would I say anything about Gordon?"

"And why would someone say you had if you hadn't?"

"I dunno. People just say stuff, don't they?"

"They do, yes. That is true. So why don't you tell me some stuff. About Saturday. About what *you* think happened?"

"I have *no idea* what happened. I swear. We were just in the playground, then Pip came running by, then it all went crazy."

"And what were you doing in the playground?"

"Just what we always do. You know. Hanging out. Mucking about."

"Pushing people off swings?"

"Yes. Well. She was annoying me."

"And what was she doing that annoyed you?"

"I can't remember."

"You can't remember?"

"No."

Adele sighed, remembering innumerable situations over the years where she'd had to question Tyler about her involvement in childish scraps. She'd always been evasive to the point of genius. "She's got a terrible bruise, you know."

Tyler shrugged, squaring the menu up against the corner of the table. "Sorry," she said.

The waitress brought Tyler's potato, steaming through a mountain of cheese and baked beans. Tyler immediately picked up her fork and began to eat, blowing the steam of the too-hot food from a mouth made into a circle.

"Where was your mum on Saturday?"

Tyler unfolded a paper napkin and wiped her mouth with it, picked up her Coke and took a slurp. "At his."

"Who's 'his'?" She remembered the date Cece had been going on when they'd met in the street a couple of weeks back.

"Her boyfriend. She's there all the time."

"Oh," she said. "And who's looking after you?"

"No one. Me."

"Do you like him?"

"He's all right," she said, her fork suspended by her mouth. "He's not very chatty. And he's a bit ugly."

Adele sighed. She could not imagine. She really could not. "Anyway," she continued. "Going back to Saturday night. Do you remember seeing anyone else, apart from your friends? Anyone you wouldn't expect to see in the garden at that time of night?"

"Saw Gordon," she said, "hobbling about. Saw Leo. With the dog. Saw Rhea on her balcony. Didn't see anyone else. No weirdos lurking in the undergrowth."

"You know, Tyler," she said. "They've run blood tests on Grace. She was given an overdose. That's what caused the coma."

She watched Tyler chewing a mouthful of food, loading up her fork again, putting it in her mouth.

"You don't look very surprised."

"Not really. It's just history repeating itself. Isn't it?"

Adele turned her teacup around on the saucer. "You mean Phoebe?"

"Yes. Phoebe. And Gordon. My mum told me that it was him. That he'd been abusing her. And she threatened to tell. So he killed her."

Adele felt anger building within her. "Right. Tyler," she said, firmly, "it is absolutely *not OK* to talk like that about people. I have no idea where your mother got this ridiculous notion from, but it's utter rubbish. And neither of you should be going around saying things like that."

"Yes, but it's *relevant*, isn't it? Grace was drugged. Phoebe was drugged. Gordon was in the garden." She shrugged as if to say: *Dur.*

"Right. Fine," said Adele. "Let's just drop this for now. But seriously, Tyler, when the police come to talk to you later, you have to be very careful what you say. Because if you start shooting your mouth off with all this nonsense about Gordon, you'll be distracting them from the real issue. And the real issue is Grace. And what on earth would Gordon have to do with Grace?"

"I don't know," she said. "Maybe he's a paedophile?"

Adele's thoughts returned to Rhea's words the other day: that she wouldn't feel happy having Gordon in her home with young girls. "Don't be silly," she said. "Of course he's not."

"How do you know that? How do you know anyone's not a paedophile? How do you know *Leo's* not a paedophile? I mean, he went out with my mum when she was only thirteen!"

Adele recoiled. "God, Tyler," she said, aghast. "How on earth do you know about that?"

"Because my mum told me," she said. "She told me everything. That she was obsessed with him. For years. I know all that. And you know something else?" Her eyes narrowed and she put down her fork. "I used to think that Leo was my dad. I really, really did. Because my mum let me believe that he was. She let me believe that for years and years and years. She never said he was. But then she never said he wasn't."

She slid her fork back and forth across the side of her plate. Adele could see a film of tears across her eyes. The fork was moving faster and faster, making an irritating, rasping sound. She resisted the temptation to grab Tyler's hand and stop it. There was something colossal happening here and she didn't want to scare it off.

"But why?" she began gently. "Why would you think he was your father?"

"Because —" She stopped. She looked up at Adele. "Because once, when I was really little, when I was about four, five or something, I saw them kissing each other."

Adele laughed. She couldn't help it.

Tyler looked at her, affronted. "I don't know why you're laughing. It happened. It really happened."

Adele cast her thoughts back through nearly a decade of memories. Nine years ago. Willow was one. Fern was four. Catkin was six. Leo's consultancy was just taking off. Adele was not yet used to juggling a baby with two home-schooled children. Life had been quite stressful. Things between Leo and her had been almost dark. She'd wondered back then if Leo might be tempted to find some light somewhere out of their home. Find someone to be nice to him when she was incapable of doing so. But still — Cece Rednough? She was hardly a ray of sunshine. She was a whole other kind of dark.

"Does your mother know you saw them?"

"Don't know," she said. "It was in the Rose Garden. I was looking for Dylan. I don't know if she saw me. I never talked to her about it."

"Are you sure that's what you saw, Tyler? Because you know Leo, he's very touchy-feely, very affectionate. Maybe he was just hugging her?"

"I don't know. I was *four*. I know what I think I saw and how what I think I saw made me feel. And it made me feel like Leo must be my dad because only dads kissed mums and it was the best feeling I ever had because I wanted it so much. Because I wanted to be part of your family more than anything."

"Tyler, you *are* part of our family. You've always been part of our family."

"No," she said, "no I haven't. Not properly. I thought I was. I really believed it. But then . . ." She stabbed the skin of her potato with the tines of her fork. "Mum told me. Last week. She told me who my dad really is. I met him." She looked up at Adele with horror. "I met him last week. And he's a . . . literally a nobody. He's a loser. I mean, do you know where he's been all my life? All the thirteen years that I've been alive?"

Adele shook her head.

"In prison. My real dad. In prison. For beating up his girlfriend. Beating her up so badly that she's blind in one eye."

310

Adele clasped her throat.

"Yeah. Exactly. So. Imagine that. All these years thinking that Leo was my dad. Thinking I had his blood in my blood. Thinking that your children were my sisters. And it turns out that I've got nothing to do with you. And that this ugly little rat of a man with tattoos on his hands and dirt under his nails, this little man who hasn't even got a proper home, this man who hurts women — *he's* the man who made me."

"Oh, Tyler . . ."

"His name is Wayne. Imagine that. My dad is called Wayne. Wayne the Wife-beater. *God.*"

Adele couldn't speak. She stared at the little scratches up and down Tyler's scrawny arms. The scratches she said she'd got retrieving a football from a blackberry bush. She looked at the dull, greasy roots of her hair. She thought of the heaviness of the atmosphere between all the children these last couple of weeks.

"It's not . . ." she began. "The man your mum's dating — it's not him, is it? It's not your father?"

"No!" She looked appalled. "God. No! Mum thinks he's disgusting too. Mum hates him. And you know, all those years that she let me think Leo was my dad, even though she knew he wasn't, I think I get it. I think I do. Because she was in love with Leo. All along. Just like me. We were both in love with Leo. Both of us. We both wished he was my dad. And he's not. He never was. And now he's . . . All of you have . . . It's all . . ." She was crying properly, tears pouring down her cheeks.

"Tyler . . ." Adele put her hands out to Tyler's, but Tyler snatched them back. She pushed back her chair and she collected her schoolbags. "I'm sorry," she said. "Thank you for my tea."

And she half ran from the café, away from Adele, knocking into people as she went.

Grace's room was washed in golden light. The three of them sat around her bed watching the sun's rays, filtered through the branches of a tree outside, flickering over her face. Pip wondered if she could feel it. Wondered if she could see the strobes through her closed eyelids. She wanted her to wake up, right now, like a princess from a fairy-tale slumber and then she wanted to say to her: *Tell me tell me tell me. What happened in the Rose Garden?* Because there was a question nagging at her in the darkest corners of her mind. A question she hadn't asked Max earlier on. A question that hadn't even occurred to her at the time. Something so obvious and so awful that maybe she hadn't allowed herself to think it.

She looked at her beautiful sister, so still, so separate. Grace had been a baby when Pip came along. She'd never known a world without Pip in it and Pip had never known a world without Grace in it. They were as intrinsic to each other's beings as their own shadows. And yet, in the black hole left behind after their father burned down their house, Grace had found a way to fill the void that didn't include her. Another family. Another father. Another soul-mate. She hadn't needed Pip at all. But now there was something Pip could do

312

for her that nobody else could do. She could ask Max the question. The question that might provide the answer to who'd done this to her sister. And why.

She touched the sleeve of her father's soft pink shirt and said, "Daddy. I need to do something. Will you come with me?"

She saw him immediately. He was still in his school uniform: grubby white polo shirt, navy trousers, scuffed, end-of-term leather shoes. He was playing football with his dad. He looked so happy, the very particular happy of a boy whose dad had come home from work early and said yes when asked if he'd come out and play football. It was the happiest she'd ever seen Max.

She felt guilty for a moment, to be interrupting Max's special time with his dad, but there was no other option. She didn't want to leave Grace at the hospital for any longer than necessary. She couldn't bear not to be there when she opened her eyes. She wanted to be the first person Grace saw. She wanted to start everything all over again with Grace, to be once more her beginning and her end.

"Max," she called out. She saw the look of joy fall immediately from his face. "Can I ask you something?"

Max looked curiously behind her at her father. She hoped he'd know without thinking too hard who he was. She hoped that the physical similarity was striking enough.

"You know, on Saturday? You know when you were playing football? When you went up the hill to get your ball? And you saw Grace on the grass?"

He nodded, staring at his shoes. "Yeah."

"You know, before you came up? Can you remember who was in the playground?"

He looked at her strangely, as though the question didn't compute. "What do you mean?"

"I mean, that night, when you were playing football. Who was in the playground?"

"There was no one," he said, flatly, as though it was so obvious it didn't need to be said. "There was no one in the playground."

"No one?"

"No one. It was empty." He shrugged, apologetically.

Pip nodded, her head spinning with a sudden, awful rush of knowledge and understanding.

"Thanks, Max. See you later."

"Yeah. See you later."

She turned to her father, her face set hard. "OK," she said. "We can go back now."

"You got what you wanted?"

"Yes," she said. "I got what I wanted."

CHAPTER
THIRTY

The atmosphere in the Howeses' flat by the time the two PCs returned at six o'clock that evening was charged with so many different kinds of energy it was virtually electric. Adele had had to give Willow a dose of Tarentula hispanica, a homeopathic aid with indications towards calming hyperactivity in children. So far it didn't seem to be working.

She offered them home-made hummus and bread-sticks. Then she felt worried that the Greek PC would think she was patronising him, so she offered them, rather randomly, some pasta salad.

"So," began PC Michaelides, "we've spent the day talking to various people, as you know, although we still haven't managed to get hold of . . ." He consulted his notes. "Cecelia Rednough."

"No," said Adele, wishing that Willow would stop bouncing up and down on the footstool. "She doesn't tend to get home from work until quite late."

"Maybe we'll give her another try after we've finished here then." He smiled, and then turned to Leo. "So, Mr Howes?"

"Leo's fine."

"Leo. Thank you. I wonder if we might be able to talk to you first? Possibly without the children?" Adele looked up sharply, glancing from the PC to the WPC and then at her girls.

The WPC smiled reassuringly. "Just a couple of little things," she said. "Won't take a minute."

Adele gestured at the three girls to leave the room, which they did with varying degrees of grace.

After they'd gone all four turned and smiled at each other, nervously.

"We were wondering", said the PC, "if you could tell us a bit about your impressions of Grace Wild?"

"My *impressions?* Gosh, well . . ." He stroked his chin, making himself, in Adele's opinion, look thoroughly dodgy. "She's only been living on the garden for a few months, so I haven't really had a chance to —"

"I suppose", the WPC cut in, "what we mean is: what was your relationship with her? Are you close?"

"No," Leo replied, too fast, too firm. "Not at all. I mean, there are children on the garden who I've known since they were babies and I'd say I was close to them. But not Grace. She is just a friend of my daughters."

"The reason we're asking, Leo, is that we've had our analysts going through the CCTV footage from Saturday night, from the cameras situated above the communal gates? And there is clear footage of you, at approximately nine twenty-five, approaching Grace Wild by the gate, engaging her for a while in conversation and then . . ." He pulled a print from a folder on the sofa next to him and passed it to Leo. ". . . embracing her."

Adele flicked her gaze to her husband, reptile fast. Then she looked down at the photo in her husband's hand. It was almost a bird's-eye view. There was Grace, her bare arms wrapped around the waist of a dark-haired man. A dark-haired man attached to a medium-sized golden dog.

"Ah," said Leo, not making eye contact with Adele. "That. Oh. God. I mean, that was . . . She was standing there. Waiting for her boyfriend to come back. You know, I must be honest right now and say I wasn't sober. You know, a big family day. Drinking since two p.m. So I don't entirely remember what happened here. But I do remember seeing her standing there and me saying she should probably go home, because her mum wasn't well and her sister was there on her own. And then, I honestly don't know why, but she launched herself at me. I mean, if you watch the footage you'll see it. You'll see what happened. Look here, at my arm." He pointed at the photo. "It's kind of hanging loose, see."

"Mr Howes — sorry, Leo. No one is accusing you of anything here. We're merely trying to ascertain the nature of your relationship with Grace so that we can put all the jigsaw pieces together. And from this footage it struck us that maybe you and she were close. Maybe you had an insight?"

"You know," he said, his eyes too bright, his body language all wrong, "it strikes me now, now that I think about it, that maybe she was missing her dad. It was her thirteenth birthday; she hasn't seen him for such a long time. It's possible she saw me for that brief moment as a father figure? Or that I reminded her in some way of her father? I mean . . ." He shrugged and rubbed his chin again.

Stop talking! Adele wanted to scream. *Please stop talking!*

Who was this man? This man who kissed thirteen-year-old girls? Whose own father believed he'd been involved in the death of a teenager? Who may or may not have kissed their neighbour in the Rose Garden nine years ago? Who fuelled other people's daughters' fantasies about him being their Real Father? And who hugged other people's daughters in dusky alleyways? Why hadn't he told her about the interlude? Moments after this had happened, he'd been back at their flat, saying goodbye to Zoe and her family. Why hadn't he said: *God, you won't believe what just happened. Grace Wild just hugged me for no good reason!*

The PCs stayed for an hour in the end. They talked to the girls, their questions yielding no more information than Adele had already extracted from them during the course of the day. They sat with Gordon for a while. Adele tried to hear what was being said but could catch very little. They'd briefed him very carefully beforehand to say nothing just yet about the missing sleeping pills. He'd said he'd be economical with the truth but that he wasn't prepared to out-and-out lie.

318

When they'd finished interviewing Gordon, the PCs appeared in the kitchen doorway with their empty water glasses and the half-finished hummus.

"Well," said PC Michaelides, "I think we've got as much as we need for now. Thank you so much for your valuable time. We'll let you get back to your lives now. And if we need to ask any more questions, would anyone be around tomorrow at all?"

Adele nodded, putting the hummus dish in the sink. "We'll be here. All day. Every day. Just knock." She was trilling. She knew she was.

After they left the atmosphere flattened out immediately.

"Well," said Gordon, "that wasn't too bad. No mention of the sleeping pills. Think I might have a quick lie-down before supper. Assuming there is any supper? Mrs H.?"

She looked around her at the kitchen, at the fridge full of things to be cooked, at the pantry full of other things to be cooked. She looked at her daughters, at scruffy dreadlocked Catkin, dark-eyed, shaven-headed Fern, at Willow, with her wild eyes and misplaced energy. She looked at Gordon, the former scourge of the gardens, staring at her with hungry feed-me eyes and then at her husband, the teen-bothering, fantasy-dad murder suspect, and she suddenly thought, *I do not know any of you.*

"I'm not sure about supper, Gordon," she said, her voice even and slow. "I think maybe Leo could order us some pizzas. Leo?"

Leo looked at her in surprise. Pizzas were usually only allowed in emergencies, when the train was late and you got home too late to cook. They were a special treat for the tail end of days gone wrong and plans gone awry. The girls cheered, oblivious to her disturbed state of mind. Leo pulled out the menu from the drawer where menus were kept. Everyone shouted out their preferences.

"Del?" Leo called over to her. "What do you want? Fiorentina?"

She nodded distractedly and left the room.

It was finally growing dark beyond the walls of the Royal Free. It had been light for so long and she'd been awake for so many hours that Pip felt almost as though she might have skipped a night. But now the lights on the ward were going on and at last this day was coming to an end. And then, just now, a second ago, there'd been a flicker across Grace's left eye. And then another. And then another.

All three of them now stood over Grace's bed, staring intently at her face. Her eyelids had been flickering for about a minute. The next flicker was accompanied by a full body twitch. Then a small groan. With each sign of life, they moved closer and closer until Pip was almost compelled to say: *Move back. You're going to frighten her.* Pip held her hand against Grace's cheek. Clare held her hand.

"Do you think she's waking up?" Clare asked.

Pip's dad nodded. "Should I get a nurse?" he asked.

"Not yet," said Clare, her eyes never leaving Grace's face. "Not just yet."

Grace groaned again. Then suddenly her eyes were opening, the bright hazel half-moons of her irises miraculously visible.

She moved her mouth and Pip watched as she tried to make a word. But nothing came. Her eyes were open now, properly open, taking in the faces of her mother, her sister, and then, finally, her father. They widened and went to Clare, looking for reassurance. "Daddy's here," Clare said in the sort of voice you might use to talk to a toddler. "The hospital said he was better. That he could leave. So he's here. And it's fine. It's fine."

Pip could see her sister's expression relax. And then, as they watched, she saw her sister look from each one to each one and then she said something in a dried-out voice filled with scratchy tears and at first they couldn't make out what she was saying. But then they knew.

She was saying, "I'm sorry. I'm sorry. I'm sorry."

CHAPTER
THIRTY-ONE

5 July, 3p.m.

Champagne. Dylan had bought her champagne. Grace had opened the package in her room, after her lunch party. It was wrapped up in pink tissue, twisted to the form of the bottle, then put in a different-shaped box. So no one would guess, you see.

Grace had forced it into the too-tight confines of her bag and rushed from the flat before anyone could ask where she was going, what she was holding so close to her inside that bag.

"Tyler says to put it in her fridge," Dylan had whispered into her ear when she joined up with him again in the garden. "She says her mum's out."

They head out now, through the garden gates, on to the summer-dry pavement. Dylan holds her hand. Just like that. Just like people do. She feels amazing walking down the street with him. She still remembers the first time she saw him, at the top of the hill, waiting for Tyler. She remembers the way he pulled off his school tie and rolled it up, put it in the pocket of his blazer. Stood and waited. So tall and so assured. She'd thought then he must be fifteen, sixteen at least. She'd thought Tyler must be his girlfriend. And when she'd found out he wasn't even a year older than her, that he and Tyler were just good friends, it had been like something amazing being handed down to her from the universe.

They stop at the entrance to Tyler's mansion block on the corner. She feels Dylan's fingers running up and down the backs of her thighs. "Best shorts ever," he whispers.

She shivers at his touch. She wants to touch him back but she doesn't know how. She doesn't know where. Then he throws her a smile that is so beautiful and so bad that when he looks away she raises her eyes to heaven as if she might find its source up there.

Inside Tyler's flat all the glory of them fades away. Tyler is playing happy and glad but Grace knows that she is neither. They are set again at the sharp points of their awful triangle. When Tyler's back is turned to take the champagne to the kitchen, Dylan's fingertips find the backs of her thighs again, tracing an exquisite undulation across her skin that seems to join up dots in her body she'd had no notion existed. She feels like one of those actors in a CGI suit, as if there are blobs of light all over her.

"Aw," says Tyler, coming out of the kitchen, catching the glittering comet tail of their longing, "you two. You are just adorable. You should get married and have babies."

"Yeah yeah," says Dylan.

They stay for too long. Outside are the sounds of children and summer. In here it is dark and hot and they are only here because they have all somehow decided that it is more grown-up to be indoors in a flat with no adults than to be outside at a boring babyish old *garden party*. Grace wishes they would leave, and is relieved when her mum calls just after four to tell her off for disappearing. "We'd better go," she says to Dylan.

Dylan gets to his feet, says, "Can I use your bathroom?"

Tyler nods. Dylan leaves. Then they are alone.

"So," says Tyler, her voice flat. "Are you having a lovely birthday?"

Grace nods.

"My thirteenth birthday was shit. Everyone forgot. Except Dylan. He bought me roses. Pink ones." She looks at Grace as if to say *beat that*. "You know" — she brings her face closer to Grace's — "you know that he's the best person in the whole world, don't you? And you know that you totally don't deserve him."

And for some reason, because it is her birthday and because Dylan's touch has brought her somehow to life and because Tyler appears somehow smaller and less significant in the overcast surroundings of her mother's slightly shabby little flat with its empty rooms and plain woodchip walls and because she is so sick of Tyler always being there, always with that face with its peaks of disapproval and dips of envy, Grace finds herself saying, "No, actually, I think you'll find *you're* the one who doesn't deserve him. If you were a real friend you'd be glad for him, instead of walking around the whole time with that *look* on your face."

324

The look appears, right on cue. "Christ, you're a bitch," Tyler says. "I honestly don't know what he sees in you."

"And I don't know why he'd be friends with a loser like you. You're like a leech, just sucking off him. Sucking the goodness out of him. Because there's none inside you. Because you're all hollow inside and without him you're just *nothing*." Grace inhales, sharply.

And then, in the smallest, deathliest voice, from lips twisted and contorted against tears, Tyler says, "I hate you."

Dylan reappears.

"Take her away, will you, Dylan? I don't want to look at her." Tyler turns and stares from the window, out across the trees and the tops of gazebos and marquees, her fist held hard at her mouth, her body rigid with fury.

Dylan tries to say something but Tyler raises her arm in the air and repeats, "Take her away. Now."

They catch the lift down, even though it's only two floors. Dylan pulls across the shiny brass concertina doors; then he turns. He's about to say something. Something about Tyler. But Grace does not want to talk about Tyler. She wants to do something to erase Tyler from Dylan's thoughts forever. As the lift straddles floors one and two, Grace does something she saw on a TV show once. She presses the emergency-stop button. The lift bounces gently in its cradle, making a mournful humming noise.

She takes Dylan's hands and she leads his fingers up and down the backs of her legs until she gets that feeling back. That feeling from before, that she was all and she was real and she was ready. Dylan drops his face into her shoulder, his breath against her skin warm and surprised. Her hands find the button on his jeans. He makes a noise into her hair. She knows that it is a noise he has only made alone before. That she will be the first person to make him feel this way. She feels empowered, unassailable, thirteen. She sinks, slowly, as she's seen them do on screens, to her knees and does the thing that they do on the screens and she has no idea if she's doing it right or doing it wrong and the smell is odd and sweet like stale drawers and candyfloss and Dylan's hands press into her hair, and then it happens and he says, *I love you, Grace. Oh God, I love you.* And he looks shocked and awed and she feels strange and euphoric. She reaches back up his body to his face and his mouth and his hair, to the familiar parts of him, and he holds her face in his hands and his eyes burn with gratitude and adoration and amazement, and she knows. She knows that she has won.

Her eyes look up through the lift shaft. And there is Tyler, pale eyes on hers. She presses the down button and Tyler disappears from view.

CHAPTER
THIRTY-TWO

Adele waited, heart racing, for the sound of her husband coming to bed. She was so awake, so alive, so wired into the dark, dizzy, fast-pulsing core of everything that she felt as if she might never sleep again. Finally, just gone eleven thirty, he appeared. He had lost some of his sparkle, some of his lustre. He looked tired and overwhelmed.

The words that had been swirling inside Adele's head all day didn't take long to find their way to her tongue. "We need to talk," she said, patting his side of the bed.

"I promise you," he said, "we'll go to the station, we'll look at the CCTV footage. You'll see what happened. She was upset. I don't know why. And she hugged me. I did not initiate it. And nothing else happened. I prom —"

"I don't mean about Grace. I mean other things. Come to bed."

"Yes," he said, robotically removing his clothes.

She stared into the middle distance as he did so. She couldn't bear to watch him naked and vulnerable. Her perfect husband.

He slid in beside her. She heard him exhale slowly. Then rub his hands down his face. There was a denseness to his movements, where usually there was light and energy.

"I spoke to Tyler earlier," she began. "I took her out for her tea. She hadn't had lunch because Cece hadn't topped up her lunch card." She sighed, still sad at the thought of it. "Anyway. We had a very revealing conversation, Leo." She paused for a beat before continuing. "Did you know that when Tyler was four years old she saw you kissing Cece in the Rose Garden?"

She turned to watch his reaction.

For a moment he said nothing, his mouth left open. Then his head dropped and he rubbed his eyes and he said, "I remember that."

Adele's already marching heart picked up pace.

"So it happened?"

"Well, yes, but not in that way. Not in a 'kissing in the Rose Garden' way. It was more" — he scratched his scalp — "she kissed me."

Adele stared at him.

"She was upset. She was cross with me. For some reason. Dragged me in there. Told me everything that had gone wrong in her life was my fault. Told me she was still in love with me. Told me she'd thrown away everything for me. Told me she'd . . ." He looked at her then, and she saw something so dark and dreadful in his eyes that it almost burned her.

"What?"

The look faded. "Nothing. Just that she'd only ever wanted me. And she'd made loads of bad choices because she couldn't have me. And all those bad choices were my fault. And her having a baby when she wasn't ready to have a baby was my fault. And how Tyler should have been mine. And if Tyler was mine she'd be a better mother. And how she —" He stopped. A half-smile of regret passed across his face. "How she hated you and resented my children. Oh, God . . ."

"And then you kissed?"

"She started to cry. I put my arms round her to comfort her."

"After she'd just told you she hated me?"

"I just . . . Del. You know what I'm like. Women crying. It's my weak spot. And she was crying and in pain so I held her and then she kissed me and it was so full of fury and pain. It was . . . like being sucked into a black hole. Or into the pits of hell. And I had my eyes wide open the whole time. And I saw Tyler, I saw that little girl standing there, watching. And I pulled away and Cece turned and saw her there too and then she . . ." He moaned gently, pulling at the skin of his face. "She kissed me again. Knowing . . ."

"That her daughter was watching?"

"That her daughter was watching."

"She wanted her to see."

"Yes."

"Tyler thought you were her dad for ten years, Leo."

"I know."

"You know!"

"Yes. It was obvious. Wasn't it?"

Adele thought back again through the years: the little pixie girl always in the middle of everything. Always where Leo was. Always where his children were. It was obvious. Yes. But she'd never really noticed.

"But she's not, Leo. Is she?"

She had to ask it.

"What? My daughter?"

Adele nodded.

Leo turned fully now, finally seeming as though he was hers again. "No. God, Del. No."

She nodded, believing him. "She told me, earlier, she met him. Her real dad."

"The woman-beater?"

"You knew?"

"Yes. Cece told me. Years ago. Made me promise never to tell a living soul."

"And you didn't?"

"I didn't."

Adele looked at him curiously. "What was it?" she said. "Between you and Cece. All these years? All these secrets?"

Leo shrugged. "Just a garden thing. Just history. Just . . ." He paused. ". . . the stains of childhood."

"Leo," she said, quietly. "What happened to Phoebe?"

Grace held the mirror up to her face. Turned her head this way and that way. Grimaced.

"It's not too bad," said Clare. "They reckon it'll set straight. You were lucky."

Grace nodded miserably and then put down the mirror.

330

She claimed not to know how she'd broken her nose. She claimed to remember nothing. But Pip knew; she knew without a doubt that her sister was lying. She knew that it was only a matter of time before Grace "remembered". But there was something, something else underlying the happiness of Grace's awakening. Something her mother knew, that her father knew. Something they weren't telling Pip. Conversations that stopped when she entered the room. Concerned looks. Snatches of words spoken as whispers into each other's ears. Pip was beginning to believe that there something more than a broken nose and a drug overdose in the story of what had happened to Grace on Saturday night. Something to do with the yanked-up top and pulled-down shorts. Something to do with the special nurse who'd seen Grace yesterday. Something to do with sex.

She pulled at her father's arm. He looked down at her. "I want to talk to Grace, on my own."

Clare nodded at Chris, and they left the room. And then it was just the two of them. The Irish twins. It was awkward at first. As though they were new to each other. Pip sat in the plastic chair, still warm from her mother's body. She stared for a while at her sister. "Where've you been?" she said.

"In a coma."

"No," said Pip. "I mean: where've you been all these weeks?"

Grace frowned at her.

"You've been in another world."

"What the fuck are you talking about?"

"I don't know. It's just, since we moved on to the garden, since we met the others, it's like you've been taken over."

Grace shrugged. "It's not just the garden though, is it? It's everything. New school. New house. New mum. *Dad*."

"He's back now."

"Yeah. I'd noticed."

"Are you happy?"

Grace shrugged again. "Not really. Kind of. Whatever. You know, until the next time."

"He's on different medication. Maybe he won't get ill again."

"Yeah. And maybe he will." Grace put her hand to her face, to her nose, stroking the tender contours with her fingers as she'd done almost obsessively since she'd woken up last night. Then she moved her hand to her hair and grimaced. "Fucking hell, I need to sort my hair out."

"You'll be home soon. You can wash it then."

"I don't want to go home." She plucked at the white sheets of her bed.

Pip looked at her questioningly.

"I don't ever want to go back to that place."

"Was it . . .?" she began, cautiously. "Grace? Was it Leo?"

Her sister's face broke up into a splintered mask of disbelief. "What?"

"Was it Leo? Who hurt you?"

"Oh my God. What? Seriously? What are you asking me?"

"Leo! He's weird. I've seen him, with Tyler, acting weird."

"Oh my God," she said again. "Are you crazy? Leo's, like, the best person in that garden. He would never —"

"So who did? Who did?" Pip said, words tumbling now. "The others. They said they were in the playground when you got hurt. But they weren't. And Max says he heard stuff, voices and stuff. And then he saw you. On the ground. And heard people running away. And your clothes, Grace, they were all pulled up. I had to cover you, because you were showing. You know. *Showing.*"

Grace's face flushed. "That's not true."

"It is true, Grace. Someone hurt you. Someone drugged you. Someone tried to take off your clothes. And I don't believe that you don't know who it was. I don't believe you. And I don't understand why you would lie."

"I am not lying. I don't remember anything."

"Yes you do. How could someone have given you a drug overdose without you knowing? Someone must have given it to you. Someone must have."

"I really, really don't remember. I promise you. If I remembered I'd tell you. But I don't."

Pip brought her face close to her sister's. "What if it was me, Grace? What if that person who gave you those drugs did it to me next time? Because you didn't tell?"

"They wouldn't," she said.

Pip felt a pinprick of triumph. "They?"

"Whoever it was."

"How do you know?"

"Because it's not about you, Pip. It's about me."

"So you think it was someone you know?"

Grace's pale, bruised face lit with a small glow of remembrance. "I know who it might have been. I know who might have wanted to hurt me. But it's not a man. It's a girl."

CHAPTER
THIRTY-THREE

5 July, 9.17p.m.

Grace watches Leo heading away from them, with his dog, heading away from Catkin and her. And now they are on their own in the Rose Garden. And she feels a bit awkward. She doesn't know Catkin that well. Finds her intimidating. She's one of those girls with a chip of ice in her heart. One of those girls who make you feel as though everything you do is a bit silly. As though her way is the one true way. For a moment or two they don't talk. It's an uncomfortable silence and Grace wants to fill it, but all the things she can think of to say are pointless and dull.

"I think", she says after another moment, "I'll go and wait for Dylan. By the gate. Say goodnight properly."

She gets to her feet and Catkin nods, gives her a knowing look, and then speaks. "We all know," she says. "We all know what you did to him. It's sick."

"What are you talking about?"

"Tyler told us. About you and Dylan. In the lift. You're thirteen. Do you know how sick that is?"

Grace feels a thick fog of shame crawling all over her. She can still taste him in her mouth.

But then she looks at Catkin, with her dreadlocked hair and dead eyes, thinks about all her secret longings and night-time worlds. She thinks of the novel Catkin has been writing for all her childhood and never finished. She thinks of her home-schooling, in a house full of girls. And she thinks: *She's jealous.* Catkin is jealous because I'm younger than her but I've done more. Because she wants to know how it would be to stop a lift, to undo a fly, to do the thing that she had done, to have a boy say *I love you* in that desperate, strangled voice, as though you had unlocked the very essence of him and given him the key. She wants to know and she doesn't and she can't because she is trapped here in this garden. Trapped within all these staring eyes of windows. Trapped in this place that has not let her grow, has not given her the space to be something more than her parents' daughter, her sisters' sister. And she is scared. Because she knows all this. And here am I, thinks Grace — thirteen years old. *Thirteen years old.*

And Grace turns to Catkin then and looks into her dead eyes and says, "You're just jealous. All of you. You're freaks and you're losers and you're jealous."

She walks away, leaving Catkin on the bench, staring at her darkly.

By the time she reaches the garden gate Grace has lost some of her bravado. Her hands are shaking. She can feel tears building in the back of her throat. She stands for a moment, her back against the wall of the alleyway, breathing heavily.

"Grace?"

It's Leo. He's tying a knot in a dog-poo bag. He drops it in the dog-mess bin and walks towards her. "You OK? I thought you were going in?"

"I am," she says. "I was just waiting for Dylan. Waiting to say goodnight."

Leo looks up and around. "I really think you should go back. Your sister needs you," he says. "I can wait here for Dylan. Tell him you said goodnight."

Grace shakes her head. "Thank you, but I'm happy waiting."

Leo smiles, that smile of his that makes everything OK. "Well," he says, "don't talk to any strangers."

"I won't," she says. And then suddenly, unexpectedly, she needs to hold him. She needs to feel the warmth of him and the depth of him and the goodness of him all the way through her. She throws her arms around him and squeezes him, the way her dad used to squeeze her. Hard and proper. "Thank you," she says, her face burrowed into his shoulder.

He laughs a little uncomfortably. "What for?"

"I don't know," she says, letting him go. And she really doesn't. She laughs nervously and he laughs nervously and then the dog starts to pull at the lead and Leo says, "Don't hang around here for too long. If he doesn't come in the next few minutes, promise me you'll go home."

"I promise," she says.

She watches Leo leaving again, moving towards the light of his house.

And then Grace waits in the dark for the tall boy who loves her and as the moments pass she wonders if she loves him back, and she wonders if any of this is what it's supposed to feel like and if she's done any of it in the right way and if the girls will ever talk to her again, and she wonders what Dylan is thinking right now and what Tyler is thinking right now, and she thinks of her mother, drunk in bed, and Pip, alone, in that small, dark flat that has never been her home and then of her real home, which is carbon-black and death-shrouded, and she thinks of her father in the wetsuit and Leo in the shadows and the smell of him and the feel of him, and then she hears the garden gate click open, click closed and she turns to look for Dylan but there's nobody there and then she hears: "*Psst, Grace.*" And she turns towards the voice although she's sure it isn't Dylan and there is a pain, sharp in her shoulder.

She slaps at the pain, as though it was an insect. And then for a moment or two she reels around and around like a dying fly and there's no one there and then there is the ground and the feel of her nose splitting in two like an axed log.

Then there is nothing but dreams.

CHAPTER
THIRTY-FOUR

Adele awoke the following morning with a start. Leo stood over her bedside. To his right was Fern. To his left was Catkin. She looked at the time. Seven thirty-five.

"What's going on?"

"The police just called. They want us to bring the girls into the station."

"What! Why?"

"I don't know. They just said something came up on the CCTV footage and they need to ask them some questions. You coming?"

"What about Willow?"

"Dad says we can leave her here with him."

Adele pulled herself out of bed. She rubbed the sleep from her face with both her hands. She didn't wash. She put on yesterday's clothes. Then she headed down the hallway and knocked at Gordon's bedroom door.

"I'm not decent," he called out. "Please do not enter."

"Gordon, it's me. I need a word."

"I am not wearing underwear."

"Do you have a dressing gown?"

"Give me a moment."

She heard him bumbling about and then clearing his throat. "Enter."

He was sitting on the side of his bed, otherworldly bare legs dangling from a once-grand red silk gown, ripped in places, stained in others, barley-twist piping. "What can I do for you, Mrs H.?"

"The police have called."

"I know."

"They want to see the girls."

"I know."

"Leo told me things last night. About Cecelia."

"Now, remind me. Which one was Cecelia?"

"The one who didn't die."

"Yes. Yes. Gorgeous little thing, she was."

"Leo went out with her."

"I know. And the other one." He ran his hands down his leg, massaging it as he went. "That was a long hot summer, if ever there was one. All sorts going on that summer."

"You said something before. About your boys. You said they had something to do with Phoebe's death."

"Did I? Did I really? Doesn't sound very likely, does it?"

"Well no, exactly. Which is why I was wondering what you meant."

"I suppose I just meant that they were a terrible bunch of scoundrels, going around the garden, breaking young girls' hearts. I suppose I just meant that if that poor girl killed herself, which, as you know, was never proved, then they all played their part in that." He looked at Adele curiously. "Old girl," he said, "you

340

haven't been going round all this time thinking your husband was a cold-blooded killer, have you?"

Adele shook her head. "God. No. Of course not. I suppose, with all that's been going on, I just wanted to have a clear view of everything, that's all. Especially if we're talking to the police today."

"You know what wouldn't surprise me, Mrs H.? Wouldn't surprise me in the least if it turned out to be the sister. She was a green-eyed devil when it came to Leo and Phoebe. She really was. I used to look at her sometimes, the way she watched them together. Like she wanted to kill someone. And maybe she did in the end. Maybe she did."

"There," said PC Michaelides, moving slightly so that everyone got a good view of the screen. "Look. See how Grace is standing there for a few minutes after your dad goes. And then see how she turns, like she's heard something? And then comes around the corner, away from the camera. Well, look at this. Just here. A few minutes before. The gate opens, then closes, yet nobody comes in. We thought at first it was just the wind. But then look at this, just before Grace goes out of shot. Can you see that, just at the bottom of the screen? It looks like the top of someone's head. Doesn't it? And we've zoomed in on it, as much as we can. And it looks, as far as we're all concerned, like a ponytail. So what we're thinking is that someone came in through the gates and crawled on their hands and knees. Deliberately avoiding the camera. And that it was a female, with blonde hair. So . . ." PC Michaelides

341

paused the video and smiled at the two girls. "You two were in the garden around this time. The question is: did either of you see a blonde female with a ponytail? Behaving strangely?"

Adele bit her lip, waited what felt like an eternity for one of her girls to reply.

"Well," said Fern, sharing a glance with Catkin. "I mean. Tyler has a blonde ponytail."

Catkin nodded. "Yes. She does."

"Tyler Rednough?"

They nodded.

"But according to your account of Saturday night, you and Tyler were together the whole time, between nine and ten p.m.?"

"We were," Catkin replied, steely, but with a nervous gulp.

"So it can't have been Tyler crawling along the alleyway at nine thirty?"

The girls exchanged another look. "Maybe it was someone else?" said Catkin.

"Yes," said Fern, a terrible flush rising up her chest. "It must have been."

Adele felt her pulse start to race. Everything began spinning around her head: the missing pills, the blonde ponytail, the looks of consternation on her daughters' faces. And something else. Something she'd barely noticed at the time, because she'd been drunk. Because she'd been so focused on Clare and the way she was flirting with her husband and the need to get her home and sober. And towards the end, when Pip came back and Clare was reaching her terrible crescendo of drunkenness and she was saying, *It's been decided. Leo is going to be your new daddy. It's been decided*, Adele remembered, now, seeing Tyler's face just beyond the terrace and she remembered the expression — of sheer rage and disbelief. And now she knew. She knew what was inside that child as she heard those words. First Grace had taken Dylan from her. And now she was taking her fantasy father too. The broken child, daughter of a wife-beater and a negligent mother, she'd found her family out here, found her place in the world. And Grace had come and Grace had slowly dismantled it and how could a half-formed child such as Tyler cope with all of this?

She looked at Leo, chin upturned, trying, she could tell, to look as though it was all terribly interesting and nothing at all to do with him when so much of it was, whether directly or not. She said, "Leo, when you were in the alleyway with Grace, did anyone see her hug you? Did . . ." She paused. "Did Tyler see her hug you?"

Everyone turned to her. Leo gave her a questioning look, almost as if he thought she was trying to catch him out.

"I don't know," he said. "Like I've said before, I wasn't sober. I suppose she might have done."

"Is there a reason for you to ask, Mrs Howes?" asked WPC Cross.

"No," she said, "sorry. Nothing. I think I was . . . Nothing . . ."

And another memory. While she was clearing up the flat. A light in the bathroom. A noise. A few minutes after Leo came back with the dog. She'd thought it was him. Knocked on the door. "Is that you, Leo?" No reply. She'd been busy tidying up, didn't bother to go in and turn out the light, to check whether there was someone there or not.

Her heart ached.

Tyler had said it herself. *History repeating itself.*

The same green-eyed monster living inside her mother had taken up residence in Tyler's soul too. Like mother, like daughter. Because Adele fully believed that a woman who would deliberately allow her four-year-old child to see her kissing another woman's husband so that she could maintain some kind of claim over him would also be capable of doing something unspeakable to her sister.

The police appeared to think that the girls had nothing more to tell them. They mentioned that they would be talking to Tyler and her mother, just as soon as they could find them both at home. Then they thanked them for their time and saw them from the station.

They drove past Tyler's school on the way home: the hard-faced Victorian monolith, source of so much mystery and obsession to her own daughters. She thought of Tyler, somewhere in there, unfed, unwashed, lost and scared. And then of her two daughters, sitting now in the back of the car, Fern rubbing her satin strip over her top lip, Catkin staring crossly through the window.

Grace was awake. The WPC had told them that. She'd woken up the night before and claimed to remember nothing.

344

Leo dropped them all home. They saw Dylan's mum leaving the building, dressed in her petrol-station uniform of green polo shirt and matching trousers. She smiled at them, politely and hurriedly, worried, it seemed, that they might want to engage her in conversation. Adele watched her striding up the hill towards the main road.

Once inside the flat, Adele made tea. Then she opened the French windows on to the garden and stood for a moment, trying to breathe it all away. "Girls," she said, distractedly, "we'll start lessons after lunch. Why don't you all go out into the garden? It's such a beautiful day . . ."

CHAPTER
THIRTY-FIVE

5 July, 9.19p.m.

Tyler can't sit still. She has too much energy burning up inside her. She pushed Willow off the swings earlier, because she had to push something and Willow was asking for it with her incessant talking. Every time she closes her eyes she sees Grace looking up at her through the bars of the lift. Looking up at her as if to say: *See. See how I've won.* And she hears Dylan's voice, all weird with sex, saying *I love you, Grace.* And all day long Tyler's head has been black and red and flashing and hot.

And all day long she's thought of what her mum said a few weeks ago when she came home drunk after her first date with her new man. When, because her mum was being all soft and loving, not quite like a mum but at the very least like a fun friend who cares, Tyler had said, "Mum. I've lost Dylan. Grace has stolen him from me." And her mum had looped her arms around her neck and stared cross-eyed into Tyler's eyes and breathed sour and sweet into her face and said, "Make her pay. Dylan belongs to you. If she wants him she has to pay." And it hadn't made any sense at the time. But it's starting to now.

She sees Leo leave the Rose Garden. A moment later she sees Grace leave too. She sees her walk towards the alleyway. She watches Leo as he waits for his dog to poo at the bottom of the hill. Then he too walks towards the alleyway and she tiptoes over and watches from behind a small tree. He's talking to someone. It must be Grace. She can't quite make out the voices. Yes, it is; it's Grace. She can see the brush of her hair, the dense curls that Dylan had his hands all over earlier. And then she sees her throw her arms around Leo, hold him to her. And she remembers what she'd heard Clare saying earlier, telling Pip that Leo was going to be their new dad. She was talking crap, obviously she was, because she was drunk. But she was trying to claim him for herself. And now Grace is doing the same. And this, this is too much. She thinks of her mum's words: *Make her pay.* And she remembers the pot of blue and white pills in Gordon's bedroom that Catkin had shown her last week.

"These are good," she'd said, nestling one into the palm of Tyler's hand. "Sleeping pills. Kind of trippy."

They'd swallowed them down with tap water and lain about in the garden all afternoon feeling swoony and silly and nice. She wonders now how many of those little pills it would take to knock Grace out. Knock her out sideways. Just for a while. Just for long enough to show everyone on this garden what kind of a girl she is, to humiliate her — completely. She pictures herself crushing some of those little pills and dissolving them in water, but she can't work out how she'd get Grace to drink them. And then she remembers seeing Adele injecting Gordon's bad leg with something the other day. She remembers the pile of dressings and hypodermics on his chest of drawers. She glances again at the alleyway, sees Leo leaving Grace there and heading back to his flat. She can see then the shadows of Leo and Adele moving about in their kitchen, clearing things away, Gordon appearing behind them. She looks behind her at the figures in the playground. Catkin and Fern. Her garden sisters even if she knows now that they're not her actual sisters. She has no time to lose. She moves fast and quiet. And then the plan comes together like a dream.

But half an hour later she's forced to abandon her project halfway through, has to leave Grace there, not quite ready, not quite paying the price. She burrows through the tunnel behind the bench and runs back to the playground. Then Dylan appears, sits there on the swing, waiting for Grace. Waiting like an idiot.

And then a moment later, there's little Pip, the sister who hasn't fucked up Tyler's life, and she comes towards them and says: "Have you seen Grace?" and they all say they thought she went home. And oh, her face, her little face. Poor Pip, not understanding. Heading up the hill. Tyler sees her cross paths with Max. They do not talk. And then it all begins.

The drunk mum comes.

Then everyone else comes.

Then the blue lights come.

Then Grace is gone.

348

And Tyler watches disconsolately from a distance, watches and thinks: *You didn't get all that you deserved. Not even half.*

Ten Months Later

CHAPTER
THIRTY-SIX

Cherry-blossom spume overhead, sugar-pink sharp against baby-blue sky. Adele had brought the girls to the Tate for a learning trip. It was too nice to be indoors, one of those spring days that made you nostalgic for a summer that had yet to begin. The girls walked ahead, light-footed in summery clothes. The Thames ran lazily alongside, like an old dog.

A woman came towards them, slow-walking in a cream jacket and cream skirt, blonde hair bobbed and fringed, tanned legs and a small smile, as though someone had just said something nice to her.

As she came nearer Adele felt a jolt of recognition. Was it? Could it be? After all these months?

"Clare?"

"Oh my God, Adele."

Hard to gauge whether Clare was pleased or horrified.

"Wow, how are you? I haven't seen you since . . ."

"Last summer, I know."

"How are your girls? How is Grace?"

"They're both fine. Really good. And yours?"

Adele pointed to her girls, standing now at the water's edge, hands gripping the wall, staring into the river. "All present and correct."

Clare smiled. "I'm sorry", she said, "that I didn't say goodbye. It was all so . . . you know. After Grace was discharged, she really didn't want to come back to the flat. So Chris found us another place, about a mile away. It was ready to move into and it all happened so quickly."

"We miss you."

"Oh, gosh." She laughed wryly. "I'm sure you don't. I don't think we were really cut out for that kind of communal living. All that . . . exposure . . . I don't think we were very good at it. We've got our own garden now. Totally private."

"So, you and your husband, you got back together?"

"Yes." Clare smiled that small, warm smile she'd been wearing when Adele first saw her just now. "Yes, we're back together. It's good."

Adele sensed that any second now Clare was going to say: *Well, I must be on my way.* She checked the girls from the corner of her eyes. They were still standing at the river wall.

"Listen, Clare," she said. "I just wondered. In those days after the garden party, the police were everywhere. Asking questions. Then when Grace woke up, it all stopped. And I wondered: What did Grace say? About that night? Did you ever find out what happened?"

Clare blanched. "Well, sort of. Grace told us that she did something. Earlier, before the attack. She wouldn't tell us what exactly, but we guessed. It tied in with the forensic evidence and of course it was all a bit shocking. But it meant at least we knew that nothing had . . . I mean, that she hadn't been attacked

354

sexually." She shrugged. "Teenagers. They think they know what they're doing. But they don't. And that's the thing with a garden like yours — there's so much leeway for teenagers to make mistakes. Isn't there?"

Adele nodded. "But the overdose. Did the police ever find out who was responsible?"

Clare sighed. "Grace said it was an accident. Someone had offered her something and she'd taken too much." Clare shrugged, clearly unconvinced by Grace's explanation but not able to push past it. "She said she wanted to put it all behind her. Get on with her life. So she begged us to get the case dropped. And we did."

"Gosh," said Adele, overawed by the gentleness of this reaction. "But she might have died."

Clare shrugged. "I know. It was a hard decision to make. Chris and I — we wanted someone to blame. We wanted someone to suffer. But in the end, we had to respect what Grace was asking of us. We had to let her choose."

Adele nodded. This echoed her liberal parenting ethos, but she was not sure that even she could stomach the not knowing. "Well," she said. "I admire your restraint. I really do."

"I don't think there's much to admire about any of it, to be honest. The whole thing was just a terrible aberration."

"And Dylan? Are he and Grace . . .?"

"They're still an item."

Adele recoiled slightly with surprise. This she had not imagined. "Really?"

355

"Yes. He's over all the time. They appear to be that rarest of things: real teenage sweethearts." Clare smiled, and then shrugged, as if to say: *We'll see how long it lasts.* "How's Gordon, by the way? Did you ever manage to get him back to Africa?"

Adele laughed. It already felt like a distant memory, and in some strange way she almost missed him. "Yes. He went back last August. Three stone lighter. Apparently he'd put it all on again by Christmas. His wife likes him fat."

"Or maybe she likes him dead."

Adele laughed loudly. Clare laughed too. And Adele felt something settle deep inside her, something that had been jumping around her gut in the dead of night for months. The sense of unfinished business. But here she was, here was Clare, pretty and bright, reconciled with the events of last summer, in a house with a garden and a husband. And maybe now Adele could forget about the other things, the unsettling things, that had emerged in the days after the summer party: the Google search for "how to fill a hypodermic needle" that Leo had found in their browsing history, timed 9.22p.m. on the night of Grace's attack. The packaging from one of Gordon's NHS-prescribed sterile hypodermic needles that she'd found buried in the bottom of Fern's wastepaper basket when she'd emptied it the next day. Dylan's expression of innocent certainty when she'd asked him if he'd brought a bottle of water out to the playground that evening; "No," he'd said, "definitely, definitely not." The awful pondering on the unknowables like: How could tiny Tyler have single-handedly felled a big girl like Grace? Pulled her up the hill? Without any help? And the terrible flicker of her girls' eyes as they watched the girl with the blonde ponytail creeping across the bottom of the computer screen at the police station, the awful heaviness in the car on the way back home that seemed full of buried words.

Because although Tyler was the girl with the broken heart and the damaged mother and the reasons to want to hurt Grace, her girls too had felt the impact of Grace's presence in the garden. And even though Tyler wasn't their sister, they'd grown up with her as though she was. And hadn't it been her choice to keep her daughters at home, forcing them to forge stronger-than-average attachments to the friends they lived amongst? Hadn't that probably warped their perspective on the nature of friendships, of loyalty, on how far you would reasonably go to support a friend?

So they'd decided, she and Leo, decided to leave it. They were sure, they thought, sure that whatever the truth of it, whatever their daughters' real involvement, they had learned from it. That they would never again allow themselves to be caught up in someone else's madness. They were sure. They really were.

And there was Tyler, emerging suddenly into the blue sunshine from the gallery. She stopped when she saw Clare and her face fell. Adele saw her hands curl into anxious fists. She smiled at her encouragingly.

"Look who it is!" she said.

Tyler unfurled her fists, raised one hand to Clare, then ran to the river wall to join the others.

"I'm schooling Tyler now too," she explained. "In fact, Tyler has all but moved in with us."

"How come?"

"Oh, you know, the old *benign neglect* getting a bit too close to plain old-fashioned neglect. Her mum's got a new boyfriend. Turned out she was barely coming home. So the minute Gordon moved out we made up the spare room for her. Told her it was hers whenever she needed it. Which seems to be all the time. So . . ."

Making amends. Paying back the universe for the sins of her children. For the sins of her husband. And for the sins of herself. After all, had she not lost faith for moments during that terrible time, faith in her husband, faith in her neighbours? Had Leo not encouraged the confidences of vulnerable people, made himself a crutch for others to lean on when he should have been paying attention to his own children? And had they not seen what was happening to Tyler, seen the physical, the emotional deterioration and not done a thing about it? Had they not both made their own terrible mistakes?

"Wow," said Clare, "that's amazing. What a beautiful thing to do."

Adele shrugged. "I always wanted four," she said, not for the first time and not entirely truthfully.

"You see," said Clare, understanding blooming across her face, "that's the difference between you and me. And that's why a communal garden is the right place for you to live. Because you're not scared of other people's problems. Because you're happy to leave the door open and let those problems just walk straight in.

THE HOUSE WE GREW UP IN

Lisa Jewell

The four children of the Bird Family have an idyllic childhood: picture-book cottage, cosy kitchen filled with love and laughter, sun-drenched afternoons in a rambling garden. But one Easter weekend a tragedy so devastating strikes the family that it begins to tear them apart. The years pass; the children become adults and develop their own separate lives — it's almost as though they've never been a family at all. Almost. But not quite. Because something happens that will call them home, back to the house they grew up in — and to what really happened that Easter weekend all those years ago.

THE THIRD WIFE

Lisa Jewell

In the early hours of an April morning, Maya stumbles into the path of an oncoming bus. A tragic accident? Or suicide? Her grief-stricken husband, Adrian, is determined to find out. Maya had a job she enjoyed; she had friends. They'd been in love. She even got on with his two previous wives and their children. In fact, they'd all been one big happy family. But before long Adrian starts to identify the dark cracks in his perfect life. Because everyone has secrets. And secrets have consequences. Some of which can be devastating . . .

young people, and their families. They provide clinical, practical, financial and emotional support to help them cope with cancer and get the most out of life. They are there from diagnosis onwards and aim to help the whole family deal with the impact of cancer and its treatment, life after treatment and, in some cases, bereavement, www.clicsargent.org.uk

Away from the business end of things, my thanks go, as ever, to my family and friends, those on the internet, those In Real Life and of course those on The Board. And also in this case to the friends who share my own version of the Virginia Crescent Gardens in the real world. So thank you to Helen, Chris, Joe, Jo, Sian, Bernard, Erica, Cassie, Patrice and all the other lovely people I live amongst who are the nicest neighbours a girl could possibly ask for.

Richenda Todd for copy-editing.

Jenny Colgan for early reading and reassurance.

Darren Bennett at DKB Creative for the beautiful map.

Further afield and equally amazing, I would like to thank:

Deborah Schneider at Gelfman Schneider in the US.

Judith Curr, Sarah Branham, Anne Badman, Kitt Reckord Mabicka and everyone at Atria in the US.

Pia Printz and Anna at Printz Publishing in Sweden.

Everyone at Ucila International in Slovenia, Novo Conceito in Brazil, Wydawnictwo Zysk i S-ka in Poland, Cappelen Damm in Norway, Mondadori Arnoldo in Italy, Blanvalet Verlag in Germany, Presses De La Cite in France and Otava in Finland.

Thank you to the booksellers and librarians I meet every year who are too numerous to mention here but who I know I could not possibly do without. And of course to my readers. God, yes, my lovely readers. All the people in the list above would be wasting their time if it wasn't for you lot. Thank you so much for buying and for reading and for turning up to events and writing me lovely messages on Facebook and Twitter. What would I do without you?

The character name of Adele Howes in this book was a winner of the Get In Character charity auction raising funds for CLIC Sargent. The "real" Adele Howes has been a loyal reader of mine for many years and has an adoring and very generous husband called Dan who bought her the name as a birthday gift. CLIC Sargent is the UK's leading cancer charity for children and

Acknowledgements

Behind every book there lies a sea of wonderful, talented and loving people. But I think it's fair to say that the people behind mine are by far the best! I've been feeling a bit paranoid lately that maybe the people who do all the work behind the scenes on my books don't really know how much I appreciate them and everything they do, day in day out. Worried that maybe they think I take them for granted. And I want them all to know that this is so far from the truth. I may not be one for grand gestures, for gifts or for thank you cards, but trust me, I am aware from the tiniest email interaction to the grandest marketing campaign how lucky I am to have you all and what an amazing job you all do. Not to mention what thoroughly lovely people you all are!

So thank you writ large to:

Selina Walker, Kate Raybould, Beth Kruszynskyj, Georgina Hawtrey-Woore, Najma Finlay, Jen Doyle, Jenny Geras, Richard Ogle, Asian Byrne, Andrew Sauerwine, Susan Sandon, Rose Tremlett, Chloe Healy and everyone at Arrow.

Jonny Geller, Kirsten Foster, Lisa Babalis, Melissa Pimentel, Camilla Young, Mairi Friessen Escandell and everyone at Curtis Brown.

I remember, Adele, I was very rude to you that night of the party. I was drunk and out of my comfort zone. I felt judged and on show. And you were so hospitable, just like you always were, and I threw that back in your face and I've been wanting to say sorry, all these months. To say sorry and to tell you: Leo is a very lucky man."

Adele touched Clare's hand. *No!* she wanted to say. *Please don't say sorry. Please don't say sorry!* But then Willow appeared, whirlwind in girl form, long hair spread all about her, words tumbling from her, eyes shining and Adele didn't know what she was saying, what she was talking about. She wasn't really listening, but she knew that her conversation with Clare was over.

They said goodbye, and then they walked away from each other, a small, blonde woman in cream, a tall, dark-haired woman in black; they walked between the sugar-spun cherry blossom and the sluggish river, in opposite directions, towards different lives, all their secrets buried safe and sound.